LV2

ACE IN THE HOLE

ACE IN THE HOLE

Jackson Gregory

Chivers
Bath, England

•

Thorndike Press
Waterville, Maine USA

Sc(olo?

This Large Print edition is published by BBC Audiobooks Ltd, England, and by Thorndike Press, USA.

Published in 2003 in the U.K. by arrangement with the author c/o Golden West Literary Agency.

Published in 2003 in the U.S. by arrangement with Golden West Literary Agency.

U.K. Hardcover ISBN 0–7540–7271–1 (Chivers Large Print)
U.K. Softcover   ISBN 0–7540–7272–X (Camden Large Print)
U.S. Softcover   ISBN 0–7862–5415–7 (Nightingale Series)

The text of this Large Print edition is unabridged.
Other aspects of the book may vary from the original edition.

Set in 16 pt. New Times Roman.

Printed in Great Britain on acid-free paper.

British Library Cataloguing in Publication Data available

Library of Congress Cataloging-in-Publication Data

Gregory, Jackson, 1882–1943.
 Ace in the hole : a western novel / Jackson Gregory.
  p. cm.
  ISBN 0–7862–5415–7 (lg. print : sc : alk. paper)
  1. Inheritance and succession—Fiction. 2. Ranch life—Fiction.
 3. Large type books. I. Title.
PS3513.R562A63 2003
813'.52—dc21   2003047356

CHIV 8 | 10 | 03

CHAPTER ONE

Old Early Bill Cole knew full well in the fullness of his years that his days, held by some filled with iniquity and general hellraising, were numbered and his sands were running fast. He had known for six months and with a sort of devilish flicker of glee in all that he did, had gone about making the final arrangements. He was a rare old lone eagle and in him was a stripe of Satan a yard wide, at infrequent times something almost saintlike, and on many a joyous occasion a dash of Santa Claus.

'Even if I got to die like other fool folks,' he consoled himself, 'I'm going to get me my mite of fun out of it! Hell's bells, yes, sir!'

With his preparations pretty well in order, Early Bill Cole of the King Cole Ranch still estimated that his course had a few weeks to run, but that was before this particular morning had blossomed in shining gold out of the pleasantly cool, shadowy dawn. It was always his habit to be astir before the new day came in, except for those periodic carousals of his which had begun when he was sixteen and endured until he was seventy. He had no great fondness for the night time. The things he loved with all that wild old heart of his were the good earth and green things growing, and

1

the earliest hours with the last stars winking out rather like the twinkle in his old, hard, steely blue eyes, and the little dawn breeze and the sunup and the glorious unfolding. And of late he was up and out of his enormous old *adobe* ranch house each morning earlier than was even his habit. He didn't want folks to see him and realize what he was up to. For each day he was telling some part of his wide spread acres, the whole of his world, a last *adios*.

For many the year he had inhabited all alone the ancient, picturesque *adobe* building which long before his days had been the home of the Spanish-California Estradas. He had acquired the home along with the Spanish grant from a simple folk who from the first had been confused by the inrush of the Gringos and their sharp ways; after forty years now, not many quite knew the details of the transaction, but those who did not like Early Bill Cole, and they were many, said he had cheated the poor bewildered Estradas out of their eye-teeth. Perhaps he had. He was ever a thorough-going old sinner; he might have come up with those innocents upon one of the times when there was no trace of saint or of Santa Claus in him.

At first, being younger and even wilder then than at the end, he had always had a house full, and very colorful accounts of proceedings under the red tiled roof and within the thick white earthen walls leaked out. But now, no. A quarter of a mile from the old *adobe,* beyond a

2

big grove of cottonwoods, were outbuildings, stables and corrals and barns and quarters for hired hands. His latter years he wanted to be alone, like an old wolf, except when he himself went out in quest of company.

Thus, this morning, he should be sure of going about whatever his own business might be, with no fear of a spying eye. He stepped along under the fading stars with his horny thumbs hooked into his cartridge belt, his battered old black hat pushed far back on his thatch of white hair, his high-heeled boots stepping briskly. He was damned if he'd crawl about like an old man, seen or unseen.

The house was on a gently bosomed site with big oaks all about it; to the west, miles away, towered the mountains, growing darkly purple at this hour; between the house and the mountains were little rippling green hills where many a tall pine and many a tight clump of young pines grew. He walked toward the nearest hill with the three nobly tall pines on its crest. Here was a place of vantage well above the slopes where chaparral and manzanita wove themselves into thickets for rabbits to hide in.

It was still half dark when he came to the one pine which, with no one in the least suspecting it, he had loved with a deep, still, fragrantly romantic love for nearly forty years. There was a reason, locked away in his own heart. In the half dark, and with no eyes to see,

3

he pulled off his hat and looked up at the one star, still bright, laughing down at him through the branches. He put his long, thin, sinewy arms as far as he could about the tree. He pressed his grizzled cheek against the bark, so rough yet to his feeling so tenderly soft—

Then a rifle shot, clear and vicious, cracked through the still loveliness of the hour, and old Early Bill Cole felt a stab of pain. For a moment he clung to the pine tree, gripping it tight for support. Then, quick and erect, he stepped free of it and as he did so dragged both of his old guns, almost as old and worn and deadly as himself, up from their loose leathers.

His shrewd old wintry eyes barely discerned a puff of smoke like a wisp of vanishing mist hanging above the thicket where a fiercer animal than brush rabbits was hiding this morning. And not waiting for any sure target he started blazing away with both guns. What amazed him was that no second shot was winged his way.

So still was the hour that small sounds carried far and distinct; he heard a man crashing his way through the bushes, and prayed through clenched teeth for a fair sight of him. None was afforded however until his assailant, having run to a horse tethered under the crown of the slope, went up into the saddle. The distance was great, the light none too good; Early Bill leaned against his old pine

4

and steadied himself and was very deliberate about his next shot. And then, with a catch in his throat, he laughed; there were times when the old man could laugh like a wolf snarling.

He had come within an inch or two of shooting the other man through the head; he had shot his hat off! That's what made Early Bill, contending with the pain of a bullet in him, laugh. The man threw up his hand and by a lucky chance caught his hat in the air—and then departed like something shot out of a gun.

Early Bill holstered his weapons, set his long, lean back against his tree and cursed, and when old Bill Cole cursed in such rage as now his words would have drawn rapt attention from a congress of mule skinners. What made him mad wasn't so much having a man try to drygulch him; hell's bells, he had been used for a target more than once in his stretch of years. But that a man should sneak up on him and hide and spy on him when he thought himself alone with memories and an old pine—

It was a wickedly wrathful Early Bill Cole making his staggering, lurching way back to the house. The return over the brief distance which had taken him some few minutes required a tortuous hour. He got his door open, got halfway into his living room and fainted.

After a time—it must have been upward of an hour, for the sun was glancing in at his windows—he heaved himself up, moved shakily to a big chair, slumped down with a grunt and closed his eyes. Presently he stiffened will and body together and got his shirt open. He had lost a lot of blood that he could not afford to lose. The wound was through his side, down low through the lower ribs. Lucky, he judged, that he hadn't already bled to death.

Without getting up he ripped off his shirt and with badly shaking hands contrived a bandage of sorts. Then, half swooning, he sat for a long time, feeling light headed yet as grim of determination as he always was to get the better of a bad deal. Finally he rose and made his way like a drunken man to the door opening upon the old Spanish *patio* whence he could look down to the cottonwood grove just beyond which the outbuildings were. He saw a faint smudge of smoke above the tree tops. He filled his lungs and tried to yell; he snorted, though feebly, in disgust at the result. He dragged out his guns; there was a shot left in one, two in the other. He fired all three shots, spacing them, and let the guns slip out of his hands. Then he sat down on the old green bench to wait. Though the earlier shots had evidently gone unheard, the distance now was less and the hour later, and he had hopes.

It was one of his Mexican hands, young Gaucho Ortega, who came slouching up the slope, wondering what was afoot, and found

6

him.

'For the love of God!' cried the boy in his native tongue.

'Get on a horse, Gaucho,' he said, thickly, 'and ride into town. Tell Doc Joe I want him real bad. Now, wait a shake! Damn you, can't you stand still until a man finishes? Then you find the Judge. I want him, too.'

'*Si, si, Señor!*' cried the excited boy. 'I'll ride Slim Jim, and I'll go like the wind! But, *Señor!* The first thing, I must get you to bed!'

'Look you, Gaucho,' said the old Bill, of a sudden patient, taking into consideration the boy's youth and excitability, 'if I've got to cash in, I can do it standing up. And if I'm going to live, what the hell would I want a bed for? Now get out of here.' A wry grin twisted his hard old lips, and he added, 'I'll be here when you get back.'

CHAPTER TWO

The little town of Bald Eagle, squatting untidily in its place in the sun with the cattle country lying to the south and southwest, and the hectic mining country in the broken lands to the north, was as lively as any cricket most nights and many a gala afternoon, but profoundly somnolent before what conventionally termed first drink time. This

7

morning you wouldn't have seen a horse tied to any of the hitching rails, nor a puff of dust in the road not playfully stirred up by the half-hearted morning breeze, nor would you have heard anywhere the echoing thump and jingle of spurred boots on the crazy wooden sidewalks. But on the porch of the Bald Eagle Hotel two old men sat in their rocking chairs and smoked their after breakfast stogies and looked with mild, complacent eyes across all that was to be seen of their town's stark ugliness.

These were the two men for whom Early Bill had sent, two of the most famous porch-sitters in a vast area centered by Bald Eagle. They were alike in many respects and in some were like old Bill Cole himself, though they never could measure up to his stature. Younger than Bill, they were, too, by some few years. 'Doc Joe,' who had been christened Joseph Daniel Dodge; the 'Judge,' for the other, Bald Eagle's one and only lawyer at the moment, banker besides, and christened Arthur Henry Pope. Like old Bill, though some inches below his six foot two, they were lean and wiry and gray. Doc Joe was as bald as a door knob, the Judge's glinting white hair was long like a mane, and both wore fashionable flowing white mustaches. One an old bachelor, the other a widower for so many years that it was as though he, too, had never known a home life, they lived at the hotel, had

8

their three meals together, and did their porch-sitting in the two chairs which the community conceded were their particular property by right of homesteading.

They were sitting brooding, smoking ruminantly and digesting their hearty breakfasts when the Mexican boy from the King Cole Ranch came racing into town. He saw them as he turned into Main Street, and began yelling at them before they could hear a word that he said.

'Hmf!' grunted Doc Joe. 'Something must have bit him.'

The Judge sat a trifle straighter.

'It's that half-breed from Early Bill Cole's place,' he said, with his shaggy brows perked up. 'And he's riding old Bill's favorite saddle horse. Must be something wrong, Joe. Else Bill wouldn't let any breed that ever lived fork Slim Jim.'

Gaucho slung himself out of the saddle while his horse was sliding to a stop in a great cloud of dust, and poured out his story in a deluge of words. The two old men didn't stir, didn't say a thing until he had finished. Then Doc Joe said quietly, 'Take it easy, Gaucho. Now tell me—' And this time he got the essentials. He and the Judge regarded each other with poker faces, and for a time no one spoke. Gaucho, jerking about, started to tell the whole thing over when Doc Joe interrupted him.

9

'Here's four bits, kid,' he said. 'You go buy yourself a drink. You'll want to let your horse blow ten minutes. Then you ride back to the ranch and tell your boss that we're coming. *Pronto*, kid.'

'*Si, Señor*,' said Gaucho and touched his hat and moved away.

And still the two old men sat as still as the ancient hills behind Bald Eagle. They didn't look at each other again.

The Judge cleared his throat; sounded as though some of that dust had settled in it. He tossed his cigar away, only half-smoked though it was, and gnawed off a hunk of his plug cut.

'Looks like the old buzzard must be in pretty bad shape, and knows it,' he offered. 'Well, the old fool didn't have much longer to live anyhow. I always told him I'd outlive him; fact is, we've got a bet on it.'

'I know,' muttered Doc Joe. He looked his cigar over carefully, but instead of throwing it away started chewing it. 'Same with him and me; we've got a bet. Five hundred, like yours.'

Then he did stand up and hurl his cigar clean across the street.

'I'll go get my little old black poison bag,' he said cheerily. 'You better fetch pen and ink and papers and any other legal junk a dying man might want.' Then he let out a whoop, calling back Gaucho Ortega who had progressed only as far as the near-by saloon door. 'Get along first to the livery stable,

10

Gaucho. Tell Luke to let me have those two young grays to a light buckboard.'

*   *   *

That team of livery stable grays could carry a light buckboard at a run for miles, and Doc Joe and the Judge were at the King Cole Ranch almost as soon as the young Mexican. They found four of the ranch hands hanging around the house, scraping dirt with the toes of their lop-sided boots, looking as though they didn't mean to look worried. At the sound of speeding hoofs and wheels they jerked up their heads, and one man came out of the house, a small, mahogany-brown man who looked as hard as nails and was harder than he looked, Early Bill's foreman, Cal Roundtree.

'Howdy, gents,' he said, and sounded surly as though he resented their coming. 'Come on in.'

'Got the old fool in bed, Cal?' demanded Doc Joe.

Cal started to speak, glared at him and turned on his heel. The only sound from him was the bugle blast when he blew his nose.

They went in and found old Early Bill sitting in his big chair. He looked more dead than alive.

'You damned old fool,' snorted Doc Joe. He put his bag down, took off his coat and rolled up his sleeves. 'What did you shoot

11

yourself for? Or, far as that goes, why the hell didn't you do it long ago? Think I like to go skallyhooting all over the country for the likes of you?'

'Howdy—Judge,' said the old man, by way of most beautifully ignoring Doc Joe and all his words.

'I've got to get you onto a bed, Bill,' said Doc Joe. 'I can't get at you right, this way, sitting on a chair.'

'I ain't going to bed. Most likely, working me over, you're going to kill me anyhow, and if I've got to get murdered I'd like it better sitting up.'

There were a few good pieces of furniture in the big, low-ceilinged room, good because they were plain and sturdy and honest: big chairs, benches, a couple of tables. Of the tables one was of the refectory type, massive oak, eight feet long.

'If the old buzzard won't go to bed, Judge, being that superstitious and scared of dying because of the devil waiting to grab him,' said Doc Joe, 'lend me a hand to heave his old carcass up on this here table. Now, Bill, you come off your high horse and do as I say or I'll bat your brains out.'

'If I had any brains, you pill-roller,' grumbled Early Bill, 'do you think I'd let you put your murdering hands on me?'

The two helped him to stand and, with what small aid he could give them, got him

12

stretched out on top of the table. Doc Joe's skilful hands, whether or not murderous, swiftly denuded him from neck to belly-band and removed the make-shift bandage. Then for a time the physician—and there was not a more skilled within riding range of Bald Eagle—kept his tongue in his mouth and gave himself shrewdly to his work. The Judge stood by, watching in a detached sort of way as though willing enough to stick around in case a hand were needed, but mildly bored. The men outside stood looking in at the open door; only Cal Roundtree came in; he didn't know that he was walking on tip toes.

*　　*　　*

Sometime later when Early Bill Cole returned to a misty sort of consciousness he made out that he was in his bed, undressed, bound about with what he judged to be a couple of miles of bandage, and stuffed into one of his long-tailed night gowns. At the moment somehow he didn't care.

He had stirred very slightly and on the instant the two old cronies of his popped into his room.

'Well?' he demanded as sharply as he could manage.

'You sure bled like a stuck hawg,' Doc Joe told him. 'Who shot you, Bill?'

'I wouldn't know, Doc; that's the hell of it.

Say! If you boys happen to see a feller wearing a light-colored Stetson with a hole in it—or wearing no hat a-tall—or one brand new out of the store—But let's take up business before pleasure, as the feller says. Got my come-uppance for certain this trip, huh, Doc?'

With most folks Doc Joe, tough old specimen that he was, would have hesitated or hedged or lied straight out. With old Early Bill it was different. Still he strove toward modulating his answer, toward making it fittingly euphonious.

'I sort of reckon, Bill,' he said, pulling at his lower lip, 'that it won't be all-fired long now before this is a better, cleaner world—and me and the Judge will be winning a couple of bets.'

'Hmf!' said Early Bill. Then that crooked and somehow endearing old grin of his came back, just a ghost of what it used to be but still there, like a flicker of winter sunlight. 'Might be you lose out yet, you two scums of creation. Might be your horses run away and break your damn necks before I check-out!'

Nobody said anything for a little while. Early Bill was resting, Doc Joe stepped out to bring him something to swallow, mostly hot whisky, and the Judge appeared to be taking matters judicially under advisement. They lifted Early Bill and got his drink down him. Then they had one apiece.

The draft brought the sick and wounded

14

man a flush of strength. He spoke more clearly.

'Squat, you boys, and listen. Me, I'll do the talking.'

They dragged up chairs, both on the same side of the bed so that he wouldn't have to turn from one to the other, and sat down.

'First, Doc, let's know where we stand. I need a little time and a mite of stren'th. I'm not going to pop off in a hurry like a candle blown out, am I? I feel pretty good after that drink.'

'You're a tough old devil, Bill,' said Doc Joe thoughtfully. 'If you hadn't been on the skids anyhow, this thing wouldn't have done you in. It's just hurrying things along some. No, there's no hell-fired rush. Say the word and I can keep boosting you along—Oh, hell dammit, how do I know? Anyhow, shoot the works and take your time.'

'Fair enough and *gracias, amigo*,' said Early Bill. 'Here we go.'

It was a fairly long, one-sided talk, with Bill Cole now and then forced to silence and rest, and before the conference was over every man of them had taken several drinks. And pretty nearly every time that Doe Joe went for the drinks the Judge got up and went outside, and nearly every time the Judge played Hebe, Doc Joe stepped out into the *patio*.

Fortunately both Doc Joe and the Judge knew pretty well what Early Bill Cole had in

15

mind and in one way and another had had in mind for months, though the definite thing the old fellow was going to do had yet to be told. Merely taking into consideration the facts of the case, the whole thing should be simple enough, since it was merely the making of a will. But they saw the old familiar gleam in Early Bill's eyes and were dead sure that right up to the last he was plotting some sort of devilment. Hadn't he said to them on one occasion, with that famous chuckle of his, 'Sure, folks say better have you your fun while you can, seeing when you're dead you can't have any fun. Shucks, they're crazy; me I'm having me a barrelful of fun when I'm dead.' Both his listeners remembered that remark and were to recall it more than once in days to come.

They figured that they knew Early Bill Cole pretty well, though they had to admit they'd had the pleasure of his friendship for a comparatively short time—something like twenty or twenty-five years only. And that much longer ago than that he had had two friends who had meant much, very much to him. Forty years before, and more, there had rioted through the mountains a small company known far and wide as Hell's Triplets: Early Bill Cole, Busty Lee, Buck Cody. Busty Lee and Buck Cody were haply dead these many years, having been swept away together in a night of violence, and about all that they had left behind them was their various offspring. Busty Lee had left a daughter with little dower save her loveliness, and Buck Cody had bequeathed to the world a son and not much to go along with him. They knew that little Ann Lee was teaching school somewhere or another and living with her Aunt Jenifer—her aunt living with her, rather; and that young Cody was trying to make a mining engineer out of himself. All this they knew because old Bill had told them—and that, with the first creeping of the shadow over him some months ago, he had piled into the stage and had been away for a couple of weeks—and had come back with that devil-saint-Santa Claus gleam in his eye.

'I looked 'em both over,' he announced triumphantly. 'I even met up with the two of them, one here and one there. And they didn't know me from Adam's off ox either, because I didn't happen to speak up. They're aces, Busty's and Buck's pups, and me, I'm going to have me some fun with them!'

'After you're dead!' they grunted at him.

'Yep!'

And now he was getting ready for his fun.

'In a minute, Judge, you're going to make me a couple of wills—'

'Hold on there, Bill! Just because there are two legatees you don't need two wills!' He looked at Early Bill narrowly; maybe the old devil was too far gone already to know enough

17

to make any sort of will! Then in that case, every thing, lock, stock and barrel would go to Rance Waldron as nearest of kin—the only kin, so far as Early Bill knew, though luckily distant.

'Who's doing this?' Early Bill grunted. 'Just keep your *camiso* on, Judge, until I say so. Now, I'm leaving everything I got to young Cody and the Lee girl. He's an upstanding young he-wildcat and she's the damnedest cutest trick and the nicest and—well, dammit, the sweetest you ever laid eyes on. So they get the works. The whole of the ranch and the whole of the cash. You boys know how I've been gathering a few dollars here and there, account of my expected one-way trip and how I've sold off some stock, not figgering these brats, hardly dry behind the ears yet, and one an engineer and the other a pretty young girl, would know how to manage. The money's in your bank, Judge, if you haven't stole' it yet, anyhow a couple of hundred thousand dollars—about two five now, I reckon, in case the interest hasn't et up all the principal, or you haven't been losing heavy at draw!'

The Judge, eyeing him, thought, 'He knows what he's talking about.'

'Now,' went on Early Bill, 'I've got a job for each one of you horn toads, and I'm paying each one of you a dollar a day and found, high wages for you two. Judge, you go in there and hunker down at the table and write me those two wills. Make 'em just the same, giving, granting and disposing and so forth all I got. In one will, give everything to her. In the other give everything to him. And you date 'em both the same, as of today. You, Doc, you move that old trunk of mine to one side and yank up a couple of loose boards and hand me what you find. Let's go! Wages start when you start getting busy!'

The puzzled Judge did his bit of round swearing, had a copious drink and went off to his will-making: Two wills of like date bequeathing identical property to two different people! Dammit, old Bill must be off his head . . . Just the same he did as instructed and made a nice clean job of it to boot.

Doc Joe shoved aside a battered old leather trunk, scrabbled in the corner, got a couple of loose boards up and after some further scrabbling came up, red-faced with a small iron lock-box in his dusty hands. The box was some eighteen inches long, about six inches in the other dimensions, and was provided with two locks, each set about six inches from the end. Early Bill, seeing it, chuckled and then swore under his breath; chuckling came dearly right now.

'I think it was that damn box of mine put the whole idea into my head,' he said. 'Having two locks like, notice? Look at 'em good, Doc.'

'What about 'em,' demanded Doc Joe. 'They're just two locks—'

19

'By the way,' said Early Bill, 'when you boys go out, send Cal Roundtree to me. Tell him to bring Gaucho. I've got me a great hunch! It's my ace in the hole!'

His grin grew broad; he seemed carefree, happy—even zestful.

'You're crazy like a hoot owl,' snorted the Judge. 'Doc just asked you a question: What's this about two locks?'

'Look at 'em good!'

'I am looking—They're different, that what you mean?'

'Takes two different keys to open 'em!' said a triumphant Bill Cole.

CHAPTER THREE

To two old porch-sitters in front of the Bald Eagle Hotel came a young man on horseback. The two, watching everything that went on, smoking their after supper stogies, took stock of him when he first rode into town down at the far end of the street. In the cool of the early evening, hardly dark yet, Bald Eagle was already bestirring itself; there were horses tethered along the hitching racks, a piano was being thumped in the Last Chance Saloon and a music box had just come to life in the saloon across the road, and there were men going about their affairs up and down the plank

20

sidewalks. Yet this young man, surely a newcomer to Bald Eagle, held the appraising eyes of the two old cronies.

He rode straight to the hotel, dismounted and approached. There was ample light to show what he looked like. He was young and lean and brown and tall; that was one thing. In the saddle he had been loosely graceful; one felt that for all that seeming carelessness in his way of riding, that if his horse had of a sudden sought to leap out from under him he would still have been sitting there in the saddle, confident and vaguely arrogant. Here where men dressed as they pleased, some in dusty boots and pretty much in rags, others in what finery and display of colors appealed to them, this young man struck a note. From flashy, high-heeled boots to the silk bandana, bright red, around his brown throat and on up to his forty dollar hat, he displayed a touch of elegance. A handsome young dark devil, too, when they saw his face.

'Howdy, gents,' he accosted them, and sat on the porch, holding his horse's reins. He removed his hat and ran his fingers through his hair that was inclined toward length, rich darkness and curliness.

Civilly they returned his greeting. 'Howdy,' they said.

'I'm a stranger here,' he told them. 'You look like you belonged here. Maybe you can tell me the way to Bill Cole's ranch?'

21

They directed him, telling him it was a couple of hours' ride, indicating the short cuts to take on horseback. He said, 'Thanks,' rolled a cigarette, smoked half of it, tossed the butt into the dust and stood up.

'Only,' said Doc Joe, 'I don't know as they're wide open for comp'ny right now. Bill Cole's sick.'

'Sick? Say—What's wrong? Nothing bad, is it?'

'He ain't feeling any too good,' said Doc Joe. 'I was out to see him a couple of days ago. I stuck out there until this afternoon. No, Bill ain't feelin' real good.'

The young man eyed him in a penetrating sort of way.

'You might be the doctor?' he judged. And Doc Joe nodded. 'Well, all the more reason I should ride along. You see I'm his nephew. My name's Rance Waldron.'

The Judge, after his Howdy, hadn't stirred or spoken. Now he flipped his cigar the way Rance Waldron's cigarette had gone and reached for his plug cut.

Waldron tarried a moment as though thinking some word might be added. When none was forthcoming he swung up into the saddle again, lifting easily and somehow gracefully, a man of full strength and youth and vitality, and rode away.

They watched him out of sight.

'Hmf,' said the Judge then.

22

'He had a hat,' mused Doc Joe.

'Yep. Wasn't any hole in it, though.'

'Nope. Wasn't even a new hat, either.'

'Not light-colored, either. Black.'

'Too bad.'

Doc Joe rolled his stogie and the Judge rolled his cud. They didn't look at each other, just sat there and drew their eyelids down like two old roosters. After a while,

'Funny him showing up right now,' remarked the Judge. 'Just after that damn old buzzard gets ready to cash in his chips. Kind of funny.'

'What's funny about it?'

'Lots of things. Kind of funny, I been thinking all this while, about those two damn fool wills. If they're any good, if either one of them is any good, then Mr. Rance Waldron is out in the cold. If those two wills cut each other's throats, he comes in for the gravy, being next of kin.'

'And you haven't made up your mind yet about the validness of those wills?'

'How can I tell? I never heard of such tomfoolery. If when the heirs show up they don't look out, while they're pulling both ways at once this young feller will slip in between them and walk away with the boodle. No, I don't know any more about that part of it than you know how soon old Bill is going to kick off. I warned him; was all I could do. And you warned him to keep in bed. How much good did any warning ever do that old horsethief?' He wound up with a snort, and spat shrewdly over the railing into the road.

'Rance Waldron, huh?' brooded Doc Joe. 'Do you know, Judge, that old fool Bill Cole has something struck me as a pretty fair judge of folks. This young Waldron, I don't cotton to him much. I don't like the cut of his eye.'

'Me neither,' agreed the Judge. 'I noticed we were both sorry he didn't have a hole in his hat. Let's go get a drink.'

*   *   *

Warm as the early summer evening was, a thundering log fire was making the rocks blazing hot in the living room fireplace at the King Cole Ranch. Drawn up before the hearth in his most commodious big chair sat old Early Bill with his long legs tucked under a heavy red wool blanket, with his overcoat on and buttoned to his chin, with his hat on, too. His only attendant, the only person he would tolerate in the house, his foreman Cal Roundtree, stood as far as he could from the fire, his face glistening with sweat.

Cal mopped his forehead with a blue bandana already sopping, and had his say, not for the first time, either.

'Dammit, Bill,' he said explosively, 'I tell you you're crazy! You ought by rights to have some kind of a nurse here with you; me, I couldn't nurse a sick colt. A woman anyhow. Somebody to—'

'Dry up, Cal,' snapped the old man. 'Go get me a drink. Get yourself one, too. And quit bellering like a bull calf.'

'Dammit, Bill! Didn't Doc Joe tell you—'

'He's a murdering old fool. So're you. Better fetch the jug this trip and set it close to me where I can reach it. Then you can get to hell out of here. I don't need you nor anybody else getting in my way.'

Cal Roundtree, growling like a bear with a sore paw, started kitchenwards but stopped abruptly as he heard the lively racket of a horse's hoofs coming on to the house. The sounds stopped at the front door; then there was a lusty knocking.

'Come in, you fool!' yelled old Early Bill.

Rance Waldron stepped in, just across the raised threshold, and stopped there looking about him, taking in everything at a sweeping glance. Then his look centered probingly upon the man in the chair.

'This the King Cole Ranch?' he said. 'You're Mr. William Cole?'

'Shut the door, Rance,' said Early Bill, and all of a sudden his voice was quiet and all but toneless. One speaks of a poker face; well, his voice now was a poker voice.

Rance Waldron closed the door, pulled his hat off and came closer; standing at the side of the chair he put out his hand. Early Bill took it slowly, let it go with a degree of alacrity.

'You never saw me before,' said Rance Waldron, puzzled. 'How did you know me?'

'Oh, I saw you once, two-three months ago, Waldron. Four months ago, maybe. You mightn't remember. Me, I don't forget. Over at Bantam Springs, it was.'

Until he finished speaking it was hard to make much of his face, what with the effect of the flicker of the fire, an affair of light and shadow commingled, and with his broad hat brim pulled low. Now he lifted his head and shoved his hat back and looked up into his kinsman's eyes.

Even so for another moment Rance Waldron remained puzzled, for the Bill Cole of tonight wasn't even the Bill Cole of a couple of days ago, what with the unshaven cheeks and the sunken look to them and the great gauntness about the eyes. But Early Bill could never be anything but Early Bill, when you looked closely, and with a start Rance recognized him.

'But—but—' he stuttered. 'At Bantam Springs, that night! Of course I remember. There was a card game—we had a few drinks together—But I didn't know who you were! I didn't know your name—they just called you Bill—Why didn't you tell me?'

'Better get a move on and bring that jug, Cal,' said Early Bill, and left the young man utterly to his own devices.

26

But Cal Roundtree didn't budge; he stood stock still, staring in fascination at the visitor's face. Rance was bareheaded; the fire glow seemed to make his face ruddier and ruddier until it grew bright red. Or was it just the fireglow, Cal wondered? Yes, Rance Waldron was remembering! That poker game at Bantam Springs! An old man, a stranger, sitting in! What a run of luck the old fool had had! He had been so clumsy; he seemed only halfway to know what he was doing; he fumbled with the cards when he shuffled; he made crazy bets and lost—and yet, by some miracle, in the end he won everything in sight! And Rance Waldron lost his shirt that night; lost more than he could afford to lose, expecting with every new hand to clean the old fool down to his bootheels; had lost more than just money, because he had lost his head, too, and had flown into a rage and had said things—Just what had he said? And the old fool was Early Bill Cole, keeping his name hidden the way he did an ace in the hole—and all the time Early Bill knew who Rance Waldron was!

But this consternation, holding him tongue-tied and at utter loss, was only momentary. He was a young man of parts, was Rance Waldron, hard to down and harder to keep down. Of a sudden, startling both Early Bill and Cal Roundtree, he began laughing. He slapped his thigh with his hat and put his head

27

back and roared with laughter. He laughed until he had to wipe the tears out of his eyes. And for one second, such gay infectious mirth it was, that old Early Bill came within a gnat's nose of actually liking him!

'Bill Cole, you old heller!' he shouted when he grew articulate. 'I might have known at the time that it was you! I've heard about you all my life, the sorts of things a man might expect from you—only he'd never know *what* to expect!' He sobered. 'Me, I didn't show up very well that night, did I? Guess I must have been halfway drunk—and your style of playing drove me crazy—and to top it off, I lost pretty nearly every damn cent I had in the world. Just you wait until I can get into another game with you!'

'I don't mind waiting, being kind of patient by nature,' the old man remarked mildly. And then, still mild and innocent, he added, 'Kind of funny your dropping in on me right now.'

'Right now? Why right now?'

'Me being sort of laid up like this. You see, I don't get chairbound often.'

'I had a bit of business over the other side of Bald Eagle. I thought—'

'Sure.—Say, Cal, dammit! Where's that jug?'

'I'll go put up my horse,' said Rance Waldron.

Again Early Bill Cole said, 'Sure,' and lay back in his chair and pulled his hat brim down.

He sat there very still, looking into the fire. A queer little smile, a happy sort of smile with some strange sort of tenderness in it and a flick of humor—a flick of devilishness, too, maybe—touched his lips . . .

When Cal, first to return, came back into the room he thought the old man was asleep. So he was. Old Early Bill Cole, full of years and of wickedness and of a rare sweetness, was taking his ease in his last long sleep.

CHAPTER FOUR

It was hard to catch a glimpse of the girl's eyes, so wide and drooping was the brim of her pink straw hat, so long and inclined to lower themselves bafflingly were her lashes. Her cheeks, too, were pink, and there was a laughing dimple in one of them. She scarcely lifted her fluffy skirts an inch when she stepped up into the stage; there was just the flash of an out-peeping tiny foot, the merest suspicion of a pink-stockinged ankle, and about her a wisp of fragrance as though she had just bathed and sprinkled herself with Florida Water.

Little Miss Ann Lee, accompanied by Aunt Jenifer, fragile and tremulously smiling under her poke bonnet, had taken the first stage from Bantam Springs, arriving at the small crossroads settlement of Top Notch in the early evening. There she and her aunt tarried overnight at the very respectable boardinghouse operated by a local celebrity, Big Belle. And there they spent the following day and night waiting for another stage to take them a day's journey through the mountains to the King Cole Ranch, some miles on the nearer side of Bald Eagle.

All this, of course, was because of the letter she was carrying with her now, a most mystifying communication from a Mr. William Cole—intriguing, even beyond its mere mystification, because of the hundred dollar yellow back that had come with it. A huge sum of money—but with certain strings to it.

And, upward of a hundred miles from Bantam Springs at the trading post where he went now and then, a young man named William Cole Cody had received a very similar letter. He considered the thing some sort of hoax—but then the hundred dollar 'expense' money enclosed was real dough. It was a long trip across the mountains to Bald Eagle; he had heard of the place as had most men within a pretty considerable radius. Why the devil should he pick up and travel because some no doubt crackbrained individual beckoned? Why? Well then, because a thing like that gets a man's curiosity stimulated until it won't let him rest; because it is a simple thing for youth to scent adventure over the next hill. And, when he is handed a key, it's sheer human nature for a man to wonder what lock it fits!

So in the end Cole Cody slid into his newest boots and hat, decorated himself with his most flamboyant bandana, looked to his guns and rode through the foothills, then through Black Rock Pass, and came in due course to the stage stop at Top Notch. He stabled his horse, had supper and went to bed. In the morning he'd saddle and ride on.

But a man never knows!

He had ridden late last night and would have slept late this morning had he not been awakened by the commotion out in the yard attendant upon the stage preparing for departure. He hadn't thought anything about a stage, having a good saddle horse, and had ridden by way of Top Notch simply because it lay on his line of travel. Now, being awake, he yawned comfortably and stretched and came close to dozing off again. Then through the other, coarser sounds of men swearing at horses and trace chains jangling, he heard another sound, and he thought dreamily that it fitted far more pleasantly into the early daylight hour. Little Ann Lee, very gay and electric this morning, was laughing.

He got up then, dressed and ran his fingers through a wild thatch of dark red hair, cocked his hat on at an angle which bespoke an interest in life and full approval of it, and stepped along outside. And just as he got

31

outside the door Long Peters, the stage driver, was calling down from his high seat,

'All aboard, folks. Here we go.'

It was then that Cole Cody saw Ann Lee stepping up into the stage. He did catch the most fleeting of glances from her eyes under the long, demure lashes, and noted how the pink of her cheeks was as soft as the softest of apple-blossom colors tinting the eastern sky. She lifted her foot to the step, and looked back over her shoulder—

What she saw was a young man standing, irresolute. She couldn't help looking at him a moment, and she couldn't help wondering whether he were coming with them, and she didn't even suspect that she almost smiled an invitation. She vanished within the coach.

'Hold on there!' shouted Cole Cody, and bore down on the stage at a run. He called back to the hostler who had just lent a hand with hitching up, 'Keep my horse until I come back,' and jerked the stage door open.

'If you're comin' along, pardner,' said Long Peters, his whip poised ready for the long snaking out of the lash into the pistol-like crack that would start his team off like a shot, 'climb up here. No more room inside.'

Cole Cody didn't make out clearly who the other inside passengers were; he didn't even see Aunt Jenifer. He saw nothing but the girl with the big pink straw hat. It drooped on each side of her lovely face and there were ribbons streaming from the brim. He almost made her a bow; not quite, but he did take off his hat. She almost smiled, but then she looked away very quickly and began talking hurriedly to her companion. The driver called out a second time impatiently, Cole Cody climbed up on the high seat, the whip snapped at last and they were off.

The girl was saying softly into her aunt's ear, 'Did you see him, Aunt Jenny? Isn't he—I mean—'

Aunt Jenifer had a queer little trick of smiling, tucking in the corners of her clean, pink-lipped mouth and letting her eyes drift sideways. She spoke for her thrilled niece's ears alone: 'Yes, I know, Pet. Really quite handsome and dashing and all that. To be sure. And I noticed something else!'

'What?'

'He saw you!'

And Cole Cody, rocking along on the high seat beside Long Peters, filling his lungs with the clean, sweet dawn air, hearing music in the creak and rattle of the stage and in the clang of sixteen shod hoofs on the hard, dry roadbed, engaged the stage driver in conversation. Long Peters was willing enough; as long as he had driven stages he had never got tired of meeting strangers and finding all about them when possible. It becomes monotonous business sitting up there all alone, with nothing much to do and nothing to think about—until you got into the mountain roads where a man had his hands full and needed his wits about him if he was to bring his coach through safely and on time.

Cole Cody, generally as forthright as a flying arrow going places, was inclined to a certain circuity this morning. He remarked on the horses first of all, not being in the least interested in them, yet singling out the off leader for remark; and in return got a thumb nail sketch of that animal's career, character and pedigree. He spoke of Top Notch; of a high mountain town he knew they would pass through, Tap Rock; then of Bald Eagle. Of what a fine day it was. And finally—of the inside passengers.

'Folks that live around here? Or strangers?'

Long Peters swung his equipage around a bend, down into a shallow, dry creek, cracked his whip again and started them briskly up a sharp slope with the lifting mountains looming steep and black ahead. First disposing of those of his cargo whom he knew, he got around at last to Ann Lee and Aunt Jenifer.

'We're carryin' a couple nice ladies, too,' he said. 'Don't know much about 'em. They come this far with Hank Roberts day 'fore yestiddy; I only saw the two of 'em breakfas' time. They're a Miss Edwards, that's the old lady and she ain't real old at that, and her niece, Miss Ann Lee. They come from somewhere way down yonder; around Bantam Springs some place, Hank says. And they never been up this way before; goin' to see some of their folks. Jus' visitin'.'

'Going far?' young Cody asked casually.

'All the way through to Bald Eagle. We get there early tonight.' He eased his straining horses down to a walk as the slope steepened and the road narrowed and roughened. 'How about you, stranger? I ain't ever seen you any place.'

'Me? I'm headed on to Bald Eagle, too. No, I've never been up this way. My stamping ground's down around Dutch Skill's Trading Post.'

'Glad to know you. My name's Peters; Tom Peters.'

'Glad to know you, Mr. Peters. I'm Cody; Cole Cody.'

Long Peters proffered his hand, the taut reins still in its grip, and they shook that way.

Almost immediately they entered a great, silent and glooming wilderness. The deeply rutted roadway snaked along the brink of a shadowy ravine, winding among thickening timber; here and there stood a whitening stump where a tree had had to come down, and in three places within the next hour such trees had been used for bridges across the ravine; pines for the most part overshadowed them, though there were long gentle slopes along the mountain bases where pines and oaks made close fraternity. Then they rose to the slow and tortuous climb for more than another hour where White Rock Grade had been gouged out of the rocky mountainside. For a while Long Peters had to stop his horses, slamming on his brakes to hold the stage from rolling backwards, while the horses rested. 'Got to blow the horses seven times before we come to the Saddle, where we start down again,' he explained.

At one of those stops where a grassy strip of mountain meadow lay illogically embraced between iron cliffs, a thin stream of clear cold water flashed across the road, and there was a watering trough hewn out of a log, overspilling with water so clean and bright it made a man thirsty to look at it. There was a clump of shivering aspens, and in the deep grass by the stream some tall-stemmed flowers grew, altogether a lovely spot.

Long Peters wrapped his lines about his brake and got down, taking a bucket from the rear end of his stage to water his horses. Cole Cody's boots struck the ground as soon as Long Peters', and his eyes went straightway to the stage coach door. He was just in time to offer his hand as the door opened and a bright eager face looked out, and Miss Ann Lee's little shoe reached for the step.

'Might I help you down, ma'am?' asked Cole Cody, hat in hand and very polite and grave-faced and formal.

'Thank you, sir,' said Miss Ann, also most

36

polite and formal, but not quite so grave of face, for that quick smile of hers, as swift as the dart of a swallow's wing, was not to be denied this morning.

So for the briefest of moments her hand rested in his. For the same length of time, no longer, her eyes rested on his eyes. Then she lifted her skirts, lifted them perhaps a whole inch to clear them of the uneven ground, and ran to the trickle of water which went down through a pipe to fall into the trough.

The other passengers, all but Aunt Jenifer, got down and strolled about, had a drink of water and looked the world over from this high place. Cody paid them scant attention: Ann was hastening back bringing a full cup of water, full and spilling over. What with her running haste and her skirt in one hand and her eyes on her cup, she tripped over a root and pitched headlong—and Cole Cody saved her from a fall by catching her in his arms.

She turned scarlet. Whereas, he instinctively held her close and would have held her long, she snatched herself out of his arms in a flurry of haste. Her eyes, lifted up to his, were enormous, her mouth a ripe, round O! Her hat had been knocked far back, falling to her shoulders, held by the band about her throat, and her hair was all about her face. He smiled down at her, just a friendly smile he meant it to be. She was just shaping her lips to say something; it is even possible she was again going to say, 'Thank you, sir!' Instead some wild impulse snatched her and impelled her— she didn't know then and she never did know why she did what she did next—maybe Cole Cody's smile had some finger in the pie. She still had half a cup of water left, dribbling out of the tilted cup; she felt it drip on her dress, looked down, saw it—and flung the half cup of icy water in his face. Then she bolted into the stage's interior like a rabbit down its warren.

A bit of color came up then in his copper-tanned face, and his jaw set hard, and a stony hardness came into his eyes. He stood rigid, not turning to look after her, not stirring.

One of the other passengers, a plump and paunchy hunk of a man in store clothes, snickered. Cole Cody moved then; he turned slowly on this man and asked in a very soft, gentle and slow voice,

'Did you say something?'

The grin was gone from the paunchy man's face as though his face had been a slate with something written on it, and a wet rag had been swept across it.

'N-o—no, I didn't say nothin',' he explained hurriedly and backed off.

'All aboard,' called Long Peters.

As Cody went around the stage to climb up on his side again, he heard a sound from within. And he knew the sound for what it was: A girl's smothered giggling.

'Damn that girl,' he said within himself.

CHAPTER FIVE

Toward midday they stopped at Stage Stop in a bit of alpine valley where they nooned, ate at a long oilcloth-covered table and changed horses. There was nothing here but a long barracks of a house presided over by a lanky Alabaman and his short, blunt wife and an old Mexican who helped about the place, just a station for the use of the stage and its passengers. Cody getting down from his place strolled over to the Mexican and engaged him in conversation; he did not look back to see what the others did, not in the least caring. He and the Mexican talked together in Spanish about the day, how fine it was; and about this country, sure a great country, and there ought to be gold back in the hills, and there was some first rate stock land through here—and how was the hunting? Much deer and bear?

Young Cody was never sure that he had heard her soft, hesitant approach, but somehow he knew that she was close behind him. Maybe he read a part of the fact in the old Mexican's eyes; old eyes they were yet expressive and right now glowing with a sort of startled admiration. What else but her appearance could put a look like that into any man's eyes? Cody, given to stubbornness, resisted the urgent impulse to turn.

Her voice, subdued and with a throaty tremor in it, said ever so softly,

'Mr. Cody! Please!'

He turned slowly and stared down at her along his nose. He didn't say anything, just looked at her. She was twisting the ribbons hanging from her hat; hastily she lowered her eyes and as swiftly the ready flush came back, hot in her rounded cheeks.

'Mr. Cody—You are Mr. Cody, aren't you? The stage driver told me that is your name—Oh, Mr. Cody, please forgive me—if you can! I don't know what made me do it! I was just *wild!* I was so stupid and clumsy, and felt so ashamed of myself—and for a minute I thought you were going to laugh at me, and—'

Almost at her first word all the stubborness melted out of him and an uproarious gladness took its place. And all the glint of steel in his eyes, that had made them look hard and cold, fled to make way for the warmth and jollity of a smile. He shot out his hand to capture hers which came shyly into it.

'Miss Ann Lee, ma'am! Don't you say another word! Only you weren't clumsy and you weren't stupid, and it wasn't your fault that that pesky root caught your toe—and anytime in the world it'll make you happy to splash water in folks' faces, you just send for me! I'd be proud!'

The old Mexican smiled approvingly, pulled at his mustaches and moved tactfully away.

Ann looked up then into Cole Cody's lean, brown face, so high above her own saucily piquant one, and smiled, too. And in another instant the two of them were laughing together, and it was a moment or two before she seemed to realize that her hand, which had never felt so tiny and helpless before, was still warm in the warmth of his. She slipped it out hastily.

'But how did you know my name?'

'It's the prettiest name in the world, and—'

'Mr. Peters told you! Of course.'

'He couldn't tell me very much about you. All that I know is that you and your aunt came from somewhere near Bantam Springs, and that you are going on to Bald Eagle.'

'And so are you! Mr. Peters told me that, too. Have you ever been there? What is it like? And do you know—'

Her aunt called to her, not loudly but in a limpidly clear voice which carried.

'Ann, dear! If you don't hurry and get a bite to eat you'll get nothing until we get to Bald Eagle, and that's hours.'

'I'm coming, Aunt Jenny,' said Ann, and she and Cody walked together to the long shed-like building where the others were already having coffee and biscuits and beans cooked Mexican style and a rich venison stew with potatoes and onions in it. Mr. Cody was duly presented, and bowed over the slight little body that was Miss Jenifer Edwards, and confessed himself very greatly pleased and highly honored to make her acquaintance.

After that all was haste and flurry, and then piling back into the stage and, with a crack of Long Peters' whip, they were again on their way. On the high seat, rolling his cigarette, Cole Cody looked well pleased with the world. He had handed the two ladies up into the coach. Within ten minutes he had twice held Ann Lee's hand in his. And, no unpleasant memory now, already he had held her in his arms!

They swirled away through Fiddler's High Pass, curved hazardously along the steep sides of Indian Mountain, made a descent with brakes squealing into Long Valley, and then began climbing again, and so the bright afternoon slid away and shadows began running out across their way and, from the gloom of Dark Canyon, they saw a star.

But it was daylight again when they crested the next rocky ridge, and Long Peters, flinging out his whip and sending his horses along with a rush where there was a stretch of downhill slope, said to Cody,

'Look sharp, way down there and straight ahead, and maybe you'll see the sun flash on windows in Bald Eagle. It's only twenty mile from here. And inside the hour, when we start down the Georgia Road you'll see it again, only it'll be lamps by then. Hold your hair on, young feller!'

Once Cody thought that he did see a flash of light on twenty mile distant windows, but it was merely a wink and a glint and he might have fancied it. The sun was almost down; it was hidden by a pine-studded shoulder of the mountains as they rocketed down into another steep-sided little valley; it was gone for the day when they swept upward again, and the stars were out in earnest. Even yet there was no deep dark, a thickening dusk, rather, closing in about them, with the stars at their shining best. Cole Cody put back his shoulders and breathed deep, the glory of the oncoming night a lovely thing, the night air strong and clean and heady, the tang of pines upon it like spice. Then all of a sudden and without warning, startling him out of a reverie fit for the hour, the stage driver cursed explosively and jammed on his brakes and leaned back against his reins until he pulled his horses back on their haunches, bunched and struggling, with the front wheels against the wheeler's rumps. Quick cries of alarm burst from the coach's interior. Cody stared wonderingly at what he could see of the driver's face.

'There's a tree across the road,' muttered Long Peters. And Cody, leaning out and peering closely at last saw it; not ten feet ahead of the leaders. Long Peters had seen it first, and in time before the coach had piled up on it, it being Long Peters' business to keep his eyes on the road for—Well, for things like a fallen tree.

'Now, that's funny—'

'Sit tight! Not so damn funny, Cody. That tree didn't put itself there. It's a holdup. Some damn fool must have thought I was carrying a Wells Fargo strong box. Well, I ain't.'

A voice, a deep, rumbling, roughly unpleasant voice called,

'Take it easy, driver. It's a holdup.'

It was hard to make out where the voice came from. On one side of the road was a steep slope pitching brokenly down into the dark depths of a ravine whence rose the rush and swirl of a hidden stream; on the other side was the rising flank of the mountain, made a secret place with its timber and with clumps and thickets of manzanita and chaparral and mountain laurel. So it was clear enough that the highwayman was somewhere on the upper side, but there were a hundred shadowy spots there to harbor him.

All the while the driver had been busy with his tugging reins, and the messages from his strong hands ran along them like an electric force along wires, and little by little he quieted his team. Now his body didn't seem to move, but his hands did, stealthily. He wrapped the reins about his high hand-brake; he groped behind him and pulled a carbine out slowly and got it across his knees.

'If I could only get a glimpse of that—!' Cody heard him muttering to himself, his voice hushed with yearning.

'You heard me!' the voice called again.

'Yes, I heard you!' Long Peters called back, moving his body a little to one side and the other, craning his neck, praying for that longed-for glimpse. 'You must be crazy. This is the Bald Eagle stage, *hombre*, and there's no strong box on it. You ought to know that much.'

'I'm not after any strong box. Do what I tell you and nobody won't get hurt. You've got a passenger I want to talk to. Tell him to step along and I won't even hurt him. But he'd better bring with him what he's carrying, or I'll cut his damn ears off. It's Andy Jenkins. Get a move on and you can get goin' again.'

'Andy Jenkins?' said Cole Cody under his breath. 'Who's Andy Jenkins?'

'That little scraggy, buck-toothed feller. I don't know anything about him.' He turned slightly to call back over his shoulder. 'You, Jenkins? Hear what the road agent says? What's it all about?'

From the stage's dark interior Andy Jenkins answered gravely in a very quiet voice, cool and collected, not the least hurrying.

'Tell him, Peters, all I've got on me is about fourteen dollars, silver, and a gold watch and chain and some smoke tobacco. That what he wants? He's sure welcome.'

45

Long Peters relayed the answer. Before he had spoken the last word there was a red flash from a point high up the slope and the reverberating crack of a rifle, and a bullet whizzed a yard or so above his head.

'That's just to show I mean business,' the voice called sharply. 'Get a move on, you Jenkins! I know what you've got and where you got it and how much. Step lively.'

Cole Cody said softly to Long Peters, 'There are anyhow two of them. That shot came from higher up; not from the man talking to us.'

The driver nodded. 'I wish I could get a sight of him—'

'What are you going to do? Take this sitting down?'

'I don't like to. But we got ladies along and—Anyhow, it's Andy Jenkins' business.' He called over his shoulder, 'What's the word, Jenkins?'

Jenkins scrambled down out of the coach.

'There's nothing much we can do, is there? If we didn't have these ladies along—'

'Mr. Jenkins!' It was Aunt Jenifer's voice, suddenly sharpened, grown strangely brittle with emphasis, and surely unafraid. 'Don't you talk like that! If you've got something valuable, well then, you just keep it! And if that man wants it, let him come for it. And you boys shoot him all to pieces. I'm not scared of a ruffian like that that hides in the woods, and never was, and my niece ain't either. So don't

46

you go and hide behind our petticoats! Don't you dare!'

Cole Cody heard Long Peters grunt, and despite the driver's baffled rage, the grunt was next door to a chuckle. And then he heard Andy Jenkins saying quietly,

'Thankee, Miss Edwards. But looks like it's no use.' There was the sound of his light tread, then they saw him passing on beyond the horses, climbing over the log, stepping along briskly with something in his hand; carpet-bag, no doubt.

Neither Cody nor Long Peters watched his progress; both with straining eyes were probing into the dark among the pines, trying to locate the man who had issued his orders and the man who had fired the warning shot. The latter, they knew, would be standing well-concealed behind one of the big-boled pines. They could not make out where the other was.

The little man's figure began to blur in the darkness as he kept along in the road and when they glanced swiftly after him it took a moment or two to find him. The horses, beyond tossing their heads and stamping with an occasional snort, were quiet enough. From within the coach came voices again. Aunt Jenifer was getting down; she wanted to see whatever was to be seen. Her niece started to follow and Aunt Jenifer commanded her to stay where she was. Ann Lee paid her not the slightest attention, and in another moment was

47

in the road with her aunt.

Cole Cody started to climb down. Again the bull-throated voice roared out,

'Stay where you are! Up on the seat there! All of you, or—'

Long Peters' carbine cracked and spat fire and hot lead, and cracked again and the third time: He had spotted the other man, the one who had stood behind the pine, who now moved slightly but enough to come within range of those shadow-piercing eyes of the irate stage driver. Cody, with one foot on the wheel, whirled; for a moment he couldn't see anything, not even the little man with the carpet-bag.

Long Peters' shot drew quick answering fire from two quarters. Cody saw the spits of flame but even yet couldn't see a fair target. He heard the heavy thud of a bullet in flesh, and Long Peters gave issue to a sound halfway between a choked squeal and a grunt and dropped his weapon—it clanged against iron, falling—as he folded up on the seat. The frightened horses began again to rear and plunge.

Cody leaped down, careened into the paunchy man, said curtly, 'Grab the horses' heads or they'll be hell to pay!' He broke into a run, following the way Andy Jenkins had gone, leaping the fallen tree, stooping and running on along the road. Like Long Peters before him he was ardently if mutely praying for even a fleeting glimpse of one of the highwaymen.

He heard Ann screaming after him,

'Mr. Cody! Come back! You'll be killed!'

'Get back inside!' he shouted at her. 'Dammit, *get inside*!'

The paunchy man—his name was Bert Nevers—had the leaders by the bits and was steadying them; a man to take orders. With Ann it was different; when it came to issuing orders she'd rather be issuing them.

Then, ten steps ahead of him, Cody saw Andy Jenkins. The little man had dropped his bag and had a gun in each hand and was blazing away with both. Then he, too, dropped, just as Long Peters had folded up. And then at long last Cole Cody got his glimpse of the man with the deep voice, and saw the bulk of him, looking like a squat giant with the shadows about him.

The target was none too good, yet there was a murderous devil to shoot at and Cole Cody set to work with all the grim joy in life. The bulky man stood his ground a moment, firing back, and Cody heard the hiss of bullets fanning his ears. Throughout this he was vaguely conscious of other sounds; voices shouting behind him, Ann's among the others; the quick beat of a horse's hoofs, pounding up a small thunder. There in swift flight went the other man, the one who had fired the first shot from behind a pine tree. But Cody's present duty lay straight in front, and he sent bullet after questing bullet, striving to beat down the black bulk before him. He heard also the heavy booming voice yelling at his companion, 'Hey you! What the hell—' Cody steadied and fired again, and this time heard a cry stricken out of his man, and exulted; he had put at least one shot home! Then in the general blur he lost sight of his quarry and heard his running boots crashing through the brush, and an instant later heard the pounding of a second horse's flying hoofs. He emptied his guns into the dark, sending after them a yell of angry mockery. No further shots came back. The wild staccato of running hoofbeats died swiftly away and for an instant the starry night was filled with the hush of the vast wilderness silence.

Then there was another sound; light running footsteps coming up behind him, and Ann Lee was clutching his arm.

'You're all right? You're not hurt? Why didn't you stop when I—Oh, you were splendid!'

'Run back to the stage, Ann! We're not sure yet; there may be more of them—'

Head down, he was busy fingering cartridges up out of his belt, shoving them in hot haste into his two guns. He stood a moment, straining his ears against the silence. There was not a sound that did not come from behind him, from the stage, its occupants and nervous horses. It would seem that the party

50

was over. He was sure that one of the bandits was wounded; possibly the other, too? He walked to where the little man, Andy Jenkins, had fallen.

Jenkins was sitting up, one hand a prop on the ground, the other pressed against his side. By the time Cole Cody stooped over him, the girl was with him.

'Hurt bad, Jenkins?' asked Cody.

'Hurts like hell, yep. And I'm bleedin' buckets of blood. I'm all right though; lend me a hand to stop the bleedin'.'

Cody stooped and picked the little man up, cradling him gently in his arms.

'Get his carpet-bag and his guns,' he told the girl. 'Then run ahead and get a lantern lit.'

It was the slight and delicate looking Miss Jenifer Edwards who was the greatest help from then on. After Cody had lifted the little man into the stage and Ann had brought the lantern, Aunt Jenifer, with her skirts tucked up really scandalously high to be quite out of the way, and her poke bonnet tossed aside and her sleeves rolled up on her slim white arms—and the corners of her mouth tucked in—set to work methodically and yet swiftly, and skilfully withal.

'He'll be all right,' she said calmly as she cleared the way for action and examined and cleansed the wound. (The paunchy man, Bert Nevers, had a bottle of whisky which was used copiously both externally and internally.) 'Get

51

the driver in here.'

Long Peters brought himself in, cursing savagely at every step and sounding hale and hearty in the process. He had been shot through the gun arm; that was what made him mad!

Cody and Bert Nevers, using their hands and the stage ax, cleared away the tree; the wounded men were stowed inside; Cody climbed to the high seat and gathered up the reins—and when he called out, 'All aboard?' he saw someone climbing up over the wheel to sit with him. The paunchy man, of course. Only it wasn't Bert Nevers or anyone in the least resembling him in any respect whatever!

Cole Cody threw out his whip in a long hissing flourish, bringing it up with a snap like a pistol shot.

CHAPTER SIX

And so, at least in so far as Mr. William Cole Cody and Miss Ann Lee were concerned, all was well and the night was filled with beauty. There was little talk between them; at first just a few words referring to what had just happened, then silence. The high seat of a lurching mountain stage is at no time the ideal spot for any steady flow of conversation; further, just now Cole Cody, driving a team new to him, the horses still of a mood to jam their necks deep into their collars and take the bits in their teeth and run away, had his work cut out for him—then, too, he had to keep his eyes focused watchfully on a road none too good, full of bends and kinks and spotted with chuck holes and crossed by ridges and hollows, a tricky road by daylight to a man familiar with it, far worse than that by nightlight to a stranger.

He had buckled the stage driver's leather belt about him for anchorage; the girl kept a hand locked on the iron guard rail at the back of the seat. But whereas he had to watch the road, she was free to watch him out of the corners of her eyes. There were times when his profile was defined against the light of the stars, his hat brim blown back from his forehead and the thick red-black hair above it, and there was a little approving half-smile on her lips. At times with the swaying of the stagecoach her sleeve brushed his; she was warmly aware of the slight contact. She approved of this young man, of the way he looked and the way he walked and talked and bore himself; the way he acted. She felt a little pin-prick of guilt: To be feeling so richly content—she had caught herself starting to hum a silly little song under her breath!—with those two men so sorely wounded, certainly in pain, so close to her.

Unconsciously she drew a long, quivering

sigh—

And it was just at that moment, as the stage having rocked through a bit of starlit clearing was about to plunge into another of the dark, forested canyons, that Cole Cody put on his brakes and pulled his horses down, and said hastily—his voice sounded curt to her,

'Look here! You've got to get down and ride inside!'

'Oh!' she said. She whipped back from him, as far away as the seat allowed. She was having such a wonderful ride! The wind in her face, her hat blown back and the wind in her hair, her lips partly opened to let the cool fresh air stream across them—living only in the moment, looking less at the dark world about her than at the glitter of the heavens above. So she said, 'Oh!', an 'Oh' like an icicle.

He was still slowing his team down, not looking at her but straight ahead.

'And tell Bert Nevers I want him up here with me. You can help your aunt with the two wounded men.'

What a crude sort of beast he really was. She no longer felt the cool air against her face; her cheeks were burning hot. She bit her lip before she spoke. Then her voice sounded gay and it also sounded quite determined.

'But I prefer to ride outside. It was stuffy in there and I like the wind in my face. I was miles away, thinking—'

He had the horses at a restless standstill

54

now and turned briefly toward her.

'I've been a fool,' he muttered. 'I wasn't thinking—'

'I've heard that all men are fools,' she said brightly. 'Are you going to drive on? I am not getting down!'

'I tell you, I wasn't thinking!' He was urgent, and sounded harsh. His eyes had only flicked at her, then turned ahead again, to the road entering the deeper dark in the canyon. 'Just because those two highwaymen rode off doesn't necessarily mean that they've gone for good. They may waylay us again. You mustn't be up here! Let Bert Nevers come up; if there's any trouble he can use Long Peters' carbine.'

'You know very well, Mr. Cody, that those two cowards are miles from here by this time! Besides, you know that you wounded one of them!' She reached behind the seat and lifted the carbine from its place, cuddling it across her lap. 'And I know how to shoot. Drive on, Coachman!'

'Damn it, no!' said Cody, and really was short with her this time. He should have pleaded but instead he was commanding, hardly realizing it. The trouble with him was that suddenly he was all nerves, as nervous as a cat, because his eyes on the dark road were beginning to trick him; he could fancy he saw those two men sitting their horses there, slowly lifting their rifles—he could fancy the crack of the two explosions, the whine of lead—a bullet driven into that tender pink and white loveliness sharing the danger seat with him. He was in haste to have her inside the coach. So he said, and was sterner than he realized, 'You must do what I tell you. And hurry. We don't know that they are gone—we don't know anything. No use being fools! Hurry! And send Nevers to me.'

Hotter than ever did her cheeks burn. There was the slightest quiver in her voice as she said crisply:

'I won't do it! I am going to stay here. Whether you like it or don't like it, Mr. Cody, I am staying here!'

'You'll do nothing of the kind. Dammit! Look here, Miss Lee—'

'Don't you swear at me! And I won't look. And I won't get down dammit!'

'I'll make you get down! I'll drag you off the seat and throw you inside!'

She laughed at him, treating him to her scorn at its best.

'You just try it!'

He put one hand on her shoulder, the other busied with the reins—and Miss Ann Lee slapped his face. Good and hard. And his temper blew off the lid. Lord, Lordy, this girl was the most unreasonable little chit of a thing that was ever born to drive a man mad.

He yielded to the urge within him and caught her hard and fast in the circle of his free arm and drew her astonished body close to him—and kissed her on the mouth. Good and hard. A kiss every bit as emphatic as a slap.

She gasped and jerked away and scrubbed her mouth with her hand and then with all her might she slapped him again! The blow jarred him; after it was over he could feel the shape of her hand, fingers and all, etched in fire along his cheek and jaw. For an instant he sat rigid. Then again he dragged her to him and again he kissed her, and it was a long kiss, his lips crushing hers, before he would let her go.

'I didn't do that for any fun I get out of it,' he told her in a cold fury. 'It's just the best way I know to slap you back, you little hell cat.'

And, making sure that she saw, he scrubbed his lips savagely with the back of his hand . . .

And she slapped him! And, as he was reaching out for her she let the carbine slide off her lap and scrambled out of the seat and half leaped, half fell over the wheel to the ground.

Aunt Jenifer's voice called up, 'What's wrong? Why are we stopping?'

He took a long breath to steady himself, then answered.

'I just saw a wild cat. Oh, never mind! We'll be going right on. I want Bert Nevers up here with me. Miss Lee will ride inside after this.'

Bert Nevers came as desired, retrieved the fallen gun, climbed up beside the driver.

'What the hell's this about wild cats?' he demanded.

Cody threw off the brake and started. A scream stopped him. It was Aunt Jenifer.

'Mr. Cody! What on earth! Ann isn't even in yet.'

'That's all right, Aunt Jenny,' said Ann's voice—if it really was Ann's! 'I could walk from here.—Thank you for waiting, Mr. Cody. I hesitated because I thought I just saw a skunk!'

Then she got into the stage.

'Oh, hell!' said William Cole Cody. And from that spot on into Bald Eagle the stage horses probably made the best time they had ever made in their lives.

CHAPTER SEVEN

The two old porch-sitters in front of the Bald Eagle Hotel smoked and sat in a companionably gloomy silence. They didn't once mention Early Bill Cole. But like the Irishman's parrot who didn't talk, they did a lot of thinking. They had known for a long while that Early Bill had seen his last roundup, had watched his last spring come in and bloom out into young golden summer, and yet now that he was gone they missed him as neither of them had ever realized they could miss an old reprobate like Bill Cole. Up until the very last, up until the sod fell an him he had represented something that had meant a very great deal in the lives of these two silent old men. They, too, were getting along; they thought of that, too. There are certain men like wild Bill Cole who, no matter the hoary accumulation of years, remain so full of life, such positive, dominant characters, that it is next door to impossible getting over the wonder of the thing, that they have actually rolled their blankets and looked over their shoulders, and grinned and waved at you, and gone away for the last time.

Even Bald Eagle into which he had ridden hell-bent so many and many a time, where he had dragged his big Mexican spurs clanking along the wooden sidewalks, where he had stamped and laughed and cursed and caroused and sung—Ah, a great voice had old Early Bill when the mood was on him!—seemed a different town now, pale and insipid and emasculated.

It was early dark, a couple of hours after sunset, and fitful music blared and died in the saloons—accordion and music box and somewhere the scraping of an inaccurate, languid fiddle; men went up and down, stopping in small knots now and then for an exchange of old news; everything was quiet yet mildly expectant, for it was stage-day and time now any minute for Long Peters to swing his racing team into Main Street and pull up in front of the hotel in a great billowing volume of dust. Once in a while a man here and there looked at his watch if he had one, or asked a friend; it was beginning to be remarked that the stage was later than usual when a voice sang out, 'Here she comes!'

The stage came lurching and rocking around the bend, the four horses at the run, and pulled up at its usual place. That was because Bert Nevers had instructed the stranger-driver. Men caught the horses by the bits; Cole Cody tossed his reins far out to right and left, socketed his whip and got down. He ran briskly up the steps and confronted the Judge and Doc Joe.

'There are a couple of men in the stage who've been hurt,' he said crisply. 'Where'll I find a doctor?'

'Who the hell are you? Where's Long Peters?' demanded the Judge.

'Long Peters is one of the men that got hurt. Both of them want a doctor right away.'

Doc Joe stood up.

'Get the men inside,' he said. 'I'll go ahead and have a room ready.' He went into the hotel.

The Judge threw away his cigar and reached to his pocket.

'Bad hurt?' he asked, and stood up.'

'Not Peters. The other man, Andy Jenkins is the other, I'm afraid he's in pretty bad shape.' His eyes had followed the departing Doc Joe.

'He the doctor?'

The Judge nodded and went down the steps to watch proceedings and to direct. Already the stage doors were open, folks were getting down. He saw a couple of females, didn't pay them any attention. He watched Long Peters descend under his own power. Men standing close lifted little Andy Jenkins out; at first they and the Judge, too, thought him dead already. He was carried into the hotel, Long Peters following.

Men were asking rapid-fire questions: Just what had happened? Where? When? The two women, looking a bit bewildered as so many earnest-eager men milled about them, clung to each other and looked for escape. Upon Bert Nevers, known to many here, fell the duty of giving a running account of the hold-up, and Aunt Jenifer and Ann broke free. Some of the men, though still held here to listen to Bert Nevers, followed the two with their appraising eyes.

Cole Cody, standing on the steps leading to the raised platform before the hotel, looked down over the throng a moment. He himself was accosted and asked to tell about everything; curtly he jerked his head toward Bert Nevers.

'He knows all about it; listen to him,' he said, and moved away.

He didn't look back to see Aunt Jenifer and Ann Lee make their way into the hotel lobby.

61

Ann, looking with quick interest in all directions, saw his back; in the swing of his stride and in the set of his shoulders and even in the way he wore his hat she read something of the man's mood. He was still furious; be was impatient to be done with the stage and all it contained, all that it suggested to him. She had the swift impression that he was headed straight for the first saloon and meant to wash a lot of things out of his memory with good strong liquor. She was, in this, quite right.

Young Mr. William Cole Cody felt not only desolate and down-in-the-mouth, but mean and ugly. He made something of entering the Last Chance Saloon; he struck the swing door with his shoulder as a man aswarm through his veins with belligerence might smite an enemy. The half-door, flung violently back, struck a man about to depart and all but swept him off his feet.

This man glared and showed his teeth. Those teeth of his were as white as snow, as glistening as a hound's teeth and about as sharp. He was a small, aged Mexican-Indian, Porfirio Lopez by name, a stranger here in Bald Eagle and, tonight in no mood at all to be knocked around. His slim brown hand ran like the flick of a striking snake to his side—just under his ornamental jacket. It would have been with him just then a supreme joy and a perfectly superb relief to slit somebody's gullet from ear to ear.

And then he saw who it was!

'Don Codito!' he cried. He dropped all thoughts of his knife and caught both Cody's hands in the warm Latin way. *'Gracias a Dios!* Look, *Señor!* Me, all over, I weeshed I was thead! I ask for to thie! And now! I kees your hands, the two!' All of which meant, Thank God! When I was ready to die, here you are! *You!*

'You are drunk, Porfirio,' said Don Codito. 'Go to bed.'

Porfirio laughed like a coyote. He pulled his hair, looked at his hands, saw that he had caught some few harsh black strands between his lean fingers and tossed them upward.

'Boracho, Señor?' That laughter of his showed those teeth of his to all advantage; and still in his laughter there was the snarl of a coyote, the threat and surrender of a wounded wolf. He said quite simply, 'This is one other time, Señor Don Codito, you save my life. We are going to drink one with the other. You will honor me in this little thing, this thing that is so big, Don Codito?'

Codito, according to Porfirio Lopez's manner of thought, meant Little Cody. And Little Cody had known Porfirio since Little Cody was five. He slid his arm through the wizened Mexican-Indian's, tensed his muscles friendliwise and the two went to the bar.

Porfirio began, frank and unhidden in all he did, to cry. He whipped an enormous red-and-green bandana from his coattails, gave it a flourish which made a sort of rainbow arc of the gesture, and wiped his streaming eyes.

'Pretty soon,' he confessed, 'I am going to cry like one babee. The fines' man in this wor!', the fines' man, I am a-tellin' you, is sick; he is pretty dam' sick.' (Only Porfirio said 'seek.') 'He is goin' to die! Aie! I jump on top my bes' horse, an' I ride an' I ride an' I ride like hell, Señor. You believe me? More than one hundred, more than one hundred and twenty-five, more than one hundred and fifty (feefty) miles, I ride! An' so, here I am—an' he is already dead!' He put his head down on the bar and let his tears run at large.

Cole Cody looked at the bowed shoulders a moment, then very gently set a large hand on them. He knew his Porfirio Lopez; he knew that the little man, despite his extravagancies, was suffering from an irreparable loss.

'I'm sorry, Porfirio,' he said in voice as gentle as his heavy hand.

Porfirio jerked up his head, tossed back his black mane of hair, getting it cleared away from his burning black eyes—and began to laugh.

He snatched up his glass.

'We drink together, you and me, Señor Codito! To one gr-reat gentleman! To one of the soldiers of the good God Himself! To Don Señor Early Bill Cole! To him, forever and ever, *"Salud y pesetas!"* To Don Señor! Early

Bill Cole!'

Then Cole Cody, forgetting other things, gripped him by the thin shoulders.

'What are you talking about?' he demanded sharply. 'Early Bill Cole? Of the King Cole Ranch? You say he is dead?'

'Only two days ago, Don Codito. And so I am two days too late to see him one more time. He—'

'But I had a letter from him, Porfirio, only a few days ago! And dead now!'

'He was old, Señor, and he was sick and everbod' has sometime to die. But he was tough, too, like saddle leather! Maybe he would live another ten years, who knows? Then some sneaking *cabrone* shoots him out of the dark!' He rolled his wet black eyes heavenward, and his lips moved silently. Then he explained: 'I am praying the good God, Don Codito, that some day I find out who did that to that nice good old man!'

Here was news! Cole Cody stood frowning at nothing, telling himself that all along this had been a funny howdy-do: First the letter from old Early Bill, which he had been utterly unable to explain; now the violent removal of the only man who could tell him. Well, he'd go to the hotel over night, then in the morning turn tail and leave Bald Eagle and a lot of unanswered questions behind him. Along with a girl he never wanted to see again.

He lifted his glass.

65

'We drink together to Don Señor Early Bill Cole!' cried little Porfirio, and snatched off his hat. 'The two of us together.'

Cody politely removed his own hat and the two drank together. Then, with that darting swiftness so characteristic of him, Porfirio snatched Cody's glass and tapped it gently with the haft of his evil-looking knife, rendering it into splintered fragments. Before the bartender could bear down on him he had repeated the performance with his own glass.

'Hey, what the hell!'

Porfirio slammed down a ten dollar gold coin.

'I pay for the glasses and for the drinks, too, Señor,' he said quietly, and the bartender, having taken stock of Porfirio's eyes and of his knife, let the incident pass.

'Set 'em up again,' said Cody.

'No more wrecking glasses?'

'No.' He and Porfirio touched glasses. 'I'm sorry, Porfirio,' said Cody gently. 'Sorry you've lost a friend. What are you going to do now? Going home?'

Porfirio shrugged

'What else to do? But I am not going too quick. You see, Señor, a long time ago this Señor Cole told me anytime I liked I could come to live and die in his rancho. So this time I thought to come and stay. You know my little place, only one hundred and sixty acres? I sold him. That is why I have some money left in my

66

pocket. So there is no hurry I go back. A few days I am going to stay. Who knows? If somehow I can find out who the man was that shot him—'

'I see. Well, Porfirio, I won't be seeing you for a while. I'm off early in the morning. But first come have some supper with me. We'll talk.'

It was far too early for bed, so he and Porfirio Lopez dawdled over their supper in one of Bald Eagle's little restaurants for the better part of an hour, and thereafter set out to see the town. There was little enough of it to see, but they looked in at one bar-room after another, watched some of the games running and had a couple of after-supper drinks. Porfirio was not tonight the best of companions, but grew steadily gloomier and was eternally on the verge of tears, and Cody was about to call it a night and go off to bed when he was accosted by a lean and wiry old man with a mane of snowy hair and a mammoth, unpruned white mustache, with a broad and battered old black hat and sleek high-heeled boots and a long-tailed black coat. None other, in fact, than Mr. Arthur Henry Pope—the Judge.

'Mr. William Cole Cody, I believe?' he said sonorously.

Cole Cody looked him over, and nodded.

'That's my name, sir,' he said.

'And I, sir, am Arthur Henry Pope. I know

something about you; not much, but something. And I'd be glad to shake hands, sir.'

Cody obliged him, studied him more closely than before and was set wondering. He didn't ask any questions with his lips; his eyes however were filled with frank inquiry.

'I'd just like a few words with you, Mr. Cody,' said the Judge. 'In private.'

'I'm with a friend—'

'The matter is of importance. Also of an entirely private nature—'

'Go 'long with him, Don Codito,' said Porfirio, and began a discreet withdrawal. 'He is a man they call the Judge here. He is all right, you will see, because they tell me he was a very good friend of Don Señor Early Bill Cole.' Then Porfirio bolted, headed for the bar, again flourishing his colorful bandana.

'What is it?' asked Cody.

'I have taken a room for you at the hotel where you'll want to stay overnight. Will you step over with me?'

'Certainly,' agreed Cody, his curiosity now riding high, and the two went out together.

Not a word was spoken by either until after they arrived at the hotel. As they entered the front door Cody caught a glimpse of the girl of the stage; she and her aunt were going up the stairs from the lobby, and were escorted by a gray old man of a like vintage with the Judge's. The girl, before passing out of sight, turned

68

and looked down. She didn't look away from him when her eyes came to rest on him, nor could it strictly be said that she looked at him. She succeeded beautifully in making him feel that he merely happened to be in the way and she looked through him as she might have looked through a window.

*   *   *

A bit earlier in the evening, the Judge and Doc Joe having a few moments together on their porch after Doc Joe had tinkered with his new patients as best he could and got them off to their beds, the Judge had been led to remark with a snort,

'Old Early Bill, confound his ornery hide, having sworn by all that was good and holy he'd get him his fun after he was dead, ought to be laughing his fool head off now! It's a mess, Doc, and it's going to be a hell-sight messier, and that cussed fool old Bill Cole ought to be ashamed of himself.'

In his turn Doc Joe had snorted. 'The fools were you and me, Judge,' he growled. 'Two damn softies, a couple of mush-hearted sissies. We ought to have stood up on our hind legs and told him to go to hell.—Well, I reckon that's where he is now, and serve him right.'

All this was because before his demise old Early Bill had instructed this precious duo, laying down the law to them and exacting their

69

promises to carry out his bidding. If he died before his 'heirs' arrived, the Judge and Doc Joe were to look out for the two, and were to tell them just as much as Early Bill wanted told, not a single syllable more. Doc Joe was to explain matters to the girl, the Judge was to do likewise for young Cody. And they were tot unduly to stick their noses into subsequent happenings. 'Let nature take its course!' old Bill Cole had chuckled.

'Dammit, man,' the Judge had once started to expostulate, 'if you're trying to set a trap to make these two young folks marry each other, if you're set on bribing 'em to do just that, why not say in your will—*one* will, dammit!—that they are—'

That was as far as old Early Bill had let him go.

And now the Judge and Doc Joe, having in due course learned that both Cole Cody and Ann Lee were on the stage, were faithfully if irreverently carrying out orders.

Thus, while Doc Joe was expounding to a round-eyed, breathless girl and her quietly attentive Aunt Jenifer in one room of the Bald Eagle Hotel, the Judge was letting head and ears of the cat out of the bag for the astounding of William Cole Cody in another room.

'And that's the way of it,' concluded Doc Joe, glad to be at the end of the crazy business, and opened a carpetbag at his feet, took from it an old iron box from which long ago the black paint had scaled, and set it down on Miss Ann Lee's knees.

'But—but—' the girl sputtered. 'I can't understand it! 'This Mr. Early Bill Cole you are talking about—Why, I didn't know him! I never saw him even, in my life! I never heard of him! Of course, Doctor, there is some mistake. It must be some other girl—some other girl, maybe, named Lee. Maybe even named—'

'There may be a lot of mistakes in this whole deal,' the old doctor grunted, 'but that's not one of them. You're the girl all right.— Say, haven't you got the key!'

'The key! Why, of course I have!' She jumped up, the box in her hands, and ran to the walnut bureau; she pulled and tugged until she got the lop-sided top drawer open and extracted her purse. 'Here is the key! He sent it to me with a letter that made me terribly curious, saying some things, half-saying some, leaving out the things I was dying to know!'

'That would be old Early Bill for you,' said Doc Joe tartly. 'And I reckon that's the key all right. You might try it.'

She was all eagerness and excitement, and her fingers wouldn't behave properly. At last, however, with Doc Joe come to stand over her and her aunt sitting as still as any mouse, her hands placid in her lap, she got the key in one of the locks. It fitted! It turned easily.

'It is the right key!' she exclaimed, and tried it in the other lock. Doc Joe watched her shrewdly as she struggled with the thing, an expression of intense concentration puckering her face. She withdrew the key, looked at it, stooped over the box again, tossing her head impatiently to throw the hair back from falling over her eyes. 'Something's the matter with the crazy thing,' she said, baffled. 'Will you try it, Doctor?'

He shook his head. 'No use, Miss Ann. One thing I didn't tell you. Your key fits only one of the two locks. There's another key. It—ahem!—it's being kept by someone else. A man that old Early Bill trusted it to. You can't open your box until he shows up.'

'Why, isn't that funny! Who is this man? Is he here in Bald Eagle? When will he give me the other key?'

Doc Joe was already edging toward the door.

'You take mighty good care of that box, Miss Ann,' he said hurriedly. 'Just you remember that it's worth a power of money! The whole King Cole Ranch is in there—and a heap of gold and greenbacks besides! Just you take mighty good care of it, Miss Ann. And now, good night to you, Miss. And to you also, Miss Jenifer,' he said, and ducked out and fled.

He left Ann fairly dancing with thwarted curiosity. To have an iron box bulging with mysteries—to have a key to the darned thing—

72

not to be able to do a thing about it until the other key showed up—a key being kept by some man or other—

'I could scream!' she told Aunt Jenifer.

'So I notice,' said Aunt Jenifer mildly. 'But don't you dare.' She got up and began unfastening a lacy flounce about her throat. 'As for me, my pet, I could sleep. It's been quite a day, if you ask me.'

'*Sleep!*' wailed little Ann Lee. 'I was never so excited—' She began shaking the box, holding it to her ear. 'I bet the darned thing is empty!' she exclaimed petulantly.

'No, you won't find it empty. And when you told Doc Joe, my pet, that you had never even heard of Early Bill Cole, you maybe thought you were telling the truth but you weren't. You heard a lot of him, but it was a long time ago; maybe when you were five years old! Can't very well blame you for disremembering! He was the finest friend your daddy ever had. That's why all along I favored your doing what he said in his letter. It's my notion, Ann Lee, that he's made a very rich young woman of the school mistress of Long Valley School.' Then she actually yawned.

Her niece looked at her suspiciously. Then she left the box on the table and ran to throw her arms about her.

'That yawn of yours was pure fake, and you know it,' she cried laughing, very gay. 'You're an old fraud and you know that, too! You are just on fire, like me, to know what it's all about!'

'Shucks,' said Aunt Jenifer. 'Here, stop smothering me, and unhook me.'

* * *

And in that other room under the same roof the Judge had finished imparting to young Cody all the facts in the case which he had been authorized to make fairly clear. Cody had heard him out in silence, his eyes dark between narrowed lids, his face stilled to expressionlessness. And when the Judge, too, grew silent Cody still sat on a moment or two, pondering.

'Thanks, Judge,' he said. 'I guess that's all you've got to tell me? Wouldn't do much good to start asking questions?'

The Judge rather liked him for that. Well, old Bill Cole had liked the boy, and old Early Bill knew his onions—and his men.

He shook his head, ready to go.

'Come to me later, if you want to,' he said. 'I'm hoping that things will work out all right for you. Maybe they will. That's what that infernal old devil wanted. Nope, my boy; nothing to add. You just poke on out to the King Cole Ranch tomorrow. 'Night, Cody.'

Cody showed him to the door, then came back and sat on the edge of his bed and looked over the letter he had brought along with him, the mystifying communication from a perfect stranger, a man he did not know that he had ever seen, one of whom everyone had heard many a wild tale. Old Early Bill Cole. King Cole of the King Cole Ranch.—Cole! William Cole! And he himself was William Cole Cody—

'It's got me stumped,' said William Cole Cody. 'And somehow, though I never knew the old pirate, like Porfirio Lopez, I'm downright sad he's dead.'

Having thought again of Porfirio, he pocketed letter and key, and went out to find him. He'd keep Porfirio with him for a spell.

CHAPTER EIGHT

No, she couldn't sleep. Who could, she wanted to know, at a time like this? Though little Ann Lee got to bed alongside Aunt Jenifer, and blew out the lamp and did doze now and again, it was always to start wide awake, to sit up and stare with big eyes into the dark, to ask herself all sorts of answerless questions, to grope under her pillow for the iron box. And several times she got up and lighted the lamp, turning it low, and moved restlessly about the room, going to the window, peeking out at the stars, wondering why day was so long coming. She stood over the bed and looked keenly and

75

a thought suspiciously at Aunt Jenifer. Aunt Jenifer, as she had declared and as she had suspected many the time, was a humbug; right now, like as not, she wasn't asleep at all but just playing possum.

So it was in no wise strange that the first human being in Bald Eagle to be wide awake and up and about was Miss Ann Lee, and that the second, due to her machinations, was Miss Jenifer Edwards. The two breakfasted when it was not yet full day at the lunch counter on the corner where the Chinese cook had only brought the first pot of coffee to its amber aromatic perfection. Then in all haste to the livery stable for a buggy—and then at a good round clip for the two hours' drive out to the King Cole Ranch.

The dusty white road wound through the little hills whose still green, parklike slopes were dotted with tall pines and spreading oaks, then dived deep into a dusky ravine murmurous with the soft chuckling laughter of a secret creek, then rose among steeper hills and poured itself out upon a high valley cradled on the lower slopes of the mountains. This was Sunlight Valley, a lovely, smiling and serene Edenic valley with a wavering ribbon of racing silver water cleaving through it, with the walls of the hills about it, with twin waterfalls flashing down at its upper end. 'Glorious!' gasped Ann Lee, as the sun touched the faraway cascading waters, and did not know

76

that already she was upon the outermost fringe of the great spread of the King Cole Ranch.

Their road, narrow and crooked and steep at times, led them through a shadowy pass and brought them up upon the rim of a broad and softly undulating plateau; here again was water, plenty of it, for it was from this tableland that the creek which they had been following spilled down into Sunlight Valley, and the plateau toward the north became a sort of valley itself, with forested mountainous slopes hanging over it upon the east, with a bulwark of rugged hills, running down in a long broken spur from the higher ranges shouldering up, also black in the morning with coniferous timber in the west. A herd of horses, young mares with their colts, pricked forward their ears and watched them from a meadow deep in grass and sprinkled with the flowers which had not departed with departing spring; from afar they heard the sonorous, lusty bellowing of a bull; through a break in the timber across the creek they saw a small herd of fat cattle; as their road, a mere trace of infrequent wheels, swerved about a grove of live oaks, they saw, still a mile away, the ranch headquarters. And again the girl, athrill this morning, exclaimed as in an ecstasy:

'Look! Oh, lovely!'

After all, those first comers to pastoral California, those who came here to make their homes, not merely to wrest gold from the

77

ground and rush off with it somewhere else, the *padres* who established the missions, and the pioneer Spaniards who builded them their small, snug kingdoms, had their unrestricted choice of locations and were never satisfied until they could say, Here is the spot that has everything! A broad, unsurpassed view; a sense of space unlimited, 'elbow room,' fertility all around like a great ocean; clean, sweet water sweeping past your door; game in the hills and fish in the streams—and a song in your heart.

There, upon its gentle knoll, its white-washed *adobe* walls a snowy, gleaming white in the distance under the eastern sun, the old Casa of the Estradas, the home for many a year of Bill Cole of King Cole Ranch, was like an alabaster palace out of a fairy tale—or so declared Miss Ann Lee, fascinated, athrob with all sorts of bright anticipation. Beyond it the pines, below it the grove and the almost hidden outbuildings, the old house itself smiling welcome. And all about it, rippling away into distances, broken here and there by timber with occasional vistas through it, the verdant pattern of the far-reaching acres.

The low, massive building was surrounded by a wall akin in construction to itself, a wall of *adobe*, whitewashed, topped with warm red tiles. There was a hitching rail under an oak. The wall was pierced by narrow gateways through which glimpses of an unkempt tangle of orchard and garden, ill-kept and

78

picturesque, were afforded. Ann Lee, leading the way, her carpet-bag containing the precious iron box caught tight under her arm, threw open a gate and hurried along one of the paths radiating from the old house. And Aunt Jenifer, her cheeks almost as pink as her niece's, her eyes almost as bright, came hurrying after her.

The place seemed deserted. There was no lift of smoke from any of the several chimneys, no one stirring within sight, no sound to disturb the hush of remoteness and solitude which seemed to pervade the air. The two women came to the *patio*, a spot of ineffable charm as so many of the old Spanish *patio*s are, and stood very still; it was as though they found in the silence a gentle command for like silence on their part. Unconsciously on tiptoes the girl approached the arched doorway confronting her and lifted her hand almost timidly to the dangling bellcord. She gave it a quick tug; within the house a bell clanged, and she started back at the sound.

No one came.

In their talk last night with Doc Joe neither one of them, with so much else to think about, had thought to ask who was occupying the old home now that Early Bill Cole had left it, so for a moment they stood looking at each other, wondering about that. Perhaps he was no one here? They had glimpsed the outbuildings, barns and men's quarters, and began to think that probably anyone now living upon the ranch was domiciled there.

'Try it again, Ann,' said Aunt Jenifer. 'It's kind of early, you know. If there's anyone here they might be asleep yet.'

'I guess we are pretty early,' said Ann, hesitant now.

'What if we are? Honest folk should be abed early so they can get up early.'

She herself reached for the bell cord and gave it an emphatic yank setting the bell echoing through the house. A man's voice—they were sure they had brought him rudely out of sound sleep—called out,

'Hello, who's there?' And then, without awaiting an answer, 'Wait a shake: I'll be right out.'

'I wonder who he is? A caretaker, maybe?'

They had to wait more than a minute. Aunt Jenifer sat on the green oaken bench beside the door and folded her small, sensitive hands in her lap and looked about her, through the garden and out over the walls and to the timbered reaches of the hills with a complacent satisfaction. She thought, It's next door to heaven here. How could old Bill Cole have been all his life such a heller?

At long last they heard a heavy bar let down, and the door opened slowly only a dozen inches or so. A tall young man looked out at them. Himself in the shadowy interior of the house, they could make but little of him at

80

first; his face was scarcely more than to be guessed at under his broad brimmed hat; he was fully dressed and booted and had buckled on his cartridge belt from which two large caliber guns depended. And all this struck them as a bit queer; surely they had awakened him and he had taken time for this full equipment.

Whereas, they could not make him out over clearly, he had no difficulty in seeing what they looked like. Instantly he threw the door wide open. He spoke affably, saying,

'Good morning, ladies! This is a surprise! You're twice as welcome as the birds in spring. Come in, won't you?'

They entered just a trifle hesitantly, the house was so dark and, at the moment, somehow sinister and forbidding. But that was only because all the shades had been drawn down and it was dark in there after the sunshine outside. He said pleasantly, 'Just a second and we'll have some light in,' and went to one window after another flipping up the shades. The sunlight streamed in joyously; of a sudden, with the dark put to flight, it became a genial and friendly room, aforetime the homey and yet dignified main *sala* of the old Spanish home, the fitting lair of late years of the old bachelor, Early Bill Cole. The red and black Navajo rugs were gay and warm, the few chairs deep and intimate and comfortable, bright with their colored cushions.

And now they could see Rance Waldron clearly. He's a handsome devil, thought little Ann Lee. He looks nice and friendly though, and I like him. And Aunt Jenifer formed her own impression: How shrewdly, almost suspiciously he is looking at us! That man has got something on his mind!

He offered chairs and they sat down. Then Ann looked swiftly and a trifle pleadingly at her aunt; she didn't know just how and where to begin. But Aunt Jenifer only smiled at her and smiled at Rance Waldron and sat silent. So Ann cleared her throat and made her beginning.

'I am Ann Lee and this is my Aunt, Miss Jenifer Edwards. We had an invitation from— from Mr. William Cole to visit him here. We got to Bald Eagle only last night and now— Well,' and she too smiled faintly, 'here we are!'

'I see.' He nodded and regarded her gravely. 'You have heard?'

'Oh, yes! We are terribly sorry, of course— even though we didn't know Mr. Cole personally. But we thought we had better come on out to the ranch anyhow—'

He nodded again; he seemed, she thought, most sympathetically understanding.

'I am taking care of things right now,' he said. 'I was lucky to get here just before my uncle died.'

'Your uncle?' spoke up Aunt Jenifer. 'Old Bill Cole was your uncle?'

Rance made a little deprecatory gesture.

'I've always called him that,' he said easily. 'Not an uncle exactly, but related. I am, I believe, his next of kin; his only kinsman, in fact. I am Rance Waldron; my mother and the old man were cousins. It's because of that,' and he lifted his broad shoulders in the hint of a shrug, 'that I am staying on here. Unless there is a will, and I don't believe he ever made a will, I suppose I am the next owner here.'

At the mention of a will, Ann's lips were parted to speak up, but by the time he had added a final clause she had become conscious of Aunt Jenifer's eyes stabbing warningly at her. And so she sat very still, her foot pressed down tightly on the carpetbag she had placed close to her chair, wishing for the first time that she had made Doc Joe come along out here with them.

Aunt Jenifer said, 'It's a mighty nice place out here. He wanted us to visit him for a while. We've come a long way, too, over a hundred miles. We got to town last night on the stage.'

What she was driving at was obvious enough, and there didn't seem very much he could do about it. Had it just been the older woman alone, Rance Waldron might have been the man for putting her out bodily; his eyes, however, quitted her face while she was still speaking and drifted, openly admiring, to Ann's. He said with a semblance of heartiness,

'Well, the thing that counts is that you're

83

here now! And I am glad that I happened to be on hand to welcome you in my uncle's place. And I'll bet you haven't even had breakfast yet. I know I haven't. '

'You're a late sleeper,' said Aunt Jenifer.

'I worked late last night, going over some papers. Naturally there will be a lot to do in order to get everything straightened out. I suppose I'll have to call a lawyer in, but that can come later, after I've ransacked the place for all papers, accounts, deeds or notes or whatever turns up. The old man, I've a notion, didn't care whether he kept such things straight or not. But how about a cup of coffee and some bacon and flapjacks?'

'We had a bite before we left Bald Eagle,' said Aunt Jenifer, taking it upon herself briefly to do the talking in order to give Ann a moment to size up the situation, 'but I do declare I would like another cup of coffee.'

'I'm all alone here,' said Rance. 'If you can stand for the sort of cooking I can do—'

'Will you show me the way to the kitchen?' asked Aunt Jenifer. 'I'll be glad to get breakfast for you.'

'Say, that's great!' said Rance.

He showed them the kitchen, a room big enough for a barn, with an enormous cook stove which Early Bill had had installed here many a year ago and which had had scant use for a dozen years, and there were ample provisions, such things mostly as potatoes and beans, hams and bacon and flour, and enough canned goods in the cupboards to stock a country store. There was a big woodbox will supplied with oak wood and splintered pitch pine for kindling. Rance got the fire going while Aunt Jenifer was looking around for something to use for an apron. She didn't meant to spoil her nice new dress in anybody's kitchen.

'Now,' said Aunt Jenifer, sleeves rolled back on a pair of pretty, white arms and a clean sugar sack pinned about her waist, 'you can skedaddle and I'll call you when things are ready.'

'Fair enough,' said Rance. 'I'll go clean up a speck; haven't even washed my face or combed my hair yet!' And he hurried away; they heard his boots echoing through the big rooms with their bare floors and few scatter rugs; they heard a door close, then, from some farther room, another door.

Ann came close to the stove.

'What are we going to do?' she whispered. 'He is related to Mr. Cole; he thinks he is the owner now; he never heard of any will and— He is terribly good looking, isn't he, Aunt Jenny? I like him, don't you? And it's going to seem like stealing from him—'

'So he is good looking, is he?' sniffed Aunt Jenifer, hunting the coffee pot. 'Well, so was our stage friend of yesterday, Mr. Cody, wasn't he?'

'I would be just as glad,' said Ann bitingly, 'if you never mentioned that man to me again!'

'And you like our new friend, do you? That's real nice and it's Christian, too, to like people and strangers at your gate, and all.'

'Why, Aunt Jenny! You *don't* like him! Why?'

'I haven't said any such thing. And if you're asking why—Well, just you wait and watch, my pet. He remembers to wash his face and hands, and he remembers about breakfast—and he doesn't forget to shut doors after him—and he doesn't forget to bar his door at night and pull the shades down—and what I want to know is this: Is he going to forget to put our horse in the barn and give it some hay! You just lift up those heavy eyelashes of yours high enough so you can peek out of your eyes, and watch what happens. And are you going to keep toting that satchel of yours around every step you take?'

Ann clutched it the tighter.

'I'm not going to let it out of my sight, not for one little second, not until that other key— Aunt Jenny! Do you suppose that Rance Waldron is the one with the other key? Why, of course he is! Being Mr. Early Bill's nephew—'

'Son of old Bill's cousin,' corrected Aunt Jenifer. 'Or so he says.'

'My, it's a big house,' said little Ann, 'isn't it? It's the biggest I was ever in, and the nicest.

Just think of that strange man, Mr. Early Bill, living here all alone!'

'He wasn't so much all alone when he was younger, I've heard tell,' said Aunt Jenifer, busy beating up batter. 'Lots of menfolks are like wild animals when they get old; they like to crawl off by themselves and do their moaning and groaning in some sort of privacy!'

'I bet *he* never did any moaning and groaning—Look here, Aunt Jenifer, how do you know so much about him? Saying what he used to do?'

'Everybody's heard a lot about Early Bill Cole,' said Aunt Jenifer.

'Why don't you like Rance Waldron?'

'You'd better be setting the table, hadn't you? Right here in the kitchen. Talk about this being a big, nice house—I never did see the beat of this kitchen! What with all this room to turn about in and the sun shining in, and those deep cool windows where you could set a hundred pies to cool!'

'I bet there are twenty rooms!' said Ann. 'You'd think one man would get terribly lonesome here, wouldn't you? I wonder if they ever used to have dances and gay parties here, using that great big living room? When Old Bill was Young Bill, I mean. I wonder what the bedrooms are like, Aunt Jenny?'

By the time Rance Waldron returned to them—and again they heard the soft closing of at least two doors marking his progress—the table was set under a sunny window and breakfast was ready. He was hatless this time and had combed his hair. He smiled and said briskly, 'Ah! This is the life!' Yet it struck the observant girl, sensitive to shades of expression, that it was just his lips that smiled, and that there was a hint of sternness and of irritation in his eyes.

'So you came in by stage last night?' he said as they sat down and Aunt Jenifer poured the three cups of good hot coffee and served him his breakfast.

Ann nodded, and told him of their adventure on the mountain road, of the fallen tree and the attempted holdup, warming to the recital as all its details thrilled through her again, making much of each little happening— omitting only any particular reference to Mr. William Cole Cody. It was quite as though she had forgotten that such an individual had ever existed. But when she had finished, and her aunt looked sharply at her and sniffed, her face turned red.

Rance heard her out without interruption, then said thoughtfully, 'It's a funny sort of thing, isn't it? Why do you suppose they wanted to stick up the stage if it wasn't carrying a strong box? What do you suppose that the little man—What did you say his name was? Jenkins?—what do you suppose he had on him?'

'We didn't find out,' Ann told him. 'He was

88

badly hurt; he didn't say anything. It must have been a lot of money, though, and the robbers must have known about it somehow.'

'And they made their get-away clean? Without stopping any lead?'

'We couldn't be sure. One of the men—one of the men on the stage thought he had hit one of them. But you couldn't really believe a word he said! Most likely he was just bragging about what a fine shot he was!'

'Well, you folks came through it lucky anyhow!'

'You're not eating much for a strong young man,' observed Aunt Jenifer. 'You ought to be starved like a wolf at this hour of the day!'

He forked at his plate. 'You see I had a snack last night, late, just before I went to bed. This is good, though. How about another cup of coffee?—Who is this man Jenkins?' he asked Ann. 'Seems that I've heard his name mentioned; out here, too. Wasn't he a friend of Early Bill's? Worked for him, or something?'

'We really don't know a thing about him except that he was really very badly wounded, and that he is at the hotel in town now with a doctor they call Doc Joe taking care of him.'

Then for a time talk drifted aimlessly, and in such fashion did breakfast come to an end. As they rose Rance said casually,

'Well, now with things as they are, what do you ladies plan? It must be a terrible disappointment for you not to find your intended host here to receive you. Are you going home right away?'

Aunt Jenifer, offering no help where it was most wanted, began scraping and piling the dishes. Ann hesitated a moment, not knowing just what to say. But she did know that she meant to remain here, at least until she found out whether all that Doc Joe had told her were sober fact—No, not *sober* fact! Wild, delirious, fairy-tale fact, rather!—or the flimsy fabrication of sheer fancy. So in the end she said very quietly, her voice hushed a little yet nevertheless quite determined,

'He asked us to stay here indefinitely. We have made our plans—I suppose we will stay a while anyhow.' And then, suddenly getting those heavy lashes of hers lifted and her eyes straightforwardly upon his, she thought best to add, 'You won't mind, will you?'

In his turn he, too, hesitated. Then he exclaimed, almost yet not quite sounding cordial, 'Why, I could wish for nothing better on earth than to have you stay here for a year! But I'm afraid just now you'd find things awfully dull and dreary, and upset—there's no one here but myself you know, and—Look here! Suppose you rest up a while and later we have a bit of a chat? I want to know you and your aunt better, no matter what happens.'

He showed her the way into the *patio*, flooded now with golden sunshine, Aunt

90

Jenifer saying, 'You go ahead, Ann; I'll come along as soon as I finish the dishes. *No!* I don't want anybody in my way *helping* me!'

'Do you mind!' said Rance when they were outside, 'if I leave you a few moments? As I told you, I was going through a lot of pretty badly messed-up papers and accounts last night. Part of the mess I've got fairly well in mind right now; I think twenty minutes more with it and I could put it away shipshape. I hope you don't mind?'

He hurried away, stopped and headed back to the kitchen.

'I never tasted such coffee,' he told Aunt Jenifer. 'I'm off to my room for a little more study of those papers; I think I'll take another cup along with me.' And, carrying the full cup, he departed.

She stopped what she was doing and stood with her head tipped to one side, listening with all her ears. She had noticed something: Before he had put two spoons of sugar to each cup—this time four. She nodded complacently to herself when she heard for the third time the soft closing of doors.

'Man or woman company, which?' she asked herself. 'I wonder! And what's he scared of?'

Ann, in the *patio*, picked a yellow rose and set it in her hair. 'That's an old Spanish rose,' she told herself. 'And yonder's a moss rose. Funny that a man like old Mr. Early Bill Cole kept them alive! Oh, I wish we'd got here in time!'

Only a moment did she loiter in the *patio* garden; its beauty was all about her, steeped in the rare sweetness of the early morning and she was aware of it, yet her troubled thoughts kept darting away. Suddenly she whirled and scurried back into the house, running to her aunt in the kitchen.

'Aunt Jenny!' she cried reproachfully. 'Why don't you help me? I don't know what to do! He doesn't want us here—he has as good as told us to go—'

'Well, we're not going! Or are we?'

'Of course not! Not, anyhow, until we find out about everything.'

'I don't reckon he'll try to throw us out bodily,' said Aunt Jenifer. 'Just because he might be somehow related to old King Cole doesn't give him the right. Or does it?'

'Why do you talk like that! Always telling me something with one breath, then taking it away to ask me about it in the next! You just do it to drive me wild!'

'Now don't fly into a pet, my pet,' admonished Aunt Jenifer. 'You might lend a hand, now that you've come back, wiping the dishes.'

The girl snatched at a dish at the edge of the table in such fashion that it slipped through her fingers and crashed to the floor.

'Darn the thing!' she cried hotly. 'Darn

92

everything!'

'You're a vixen,' remarked Aunt Jenifer in her mild way. 'I guess you didn't sleep much last night, did you? And you haven't got over your mad yet at that man Cody, have you? And you're a spoiled brat on general principles. That rose looks real pretty in your hair, though. Expecting company? Or did you put it on for Mr. Rance Waldron?'

Ann began laughing and put her round arms about Aunt Jenifer's slim body and gave her a tremedous hug.

'I'll behave, Auntie,' she promised. 'Honestly I will. But I am sort of all stirred up inside. And inside, where I want to be happy, I'm sad, too! Oh, why did that poor Mr. Early Bill have to go and die?'

'He was an old man and he was sick, and on top of that somebody shot him. That's why.'

'You know I didn't mean it that way!'

'Shush! Here comes Mr. Rance again.'

Rance returned and stood in the doorway, looking in upon them gravely.

'I decided to put everything aside for a while,' he said, his eyes flicking from the girl's face to her aunt's, back to Ann's and back again to Jenifer's, as though he were for the first time really taking stock of them, as though he measured them, perhaps to decide which of the two did the thinking and deciding for both. They saw instantly that during these few minutes his mood had altered, hardened; the

93

line of his lips was straight and firm, his eyes were steady and stern.

'You see,' he went on, 'this is really no place for you people at this particular time. I couldn't pretend to make it pleasant for you—under the circumstances. What I should like very much would be for you to come back out here in a few days and be my guests. I'll be coming into Bald Eagle; you'll be staying there at the hotel for a while? I could pick you up and bring you out again.'

'My! You do sound hospitable!' said Aunt Jenifer.

He frowned at that. 'My dear lady,' he said curtly, 'just how hospitable I sound has nothing to do with it. You were invited, you tell me, by old Bill Cole. Well, he's dead and gone, and as far as I know that's the end of that invitation. Were circumstances different —did I not have so much on my hands—'

'Mr. Waldron!' cried the girl, her cheeks flaming. 'I hadn't meant to say anything like this, but I will now—'

'Count four and twenty, Tatticorum,' said Aunt Jenifer warningly.

'I won't! I've counted enough already! Mr. Waldron, it goes against the grain to come the first time into Mr. Early Bill's home and start talking like this, but how can I help it? You are distantly related to him, yes, but—Did you ever hear of his making a will?'

'A will?' He stared at her so sternly then and

94

for such a long, silent time that she felt a shiver up her back. He didn't seem exactly surprised, she thought that his eyes narrowed speculatively, and she thought there was a glint of menace in them, that was all. 'So he did make a will, did he? You don't mean that you are the lucky one?'

'Maybe I am!'

'Maybe?' He gave her a high-shouldered shrug. 'Just what does that mean? And I didn't even know that you and my uncle were old friends! Just how long and how well did you know him?'

'I never saw him in my life and you know I didn't! But—'

'This will, now? What are its terms, young lady? When was it made? And where is it now?'

'It—' But she bit the words back. She couldn't tell him, 'It's right here in this room! It's locked up in an old iron box in my satchel yonder! There are two keys to the box and I've only got one! For a minute I wondered if you had the other one!' No, none of that was to be spoken without looking ahead.

He laughed at her.

'Really, Miss Lee! Now, look here; if there's any will we'll talk about it when it turns up. As a matter of fact, I happen to know that there isn't any. Also I know that he was going to make one—but he didn't get time! He died first! Meantime, as next of kin, I am taking

95

care of things here. I'm sorry that I can't ask you to stay. Really, I am sorry!'

'We're not going!' cried the girl. 'I won't budge, for one. He wasn't your uncle, anyhow, just some sort of distant cousin or something. And he didn't like you! Neither do I! I've come over a hundred miles and at Mr. Early Bill's invitation—and here I stay!'

Rance's voice sharpened.

'Finished? Good! Now you listen to me—'

'What goes on here?' asked a man's voice, very cool and calm, almost at a drawl, yet quietly emphatic.

It was Cal Roundtree, old Early Bill's foreman. Hat in hand he came in from the *patio*, stepping softly on his toes because of his spurs.

'It's nothing that I can't take care of, Roundtree,' said Rance, very curt. 'Any time that I need you I'll let you know.'

'Thanking you kindly,' said Cal Roundtree, and then stood pulling one end of his mustache, then the other, while his serene eyes regarded the two women with the frankest interest. 'Mornin', ladies,' he greeted them. 'Me, I'm Roundtree, Calhoun Roundtree, used to be foreman for old man Cole.' He appraised the older woman at his leisure, no impertinence in his look, just unmasked inquiry, then transferred his investigations to the girl. His eyes brightened, but then most eyes brightened when they met Ann Lee's

96

eyes. 'It might be,' said Cal Roundtree, and sounded friendly, 'that you're Miss Ann Lee, come up here to see Early Bill?'

'Why, yes! How did you know?'

'I had a mite of a talk with him a few days ago, shortly before he petered out,' said Cal. 'He said as how he was expectin' comp'ny. It would be you and with you, maybe, your aunt. Miss Jenifer Edwards, ma'am?' he asked in that gentle voice of his.

Aunt Jenifer nodded.

'Pleased to meet you ladies,' said Cal then, and offered a horny, toil-blackened hand. 'You're right welcome, that's what Early Bill says I'm to say to you, and to make yourselves at home long as you care to tarry. He says likewise he's most damn sorry not to be able to be here to shake you by the hand, him Dew bein' called away to keep a date he mustn't be late at.' He cleared his throat and clapped on his hat. 'I happened to see the horse and buggy. First, I thought maybe the horse might like a drink of water and a forkful of hay; next, I says to myself, That's a livery stable rig from Bald Eagle. Comp'ny! And I reckoned it might be you ladies.'

Rance Waldron heard him out, his gorge rising, his face a hot congested red when at last he said in a repressed voice bespeaking a cold fury,

'Roundtree, when you're wanted here at the house I'll let you know. I'm taking care of things up here, understand?'

Cal Roundtree regarded him a thought distastefully, a thought humorously.

'I'm putting the buggy horse in the barn, Waldron,' he said, unruffled. 'You better step along with me a spell. You and me need a little talk together. Just the two of us.'

Waldron started to flare up; so much was obvious. With an effort he kept himself in hand.

'Come ahead,' he snapped. 'It's time to come to an understanding.'

Cal started to go, then turned and came back. 'Either of you ladies know how to shoot a gun off?' he asked gently.

'Ann there,' said her aunt, 'can shoot your eye out at fifty yards!'

Cal chuckled. 'Me, I'll make a point not gettin' ornery around you, ma'am,' he told Ann. He pulled a Colt forty-five up out of its holster, stepped across the threshold of the kitchen and dropped the gun to the table. 'Any time you want anything,' he said, 'you just blaze away with that; me, I'll be down around the corral somewhere, anyhow not too far off to hear it.—Like Early Bill said, Make yourselves to home, ladies,' and departed, stepping softly, along with a scowling Rance Waldron.

'I like *him*,' said Ann Lee when the two had gone. 'Isn't he—'

'Hmf! You like 'em all at first, then hate

'em! But shush and come here! There's something I want to find out while that Rance party is out of the way. It won't take two shakes.'

The old house was built along three sides of the deep, rectangular *patio*; a sort of corridor, roofed over with tile, skirted the *patio* along those three walls, and several doors from this corridor gave entrance to various rooms. Jenifer led the way she had seen Rance take when he had marched off with the cup of coffee down the corridor to the first door, then in. That door she had heard close after him, both going and coming. Now she hastened to it and tried it. She swung about with a gleam in her eye, a positive twinkle. It was just dawning upon Miss Jenifer Edwards that she was in for the time of her life!

'Locked!' she exclaimed triumphantly. 'Just like I thought! Him and his papers, his accounts and deeds and the like, sitting up all night together! Hmf! He's an awful liar, that man. And if he ain't anything worse than a liar, I ain't your dear Auntie Jenifer!'

They returned quietly along the corridor, back into the sunny *patio*.

'What does it all mean, do you think?' whispered the girl. 'I'm—I'm sort of scared, Aunt Jenny!'

Aunt Jenifer jerked her head about and cupped a hand to her ear.

'Here comes the rest of the world, I reckon,'

she said contentedly. 'For so far from everywhere, we sure do see folks! Someone on horseback like he was riding a race. Well, that's the way some folks always ride; just because they're young, maybe, and feel that way. That's how old Early Bill used to ride when he was young. The first time I ever laid eyes on him—'

'Why, Aunt Jenifer! You never told me that you had ever seen him!'

'There's two or three things in my life, Honey,' said Miss Edwards drily, 'that I haven't got around to telling you yetl Now who do you suppose this young feller is?'

They waited in the *patio* to find out. He dismounted out under the big oak, around the corner of the building just out of sight. Then they heard him coming on to the house—and then he came to the big arch giving upon the *patio*, and saw them and lifted his hat—

Ann Lee gasped at the sight of him, startled. The twinkle came glinting back into Aunt Jenifer's eye.

Here came the young man of the stage, Mr. William Cole Cody.

CHAPTER NINE

If Ann Lee had not been such a precipitate, hair-trigger sort of creature, a lovely little package of all sorts of unmanageable impulses, she must have marked in Cole Cody's startled expression that he was no whit less amazed to see her here than she was to see him. But she happened to be a girl who did her major thinking, when thinking seemed indicated, after the act instead of before. Right now all that she knew was that she hated this young man with a terrible, terrible hate—and that he, after having so brutally treated her, had now followed her here!

'Well!' she exclaimed, and in a flash achieved a very creditable imitation of a scornful and haughty heroine she had seen not too long ago in a melodrama enacted by a traveling troupe at the Opera House in San Carlos, a melodrama reeking with such lines as, And the villain still pursued her. 'Well!' said little Miss Ann Lee. 'Of all things! If you think for one single minute, Mr. Cody, that either my aunt or myself has anything whatever to say to you, you are sadly mistaken. Come, Auntie, let's go in the house. It's nicer in there.'

'Good morning, Mr. Cody,' said Aunt Jenifer, smiling friendliwise. 'Lovely morning, ain't it?'

Mr. Cody, having regarded her niece with his head tipped sidewise and his eyebrows cocked high, grinned back at Aunt Jenifer every bit as friendly as she.

'You're right!' he told her enthusiastically.

'Take this morning just as it is, you couldn't beat it with a ten foot pole. The sun's shining, notice? And the sky is as blue as anything. That's the way it ought to be. The air, now, it's all shot full of sunshine, and you can smell the pines and the green grass; and you just get a whiff of wood smoke out of the chimneys, dropping down lazy-like because on a still morning like this, with no wind blowing—'

'Coming, Aunt Jenifer?' asked a cool, distant-seeming Ann Lee.

Whether Aunt Jenifer exactly tipped Mr. Cody a sly wink, or whether perhaps she merely squinted an eye against the sun, looking his way, is a question. Not much of a question, perhaps, yet there is room for argument. She said meekly to her niece without in the least looking meek, 'Coming, my pet,' and followed along to the door which Ann was holding open.

'Just a minute there!' Cody called after them. 'Me, too, I'm coming in!'

Aunt Jenifer crossed the threshold, then stopped to watch events, the little muscles about her eyes crinkling. Ann stood squarely planted in the door, facing the invader like Horatius at the bridge.

'I don't think you have any business here, Mr. Cody,' she said crisply. 'You are not invited and you are not coming in. And I never want to see you again. Do you understand? Or must I say it again?'

'Can you get it through your head,' said a very rude William Cole Cody, 'that you and I, far apart as the poles in everything else, agree right up to the hilt on one thing? That we never want to see each other any more than we have to, and let's hope that today wipes the slate clean. Just the same I am coming in, and I am going to stay for a spell, and—'

'Like fun you are!' Ann cried angrily. And, stepping swiftly backward, she slammed the door in his face.

He set his hand to the latch just in time to hear her drop the oaken bar into place. He swore gently under his breath, scratched his head, jerked his hat forward and strode purposefully along the corridor edging the *patio*, hunting for another door. He found it just in time to have it slammed, good and hard. He hastened his step and heard light steps running. So he, too, ran.

The next door was already fastened. He wasted no time at all on it—those doors at the Hacienda Estrada, made long and long ago of good, honest oak two inches thick, asked for a battering ram when hospitality was not at home—but spun on his heel and dashed for the kitchen end of the house. Little Ann Lee, hearing him, ran, too, as swift and agile as anyone of the three little pigs who were not wishful for a call from the wolf, but the long-legged Cody was ahead of her by several safe yards. He burst into the kitchen and halted there, briefly triumphant, while he could hear the staccato tapping of her racing feet.

They looked at each other across the room. Cody shoved his hat back, set his hands on his hips, lifted his chin at her and gave her a look as good as a slap. She came to a dead halt, breathing rapidly, her breast rising and falling, her color high, her eyes blazing with their little fires of an inner conflagration.

'You get out!' she cried in an anger that made her beautiful for any man, not likewise angry, to gaze upon.

'Like hell I will,' said Cody, very brittle with her.

Behind Ann Lee, Aunt Jenifer appeared. She wasn't laughing; she wasn't even exactly smiling. Yet a man some degrees less than blind could have told that she was having the time of her life.

Ann Lee, close to her wits' end, remembered the recent visit of the amiable Mr. Calhoun Roundtree, remembered in a flash the gift he had made her. There on the kitchen table, in the middle of the room, between her and the detestable Mr. Cody, was Cal's Colt .45! What more could any beleaguered girl ask?

She fairly leaped upon it. She snatched the weapon up and, her eyes very bright along its barrel, looked at Cole Cody disquietingly.

'Get out!' she said again. 'I mean it. You get out or I'll kill you!'

'Better look out, Mister,' said Aunt Jenifer's gentle voice. 'Our little vixen can shoot like a sharpshooter—and she's just in the mood. Better do the way she says and come back some other time.'

Cody began to laugh. He scarcely heard the warning words, he heeded them not at all. If this fool girl would only listen to him a minute—Well, she wouldn't listen; she wasn't the listening kind. She was quite the reverse, he had reason to know; far from being passive, she was explosive. Well, then, let her explode. He had come to stay and he was going to stay.

So he just laughed at her—and took a forward step, meaning to force the gun down, to take it away from her, then to have a sensible word with the very obviously sensible Miss Jenifer Edwards.

Ann Lee, desperate now, shrilled another word or two of defiance:

'Stop! I tell you—'

In the quiet kitchen the explosion as the gun went off was as good as a cannon shot. Down at the corrals Cal Roundtree heard it, quite as he had said he would, Cal Roundtree who had failed to tell the young lady of how he had spent hours working with a file on that gun of his until it was hair-trigger. Hair-trigger? The thing wanted scarcely more than a puff of your breath to set it off! And a man could kill elephants with that Colt .45.

A queer, rigid look stamped itself on Cole

105

Cody's face. He stood his ground a minute, staring incredulously. He opened his lips to speak, then closed them again without a word. After all, what was there to say? The matter required a modicum of thought.

'That's just to show you!' the girl told him, mocking him with voice and eyes and her whole attitude. 'Next time I'll kill you!'

He thought that over, too.

'There won't be any next.time,' he managed at last. His eyes fascinated her; they seemed to catch all the light there was in the room, to focus it and draw it down to a fine point, to drive it back at her in a long, poison-tipped, altogether venomous lance. 'You see, it's like this—'

Then, when she began to feel entirely mistress of the situation, thinking that he meant to draw back and go his way, he leaped forward, taking half the room in one pantherine bound, and slapped her gun down just as it roared for the second time. His grasp wrapped about her wrist, tensing unmercifully, twisting her arm so that she screamed out in pain, and the gun dropped to the floor. He let her go, stooped and caught the weapon up and hurled it far out through the open door behind him. Then he set both his hard hands on her shoulders, jerking her toward him, shaking her back and forth so that her hair tumbled down and whipped lashingly across her reddening cheeks.

'You damn little tiger pup!' he called her.

There was a convenient chair. He dropped down into it and pulled her down across his knees; he yanked up her flounces and lifted his hand—high! She kicked wildly, her legs threshing like some fantastic sort of windmill as, on fire with this indignity, she bit and scratched and screamed at him. His hand, lifted high, came down with a smack which made even a paralyzed Aunt Jenifer shudder; that hand of his rose and fell to such effect that in a couple of minutes little Miss Ann Lee received all the thorough spankings she had missed—and needed—these many years.

It was upon such an arresting scene that Cal Roundtree, coming at a dead run, burst, gun in hand. Cole Cody, hand lifted, gazed at him frowningly, little liking the interruption just now when things were quite at their best. To make matters even less to his taste, there was another man looking in over Cal Roundtree's shoulder. Young Cody brought his hand down for the final *smack*.

'Hey, you!' roared Cal. 'What the hell!'

Promptly Cole Cody gave over what was occupying him and stood up, letting Ann Lee slide off his knees and sprawl on the floor. He stepped toward the newcomers.

'Why, darn you!' Cal Roundtree stormed at him.

Again Cole Cody emulated a springing cat, and his fist came up in a long swing, taking Cal

107

Roundtree neatly and forcefully upon the point of the chin, and such was the effect of the blow that Cal was lifted from his feet and flung backward, landing in the yard from which he had just come, flat on his back. And still a stormy Cole Cody stormed along, giving next his full attention, asking no questions, to Cal's companion, Rance Waldron. Rance, too, went for his gun, and small good it did him, for in his case as in Cal's, Cody's hand seemed to be quicker than the eye. At any rate the same fist, looking now to Ann Lee like a rock bound to the end of a war club, accomplished for Rance Waldron what it had already done for Cal Roundtree, with but a slight variation: the bronze knuckles landed with a sound compounded of thudding and squishing effects upon Rance's nose, and blood spouted, and Rance tottered backward, tripped over Cal's earthbound body, and went down ignominiously.

But already Cal was wriggling over, getting on his belly, then on his hands and knees, then surging up to his feet, and he still had a good grip on a twin to the gun he had loaned Ann Lee. And by this time there was murder in Cal Roundtree's soul; that was clear to see, just looking into his eyes.

But he had lost a precious second or two. As swift and sure ordinarily as a snake striking, just now Cal was briefly, fumblingly uncertain, and that was because of that wholehearted blow he had taken on the chin. Cole Cody, having done as well as any man could do, using the tools that nature had graciously given him, now bethought him of those other tools with which inventive man had supplemented nature's arsenal. His own gun was in his hand, its blunt, ugly nose turned Cal's way.

'Better drop it, feller,' said Cole Cody, sounding listless and not greatly concerned. He sat down as though making himself thoroughly at home. 'Might blister your fingers.'

Rance Waldron, too, scrambled to his feet. He, however, did not reach toward his hip, for he, like Cal, was being searched by Cody's unsmiling eyes.

'Look here you,' said Cal Roundtree, his hand hanging down, the muzzle of his gun brushing his boot top. 'Seems as though—'

He stopped short, biting his words off clean. He saw that the man lounging in the kitchen chair had turned white under his heavy tan, and he saw something else. He saw a tiny red pool on the floor close to one of the chair legs, and noticed the spaced drops falling down into it.

Cal said, 'I'm putting my gun away, stranger; all right?' and holstered it with Cody watching him narrowly. He turned half around and said to Rance Waldron, 'Stick your gun away, you. No more shooting. It's bad manners anyhow, shooting in a house, specially with ladies present.'

Then he stepped up close to Cody and stood looking down at him.

'Hurt bad?' he said.

'Hell, no,' said Cody. 'If you feel like finishing what we started—'

'It might be fun, at that,' said Cal, appearing thoughtful. But he shook his head. 'Some other day, though. Like I told you, there's ladies present—'

'*A* lady,' admitted Cole Cody, and looked at Aunt Jenifer. 'I ought to have had better manners,' he apologized to her. He moved as though to get up; then he thought better of it and sat back.

Cal stooped down and took his gun away from him.

Ann Lee, her eyes enormous, hot spots of red on her burning cheeks, was on her feet again and staring at the man who had just used her so, and she, too, at last saw the whiteness through his bronze, and the slowly dripping blood into the tiny glistening pool.

'I shot him and I am glad!' she exulted.

But it was hard to go on exulting while she looked at her handiwork.

Aunt Jenifer came to Cal Roundtree's side, bending over the man in the chair.

'Children shouldn't be allowed to play with shooting irons,' said Aunt Jenifer mildly. 'They're always getting hurt. If you boys, Mr. Roundtree, will get Mr. Bill Cole Cody to a bed, and if you'll bring me some boiled water and a clean sheet or pillow case, we'll try to mend him up. I don't think—'

'Mr. *Who?*' demanded Cal Roundtree. 'Who'd you say he is?'

'He calls himself Cody, William Cole Cody, and—'

'Me, I'm damned,' said Cal, and ran his fingers through his hair, then along the rim of an aching jaw. 'If ladies wasn't present, I'd say I'm double-damned.' He frowned down at young Cody. 'You Cole Cody?' he demanded.

Cole Cody, a trifle dizzy and sickish, demanded,

'Might I ask if it's any business of yours? I'm not asking *your* pedigree, am I? Suppose you leave me alone.'

'You're a nice kid, like a hornet,' Cal snorted. 'But I got to know. Unless you're ashamed of yourself, and I reckon you ought to be on general principles, you tell me whether you're William Cole—Cody or not!'

Cody regarded him speculatively. Not a bad sort, it struck him, this nosy individual. Further, he was in no mood for a lot of empty jabber. Nor had he any reason to deny himself. So he said curtly,

'Me, I'm Cole Cody. William Cole Cody. Just Cody for short. Now what? Want to do anything about it?'

Cal Roundtree stood rubbing his bruised jaw.

'Yes, I do,' he said, having duly meditated. 'Two things. I want to get your shirt off, see how bad you're hurt and mend you up again. That's one thing. The other is, I want to make you welcome to the King Cole Ranch. Old Early Bill told me to watch out for you, to treat you like home folks. That's two things. Maybe later on we can make it three: when you're all well again, I'd like powerful well to take you out behind the barn and beat you clean to death!'

He stuck his hand out.

'Shake, Cody,' he said. 'Old Early Bill says so. You're welcome; like the old Spanish used to say, "The place is yours."'

Cody looked up at him and a slow smile twitched at his lips and warmed his eyes, and his hand went out to find and clasp Cal Roundtree's. And Ann Lee stared at them with all her might. As, indeed, did Rance Waldron.

Aunt Jenifer said, growing impatient, 'You, Mr. Calhoun Roundtree, I thought you had some sense. You looked like it. Do you want to patch this old playmate of yours up? Or had you rather chin with him and watch him bleed to death? And just look at my nice clean kitchen floor!'

Cal helped Cody to stand. He said, 'There's a bed handy in that first room there,' and then was cut short by Cole Cody saying, 'Who wants a bed this time of day? I haven't even had breakfast yet! Anyhow, I'm not bad hurt; a girl like her couldn't hurt a blind cripple even if she had a sawed off shotgun to work with! On top of all that, who'd want a bed even to die in? We'll keep our boots on, kid.'

And Cal muttered, not realizing he was speaking aloud, 'Now I'm damned. Sounds just like old Early Bill Cole! And named Cole Cody! Glory be, I'm going to have my hands fulland I could break old Early Bill's neck for him, ducking out on me like this, leaving me holding the bag! I bet a man, somewhere he's laughing his damn old head off!'

So he got young Cody as far along as a chair in the living room—the same old chair in which Early Bill had sat just before he lunged up, to die standing up!—and yanked up his shirt tail and sought his wound.

Ann Lee came close after them, stood a moment looking down at the white flesh, the ugly blood-smear, the raw, gaping wound— and ran out of the room, out into the *patio*, to the old green bench in the sunshine—and sat down, her fingers twisting in her lap, her eyes traveling out beyond the girding wall, into far blue distances. She saw three tall pines standing on a gentle knoll—they filled her vision for a time—she was not conscious of them at all just then, but they managed somehow to catch and still her fugitive eyes. No one had told her yet that out there, under those old pines, Early Bill was taking his long

113

siesta.

She had overheard that funny man, Calhoun Roundtree, with the funny name, muttering— Just what was it he had said, all to himself? Something about old Early Bill—I could break his neck for him, ducking out on me like this— I bet a man somewhere he's laughing his damn old head off!

Old Early Bill—dead—she had never seen him—She stared unseeing at the still, tall pines, not knowing where old Early Bill was, and yet thought of him—laughing!

'I could love you, Early Bill!' whispered little Ann Lee, clasping her hands very, very tight. 'I could love you with all my heart! Oh, why didn't you wait for me!'

And then she had a queer, tight feeling about her heart, she felt that Early Bill, laughing all to himself, *was* waiting!

She jumped up and ran back into the house.

CHAPTER TEN

'You're not a very good shot, are you?' said Cole Cody, lazy and slow-spoken and impudent. Even his eyebrows mocked her.

'I could shoot your toenails off and never blister your feet,' she told him.

'Then why only mess me up like this, making it hurt like seven kinds of hell and at the same time do me no more harm than a hot stove lid dropped on your toe?'

'It's that darned gun of Calhoun's! It does its own shooting when it feels like it. You try it sometime, smarty!'

'Trying to apologize? Meaning you didn't go to do it?' He was still jeering at her. Maybe it was just as well then that Cal had retrieved his gun and taken it off with him.

'I can read the past, present and future,' said Aunt Jenifer, 'like something printed in a book. In big, black print, too!'

'Why, Aunt Jenifer!' exclaimed little Ann Lee.

'Take this young man, name of Bill Cole Cody, for instance,' said Aunt Jenifer. 'All you did just now was nick him in the side, miles away from his gizzard; all you broke was his skin and not even a rib. Then what does he do? He stands there like the Greek boy in the fairy tale books with the fox eating his liver; and then he gets very gay, jumping two strangers that come in, knocking Cal Roundtree galley west and Rance Waldron galley east, I guess you'd call it—him bleeding all over my floor all the time. Kind of easy, reading his present, ain't it?'

'Oh, that!' Ann Lee could shrug in such fashion to make a shrug mean whatever she chose. 'Just because Mr. Cody is strong in the back and arms, and weak where—'

'I'm telling you something, young lady,' said

115

Mr. Cody. 'Just now I had the pleasure, the privilege, the high honor, so to speak, to pull your dress up and lambaste you where a lambasting was asked for and does the most good, where you rest yourself when you sit down and where you must have gone as pink as—as pink as pink ribbons, then as red as a summer prairie on fire, and you talk about blistering me with a bullet.' His eyes made her writhe; then they drifted away to her aunt. 'Aunt Jenifer,' he said, 'I'm all ears when it comes to your reading what's in the tea leaves and things. The present, according to you, does me no great flattery. How about past and future? Just as bad? Now wait a shake and listen to this: Do what you want with the days that are gone, but when it comes to peeking into the days that are coming up, keep a girl by name of Ann Lee out of it! Do that favor, won't you, for a cripple?'

He was at his ease, as far as he could come by any ease whatever at the present irksome moment, in old Early Bill's favorite chair; Cal Roundtree had gone back to the clutter of ranch buildings beyond the grove; Rance Waldron, smoking one cigarette after the other, was walking restlessly up and down in the *patio*; Aunt Jenifer stood, half turned around, on the threshold of the kitchen door; little Ann Lee, with her arms folded tightly, was standing in front of him, half leaning against the living room table, half sitting on it.

She looked very young, very pretty and, it struck him, a very potent irritant for a man with a bullet-pain in his side. He cut her down with a glance and turned back to Aunt Jenifer.

'Well, Witch Lady, what's next?' he demanded. 'You with your second sight!'

'The past comes booming up before the future does,' said Aunt Jenifer. 'Can I help it? In the past I see a young galoot by name Bill Cole Cody, and he's always going places. He doesn't stop any place at all to pick up the pieces, he just goes rambling on. He thinks maybe the mines is the place for him, and he'll be a big mining engineer! Hoots for that; he always was and always will be just a common everyday rancher of sorts. Then he gets a mysterious letter, and he forks a horse, and he goes riding! Sure he does; I can read it in the picture shapes that keep a-shaping up in the air! And he gets to a place and to bed and sleeps a while, and noises wake him up and, before he gets his eyes clear, he sees something or other that interests him pretty considerable, and he jumps on some sort of wagon and whoops along. That's Bill Cole Cody for you—in the past!'

'Aunt Jenifer!' said Ann Lee. 'What's come over you?'

'A vision,' chuckled Aunt Jenifer.

'Go ahead, Aunt Jenifer,' said Cole Cody, and studied her more seriously than ever before. 'What's the future? Suppose you spell

117

it out!'

'Hm-m-m,' buzzed Aunt Jenifer, like a lazy bumble bee. 'The future? Well, it ain't hard for me. Most folks would bog down right now, resting up on their laurels, but—Here goes! You're headed into seven kinds of trouble, Mr. Cody. No dodging that fact. I'm almost sorry for you. Just the same, there's hope for you if you keep a stiff upper lip and can shoot straight and fast, and if you can if you can—'

She hesitated. Her wise, merry eyes trafficked with his probing ones a moment, then shifted, under uplifted brows, to her niece, then returned to his, merrier than ever.

'If,' she said, like a Sibyl, 'if you can handle the situation!'

And she hurried out, closing the door emphatically behind her.

'Mr. Cody,' said Ann, very prim and very polite, 'I am sorry, in a way, that I shot you. You see—'

'In a way? That's nice! What way?' snapped young Cody.

'There is such a thing as being humane, or anyhow human,' said Ann. 'You know very well that you are not welcome here. What's the use pretending? You and I don't like each other—for my part,' she exploded, 'I hate the sight of you! Get well as soon as you can and go somewhere else. So, what I mean by being sorry I shot you, it's just that if you weren't all shot up you could be on your way right now.'

'What did the witch woman mean by saying that I got a mysterious letter?' he wanted to know. 'Who told her?'

'And now just what do you mean? You're not delirious, are you, from a scratch on your side?'

'*Scratch!* Why, you—you—' He clamped his lips down tight and regarded her a bit sullenly. He had spanked her once, good and plenty; why was it that he felt he could go through life spanking that girl? She seemed just born and bred to make his blood boil.

He slid out of his chair, the tight bandage about his midriff irking him, and stood up.

'I'm here to stay,' he told her flatly. 'I didn't come following you, either. If I'd known you were here, maybe I wouldn't have come at all. And, not meaning to be tough with you, just the same I can ask you what the devil you are doing here anyhow? At my place.'

'Your place! Why, you—'

'We sort of find it natural to call each other "You" and then gulp and stop, don't we?' he said.

'Your place! What on earth are you talking about? Have you gone crazy? Oh, maybe you always were crazy! Of course, that's it! That explains everything!'

'Listen, and don't be so smart. You're kind of pretty, and maybe it's gone to your head. Men, I guess, seeing you at a dance, all dolled up, have told you a lot of lies, and you think you're Cleopatra, maybe, or the Queen of Sheba. Whoa! Didn't I say wait a minute? I'm answering questions right now; you say what do I mean by saying this is my place. Well, that's what it is, or anyhow going to be. Me, I'm old Early Bill Cole's heir. This is the King Cole Ranch, and it's mine.'

'Why, you—you—'

'I've told you I'm getting tired of our calling each other "You—you's." Where's your originality?'

'You—*liar*! You're worse than that man Rance Waldron. He says it's his place too—*and it's mine*! Now, Mr. Cody, will you—will you tuck your shirt tail in, and go climb a tree?'

What Mr. Cody did was scratch his head, thick-thatched with abundant dark red hair, and hold his peace a moment and do a bit of thinking, staring at her all the while. He told himself that this was a sort of funny lay-out, his running into this obnoxious girl so consistently for one thing, her making a claim like that for another, the letter from old Early Bill Cole for the first of all in a chain of events that—No chain at all, just a crazy quilt of a thing!

Pondering, he did tuck his shirt tail in. Also he produced the makings of a cigarette and very slowly, his mind on other matters, he rolled his cigarette. And in due course, lighted it. He inhaled deeply; he sent a stream of bluish smoke ceilingward.

120

'It's still reasonably early in the morning,' he said after he had driven her frantic with his leisureliness. 'You've got lots of time to comb your hair and wash your face—Go look in a looking glass, and you'll do both!—and get into Bald Eagle before noon. If the stage doesn't go where you want it to go today it'll be pretty sure to go tomorrow. So you've got time to listen while I tell you something. Mr. Early Bill Cole, rest his wild soul, Early Bill being dead now, made up his mind he wanted the right sort of man to take care of the things he had to leave behind him on taking the long, one-way trip. He nominated me for the job. He even took time to write out a will. He left every damn thing he had to William Cole Cody. And that's me. Do you begin to get the general idea?'

He had made her gasp before. He had made it simple for her to name him a liar, among other things. Now for a second he left her breathless. At last her lips parted—but he saw what was coming, and cut her down, saying swiftly,

'No you don't! No more you-you stuff, Miss Ann Lee! It does you no good. Think things over and—Why not trot along and wash your face? There's a smear on it—Cuss me down, if it's not human gore! Blood of mine? Why, Ann!'

'It's not! I wouldn't have—Oh, you—'

With an effort she got herself in hand. She

121

knew very well that if there were any smudge on her check it was only dust from a dusty old house, and that its effect would be but to accentuate the rose-petal freshness of her skin. So it was quite simple to keep her thoughts where, at a crisis such as this pretended to be, they belonged.

'When I was a very little girl,' she told him sweetly, 'I used to say that I hated things. Castor oil was one, and there were others. But, dear me, I didn't know what I was talking about. For only now, Mr. Cody, I do know now what the word "hate" means. Need I go further? Of course not. Now, suppose you tell me what, if anything at all, you are driving at? Someone has told you, no doubt, that Mr. Early Bill Cole willed everything he had to me?'

Cole Cody had a way of exhaling cigarette smoke that, she was dead sure, could infuriate anyone on earth. He did some exhaling. Her nails bit into her pink palms. But, Spartanlike, she clenched her teeth and waited.

*   *   *

Outside, in the *patio*, Rance Waldron had stopped at the side of a window, listening; one would have judged, so still and attentive had he become, that he was far and away more than merely interested. At least so deemed Aunt Jenifer, spying on him from a kitchen

122

corner!

* * *

And little Ann Lee, never overgiven toward patience, was determinedly waiting for whatever Cody might go on to say. He was making very broad and very presumptuous, evidently spurious, claims. Surely he would go on, bolstering up cloudy fabrications on still other cloud foundations! But it began to appear that this impossible Cody, having said his say, was content with silence and the expulsion of blue smoke through his nostrils. Like a devil, she averred!

At last she spoke up, and very quietly, considering who it was speaking.

'Mr. Early Bill Cole,' she said, spacing her words nicely, 'was a gentleman and a very fine man. He was a friend of my father's. He knew that he had to die. So he made his will. It's quite too bad, Mr. Cody, to disappoint you, but Mr. Cole left everything he had—to me. Yes, that's what I said. He made a will to that effect and—and I've got that will! Now—Will you get well and go!'

She spoke with conviction. Again she set him pondering. There wasn't the slightest doubt she meant what she was saying. The poor little deluded kid—

He bethought him of several things: Of a crazy sort of letter he had had from a perfect stranger, a certain Early Bill Cole: of a hundred dollar bill stuck into the letter; of a key enclosed, and a cryptic reference to a lock for the key to fit. He began to smell some sort of hoax. And he wondered if that old devil, Early Bill Cole of whom everybody in seven states had heard, had gone clean crazy in his mortal illness, and had striven to make monkeys out of various and sundry strangers—folk like Bill Cole Cody, for example, and little Ann Lee!

He moved over to the table, feeling a trifle unsteady and blurry in the head, and sat on the table's edge, one foot swinging.

'We'll soon find out about all this,' he said. 'I've got a key—a key old Early Bill sent me—'

'A key! You've got a key! Wh—what sort of key?'

'A key that's made to unlock something,' he snorted at her. 'What do you suppose, asking what sort of key? Now, when I find what it's to unlock—There's an old devil in town they call the Judge—He's crazy as a bed-bug, no question. But he knows a lot of things. Between him and another crazy old coot name of Doc Joe—'

'Doc Joe isn't a crazy old coot! He's a dear! But—but—Where did you say you got your key?'

'Forget that I've told you as much as I have! Are you and I old friends who tell each other all our hearts' secrets? Are we—'

124

'Shut up! You talk so darned much and say so little—you make me *mad!* Tell me about your key. Did Early Bill—You say that he sent it to you?'

'Well, what if he did? Maybe you've got the lock it fits! Let's laugh!'

'Maybe I have! And if you've got the other key, I'll show you! I'll show you who owns the King Cole Ranch and all that goes with it! Where's your precious key, Mr. Cole Cody?'

'Where's your lock for it to fit?' he shot back at her, and grinned his most malicious grin.

*　　　*　　　*

Suddenly they were aware of Aunt Jenifer in the doorway, clearing her throat to a warning 'Ahem!' Her eyes drifted sidewise toward the window, and managed to jerk their attention in that direction, whereupon Rance Waldron made the best of the situation, tapping on the pane, calling to them,

'What's going on in there? I thought you two, after the lady had popped a bullet into the gent, would have had enough of each other. Mind if I drop in and join in the pow-way?'

He moved away from his vantage point, and a moment later the doorway framed him. He stopped there, studying them.

'I don't think I know you very well,' said Cody, 'Do you happen to be one of my guests?'

'We met just now,' Rance reminded him, cool and insolent, as was his fashion. He pinched his chin, looking reflective. 'Guests, you said, didn't you? Whose guests, I can't but ask. You mean I'm your guest or you're my guest or—Just what did you have in mind?'

Cole Cody, drained of his strength as he was, felt a strong urge to batter all the smug insolence off the man's handsome face. As a matter of fact he experienced an all but overwhelming desire to spoil Mr. Rance Waldron's manly profile for all time.

'It's like this,' said Cole Cody, very slow-spoken. When he spoke that way he was generally saying one thing and thinking far afield; right now he was regarding Rance Waldron's empurpled nose and dallying with the thought of taking even more painstaking care of that nose when opportunity afforded. 'You heard part of what was said; I guess, out there at the window, you didn't miss a word. So suppose we go on from there. I don t know who you are—'

'Why not get straightened out at the start?' said Rance Waldron reasonably. 'Me, I'm Rance Waldron and just blew in here a few days ago. As far as I know, or anyone else seems to know, I'm next of kin to that rare old bird, Early Bill Cole. I had me a hunch that he kicked off without making any will at all, and in spite of the several mentions of wills that

126

I've heard since, I'm still of that notion. If I happen to be right—Well, then, this outfit, lock, stock and barrel, belongs to me! Got all that, Mr. Cody?'

'That's quite a speech,' conceded Cody, nodding approvingly. 'Yep, I got it. Only it's my bet you're out on a limb. Here are the three of us, you and Miss Lee and me, all putting in our claims.' He made a wry face, then wiped it away with the heel of his hand. 'Like so many turkey buzzards sitting on a fence! It makes me sort of sick at my stomach. Dammit, I got a notion to high-tail out of here and let you folks fight over a dead man's boots!'

'Scat!' cried Ann Lee. 'You're overdue some other place!'

He considered at length, then shook his head and looked stubborn.

'No. I'm sticking until I get things straight. Why old Early Bill Cole should make me his heir, I don't know and can't guess. But he might have had his reasons. I never knew him, I never even saw him. But one thing sticks out like a sore thumb: His name was Cole, and I'm Cole Cody! How's that happen? Must be that we're related, or something—'

He reached into his pocket, groped a minute and dug up a small, flat key—and did little Ann Lee's eyes all but start from their sockets!

'There!' said young Cody. 'There's the key

to the mystery, as the feller says—Maybe!
Who'll bring me a lock for my key?'

Ann Lee had a way, all her own, of getting
from the place where she was to the place
where she wished to be, that was like nothing
else on earth. Here she is, there she goes!
Gone away! Hold everything!

Here she is again!

And with her cherished carpet-bag clutched
tight. She got it open, she ran a hurrying hand
down into it, she plucked out an old black iron
box. An iron box with two locks, as anyone
might see.

'If your key fits one of these locks—This
one! Try it!'

Cole Cody chose to drive her wild. He
tossed his key ceilingward, caught it and
played with it, and he laughed at her.

'So that's it, is it?' he jeered at her. 'A strong
box with two locks, and you've got a key for
one, and are going clean crazy like Pandora
and Blue Beard's wife, trying to burglarize it!
And no can do—without the other key! Mine!
Well,' and he never spoke more drawlingly,
'there's no hurry, is there? How about waiting
until tomorrow? Maybe it might be best to
wait until my wound heals over! That's an
idea!'

And he tossed his key again, caught it and
shoved it back into his pocket. And he could
have sworn that he heard Aunt Jenifer giggle!

Ann Lee opened her hand and showed him

a key very much like his own. She tossed it up, just as he had done, and caught it; she held it between her thumb and finger—and *sneered* at him. And how little Ann Lee, when she put her mind to it, *could sneer!*

'Here, before witnesses,' she said, and her voice sounded as though she had just taken it out of cold storage, iced all over, 'if you like we'll try to open the box and see what we can find. It might be fun—for me! Or, if you like to hang on to your old key, I'm just ready to go get an ax and a cold chisel and bust this little box wide open! Then, whatever I find belongs to me. To do with, Mr. Cody,' and now her voice grew intolerably sweet, 'just whatever I darned well please!'

Don't get Aunt Jenifer wrong. She wasn't an old lady at all, really. Her age, to be sure, no one but Aunt Jenifer knew, but any man could tell by the spring in her step and the gleam in her eye and the eternally-slim youngness of her body, that she wasn't a day over sixty, and perhaps not even much above forty-five. Just one of those elusive ladies. The thing is, be her years what they were, from the day she was fifteen until right up to now, she had faithfully kept a diary! And in the diary were some surprising things—surprising, that is, if you did happen to get Aunt Jenifer wrong, as did so many. Of this day and moment she wrote—no doubt with her tongue in her cheek:

129

'Those two! He's the handsomest man in a crazy sort of way that I ever saw. Reminds me of Bobbie—Golly, I was only seventeen then! The same sort of lop-sided grin, the same sort of devil's eyes made to drive girls crazy. And this little Ann of mine! Those two! He's doing everything any man could to make her scream and pull her hair out and knash her teeth—(How do we spell k-nash, anyhow' Who the dickens cares?) And just you watch her! Flipping her key sky-high, telling him she'd use a crowbar and a stick of dynamite instead! Knowing mighty well that, no matter what else he was, he was a son of Adam, closely bound to her own Great-G-G-G etc. Grand Mother Eve!'

Cole Cody had played poker in his time. (Incidentally, though he did not know it, he had played poker with none other than Early Bill Cole.) A bluff can call a bluff any time.

'Like you say, here and now, before witnesses!' he scoffed. 'You with one key, me with the right one, let's go. Only when you read the sad news, don't ask to weep on my shoulder!'

'You!' cried Ann scornfully. And set the box down hastily, and shot her key into the proper lock. When the mechanism gave its satisfied responsive click, she looked up at him triumphantly. Little Ann Lee could crowd a lot

130

of things into one swift glance: I've done it, Mister! How about you? Just four-flushing?

Cole Cody wondered, himself. Well, here was the time to find out about things. With Ann watching his slightest move, as though she suspected him of being able to accomplish any weird sort of sleight-of-hand, not trusting him; with both the lively Aunt Jenifer and the sardonic Rance Waldron pressing close, he shot the key home.

It fitted the lock.

He turned it.

Now there was nothing to do but lift the lid and see what, if anything, the old iron box contained.

He and little Ann Lee looked at each other.

About that moment and what followed, Aunt Jenifer wrote two whole pages in her diary.

CHAPTER ELEVEN

Two old porch-sitters from Bald Eagle came skallyhooting out to the King Cole Ranch. They shared what they agreed to call a hunch. Likewise, both were scorching with curiosity. Having talked spaciously of the two newcomers, a pretty girl by name of Ann Lee and of a lean, long individual name of Cole Cody who had brought the stage in, having discussed these two at full length—Queerly, they didn't even mention Aunt Jenifer to each other, though both had taken full cognizance of her—they were impelled to travel out to the ranch at an unearthly hour, to take stock of conditions there.

They arrived early, just in time to see four people gathered about a table with an old black iron box centering their attention.

'Aha!' the two old porch-sitters said simultaneously within themselves, and came barging in.

Ann emitted a small, shrill squeal of delight.

'Doctor Joe! Oh, Doctor Joe, I'm so glad and grateful you came! I'm amongst enemies, cruel, horrid men that would steal a girl's last penny. You come watch, Doctor Joe!'

And Cole Cody, seeing the Judge, said a warm,

'Howdy, Judge. Come guard my interests, won't you? They're not only shooting me up, they're trying to steal my mess of pottage. Keep the eye peeled, will you, Judge? And I'll buy the drinks.'

They got the box open. And, all credit to little Ann Lee and some small credit to Cole Cody, they didn't grab. Their eyes, though, did grab.

They saw, first of all, two long, sealed envelopes.

'Well, Mr. Cody,' said Ann, and looked and sounded very brave, 'the top envelope is addressed to William Cole Cody. If you care to lift it out, I'll take mine!'

'So you still think that there is something in the Santa Claus box for you?' he jeered at her. 'Think that the letter underneath is for Miss Ann Lee? And that it will sort of explain, begging your pardon, why things didn't come your way?'

He had never until now quite appreciated her teeth, small and gleamingly white and—Or did he fancy it?—sharp?

'Shall I pick it up for you?' Ann said a trifle waspishly.

He lifted his hat to her, and grinned his further jibes. And then very deliberately he took the long, top envelope out of the box.

Underneath was the one addressed to her. She snatched it, ran her excited eyes over it, flaunted it in his face. Then she tore it open as fast as any envelope was ever opened in all the world, from the time of Rameses, if they had envelopes then, to this current *Anno Domini* year. Her eyes, racing faster than light travels, that rapid traveler, were shining. A glance told her the tale, the fairy tale, the story that she *knew* would be there! 'To Ann Lee I give and bequeath—all my belongings—the properties known as the King Cole Ranch—' and so forth—

'Come, hurry, Doctor Joe!' she cried. 'You were right! Look!'

Cole Cody nailed the Judge with his eye.

133

'Hey, Judge!' he called cheerily. 'Step over, will you? We maybe are going to need arbitration, and I pick you for my sponsor! Ten percent of the net proceeds, if any, goes to you. How about it? Let's both ride lucky!'

The Judge and Doc Joe looked at each other. One was thinking, 'Here's where a lot of fuss and feathers starts, with maybe hell tied to its tail.' And the other was thinking, 'That confounded old cuss, Early Bill, he ought to be here to see the thing through, being that it was him that started it.' Accustomed through the years to traffic mentally through long silences, they caught each other's thoughts and, beginning already to take sides, glared at each other.

'What in the world is this?' exclaimed Ann Lee. She waved a sheet of paper; there was a bank note pinned to it. 'Listen! It says: "Little Ann Lee, I sort of kind of liked you. You were mighty sweet to me, little Ann; you were like a flower and I bet you make yourself a lot of trouble though, but all live gals do such! Do me a favor, will you? I made a bet with a crazy galoot name of Josephus Daniel Dodge, generally known far and wide, mostly in low dives and disgraceful places, as Doc Joe. I made the old fool a bet, five hundred dollars that me, I'd outlive him. And here I am as good as dead already! Wouldn't that make you mad, l'it—!"'

She began to cry, dabbing furiously at her

eyes. But she jerked her head up and let the tears run as they darn well pleased, and kept right straight on reading:

'Wouldn't that make you mad, little Ann Lee? Well, it makes me mad, but I lose and I pay. Here's five hundred dollars. Suppose you hand it over to Doc Joe and tell him that anyhow I'll get me my laugh, sitting up on a big white cloud with nice pink trimmings and playing *Home Sweet Home* on my harp, while I peek down pretty soon and spy on him sizzling down in hell! Thanks, little Ann—and you keep your hair on, and maybe you'll ride lucky! Yours, Bill Cole.'

'I'm damned,' said Cole Cody softly.

He held up a similar sheet of paper, bank note attached. He read,

'Hi, Bill Cole Cody! Sorry I missed you; couldn't wait, having other places to go. Now look here, kid, I sort of liked you; anyhow we had fun together. So you remember old times and do me a kindness, same as I'd do you at a pinch. I made a bet with a dirty dog name of Arthur Henry Pope, commonly known in and about Bald Eagle as the Judge, five hundred bucks that I'd outlive him. I just simply got tired waiting for the old fool to die, so, dammit, kid, I lose and here's the five hundred, and you hand it to the Judge for me, and tell him it was fun dying, just that that way I could make sure him and me would never, never-no-more meet up again—for he's hell-bound along of Doc Joe, and me I'm always for the High Places! Yeee! On handing it to him look out he don't claw your hand off, the money-grabbing old coyote. And tell him I hope him and Doc Joe, barging into town to get drunk together, both chokes to death. Luck, kid. Yours, Bill Cole.'

And Bill Cole, no sissy like Ann Lee, didn't weep. He blew his nose and glared stormily.

'I—I don't understand,' gasped Ann. 'I never in all my life once even laid eyes on Mr.—Mr. Early Bill!'

'Me, too,' said Cole Cody. 'He says here— It's a funny thing. I never knew Bill Cole, never saw him!'

The Judge and Doc Joe looked at each other.

'Don't you kids be fooling yourselves,' Doc Joe said crustily. 'I don't mean any disrespect to the dead—or do I? Come to think about it, I never could see why a dead dog was any nicer than a live one. Well, be that as it may, and no disrespect meant, old Early Bill Cole was a jackass if ever there was one, a no'count rambling wreck of wickedness and sin; the same dirty dog he names this here gent, Mr. Arthur Henry Pope. Just the same he warn't no liar. If he says to Miss Ann she was sweet to him, then she was sweet to him, and somewhere he knowed her. If he says to this young Cody that they had fun together, well they did. Am I right, Judge?'

136

'Right as rain, Doc,' said the Judge. 'Hell taking old Early Bill to the contrary notwithstanding, you're right.'

'What's all this about wills?' said Rance Waldron, as sharp as a new tack.

'You shut up!' cried Ann Lee. 'You and your wills! We're talking about—' She spun on her heel like a small whirlwind. 'Doc Joe! Here's your five hundred dollars! Golly! Here—here's your five hundred dollars, Doc Joe!'

'Thanking you kindly, Miss,' said Doc Joe, and took his rightful winnings.

'Well,' said Cole Cody, 'here's yours, judge. Like Early Bill says, I'm hoping you and Doc Joe choke to death.'

The Judge cleared his throat, accepted the bank note, cleared his throat again. Beyond that, being both lawyer and banker, he would not go.

'I wish Early Bill could be with us now,' said Cole Cody. 'He—'

'He *is* with us!' That was little Ann Lee, always getting away ahead of the gun. 'Can't you *feel*—Can't you—He never really died! Not the way other people do. He *couldn't*!'

'I wish,' said young Cody, very austere, very contemptuous of silly girl-things, 'that old Early Bill was here with us now, Judge. Because you sound already like a man choking to death! He'd get him his laugh—'

'He was always laughing, the damn old fool,'

snorted the Judge.

'But, like I was saying,' Cole Cody went on, 'having done with wishing, here is the tall, straight and shining fact of the matter. I've got in my hand a legal-looking paper. It calls itself a will, last will and testament. It gives and bequeaths and etcetera, all his belongings and properties and accessories—with some to wits and some more etceteras—the King Cole Ranch thrown in—to a certain gent name of William Cole Cody, which is me! And could you tell me, Judge, without straining yourself—whose time is it right now to laugh? To laugh, my good friend and counsellor, like a whole pack of hyenas? Mine? You're damn shouting! Haw!'

'Why you—you—' stammered little Ann Lee.

There it went again, that you-you thing.

'Let's look it over,' said the Judge, very judicial.

Once again he and Doc were looking at each other. Once again they said behind their lips; 'Damn that old devil-raiser, King Early Bill Cole.'

Rance Waldron was as interested as any. More interested than the others, from the look of him. He said, speaking smoothly,

'I might help you folks out, maybe. My uncle—Mr. William Cole, you know—was pretty old. What's the word for it? Senile? It's my thought that he was dying and was out of

138

his head—what you call *non compos mentis*—in plain English he was as crazy as a bed-bug when he wrote those wall-eyed wills. He told me.—Hell's bells, he told me fifty times that all he had was going to be mine! Now here's Miss Lee and here's Mr. Cody, both of them saying they've got a will, giving them the whole shooting works! That sounds kind of funny, don't it? It might pay to see how these wills were dated, and how they were witnessed and all that. Whether, maybe, they were made while the old man was dying, and was so clean off his nut that both wills are worth about—'

He did a nice job of snapping his fingers.

Cole Cody laughed.

Ann Lee smiled; it was a tight little, slight little, bright little smile that spelled Triumph.

'I'll be glad to have you read this paper, Mr. Waldron,' she said.

'Here's a document for your eye,' said Cole Cody.

And, though both Ann Lee and Cole Cody were speaking to Rance Waldron, they were looking straight at each other.

Waldron, his eyes become like gimlets, looked at one will, then at the other. In one everything on earth that Early Bill owned was bequeathed to Ann Lee; it seemed, and was, properly drawn; witnessed by Josephus Daniel Dodge. The other also seemed and was properly drawn, duty attested by Arthur Henry Pope. The queer thing was that the two wills

139

were of the same date!

Waldron laughed; it wasn't exactly pleasant laughter, but it did ring out with a mocking sort of joy.

He flung the papers down on the table.

'They're not worth the price of a torn cigarette paper,' he said, full of confidence. 'Any court, any man not altogether drunk or altogether an idiot, will tell you that the old man was clean crazy when he signed them.' He wasn't looking at either Ann Lee or Cole Cody, but his eyes flickered back and forth between Doc Joe and the Judge. 'You two witnessed these documents; well! You know that when a man gives all he's got to one person, *and at the same minute* gives it all to another person, he don't give anything to anybody! Am I right?'

The Judge cleared his throat and pulled at his abundant white mustache. Dot Joe touched his bald head meditatively with his finger tips, then gave his own white mustache a gentle tug. Beyond that the two did not go.

'Well?' demanded Rance Waldron.

When no one else seemed to have anything to say, Aunt Jenifer spoke up brightly.

'Have all you gentlemen had breakfast?' she asked. 'Wills and things, you know, can wait longer than appetites.'

The Judge's laugh, when he turned it loose, was a jolly sound to hear.

'Wisdom speaks when Miss Jenifer Edwards

140

opens her lips,' he announced with relish. 'Now, take me: I like a great big cup of coffee with four spoons of sugar and a dash of milk, and I've oft noted that after a man hath partaken thereof, thoughts become clearer and abstruse problems simplify themselves. And anyhow coffee is coffee, especially in the morning!'

She went in her sprightly fashion to make a big pot of coffee. Young Cody drew the Judge aside with a look, and the two stepped out into the *patio* to talk. Little Ann Lee, watching them, hurried to Doc Joe and slipped her hand through his arm. And Rance Waldron, looking from one of them to another, left the room, going hurriedly back to that part of the house where he had locked a door or two.

CHAPTER TWELVE

Before departing with Doc Joe, the Judge had cleared his throat a couple of times and had gone so far as to say,

'Speaking of evictions, seems to me as though Cal Roundtree might just possibly be within his rights to throw out the whole kit and caboodle of you. But as to any of the rest of you evicting anyone else—well, I reckon it would have to be like the Irishman playing the fiddle, by main strength and awkwardness.

Better sit in at a poker game and play for it.' And in haste the Judge caught up with Doc Joe, and a cloud of dust showed the way the two had taken—each with an honestly earned five hundred dollars in his jeans.

Old Early Bill's house was big enough to accommodate a score of people; consequently its present inhabitants, little Ann Lee and Aunt Jenifer, Cole Cody and Rance Waldron could all dwell under the one roof without running into each other all the time. Ann was swift in selecting a bright little room at the southwest corner, a room with a delightful, sunny outlook across the valley; a room, by the by, which somehow made her feel that once upon a time it had been inhabited, if only briefly, by some young and lovely lady. It was none of her affair; perhaps it was only imagination but nonetheless she resented the fact, if fact it was. Aunt Jehifer bestowed her portable lares and penates in a four-square room adjoining.

So Mr. Cole Cody, with his bag in hand, strode through the house to the northeast corner, having computed geometrically that that was as far as he could get from the southwest corner. And Rance Waldron maintained his present quarters, namely in the region of the locked doors, which was to say at the northwest corner. The middle of the house was abandoned, dining room and living room and a sort of den where a few old books, a congressional record, a dictionary, a pair of boots and a dismembered Mexican saddle, with straps and buckles, were silent reminders of another era.

Thus for a time the big house was divided against itself, and all was outwardly peaceful in an atmosphere reeking with watchfulness and suspicion. Rance Waldron was locked up in his own quarters, ostensibly concerning himself with various papers and accounts he had found there. Ann devoted hours to investigating the house, its various rooms and closets, making a thoughtful study of any little chance object which seemed to her somehow foreign to this locale: In a drawer a gold chain with a locket which she could not open, because a tiny key was required and the key was nowhere to be found though she sought hours for it; in an ages-old album with purple, padded covers were a curl of dark hair and some pressed flowers! How on earth came such things into old Early Bill's house, into his life? Oh, how she wished with all her heart that he had sent for her a week earlier! She kept stepping softly; she kept peering into rooms as though she fully expected to encounter him in the flesh—and she was perfectly sure that he would be wearing a heart-warming grin.

As for young Cole Cody, he left the house as soon as he had stowed his few belongings in his room, and went down to the outbuildings along the creek, by the barn, seeking Cal

Roundtree. His wound irked him and he sidled gingerly like a crab, but the bullet had not plowed deep and he found it no great effort to make his way down the slope. Nor had he any difficulty locating the man he sought; though there are always plenty of things crying out to be done on a ranch like this, Cal Roundtree was for the moment paying their clamorous voices not the slightest attention. He was sitting on a log that had been hauled up to the woodpile, smoking contemplatively, with his wreck of a black Stetson pulled down over his eyes. His head came up with a snap as he heard footsteps.

'Mind if I perch alongside you?' demanded Cody. 'I've just had a long walk and am sort of leg-weary.'

'Squat,' said Cal Roundtree. Cody lowered himself to the log and reached for his own papers and muslin bag of fine-flaked tobacco, Roundtree eyeing him narrowly all the while. 'What's on your mind, Cody?' he asked bluntly.

'Plenty,' Cole Cody told him, and licked his cigarette and lighted it. 'I think I own this outfit now; I'm not sure of anything. That girl up at the house—'

'She's the prettiest specimen of the girl species I ever clapped eyes on, and in my time I've seen some of 'em cute enough to take prizes. And she's got as much spunk as anybody needs, with maybe a little extra

144

thrown in.'

'She's not bad looking, that's a fact,' agreed Cody without enthusiasm. 'As for spunk, she's got as much temper as you'd find in two wild cats with their tails tied together. What I was going to say, here's a funny mix-up: I think I own the place and she thinks she owns it. On top of all that, there's that Rance Waldron fellow who puts in his claim. Funny, ain't it, Cal?'

Cal agreed with a thoughtful nod. Yes, it was funny. He looked at Cody narrowly, he squinted his eyes against far distances, he looked down and scraped a small neat trench in the dirt with the toe of his boot.

'You see,' Cole Cody continued, 'I never knew Early Bill Cole. Or if I did know him, as Doc Joe and the Judge seem to be sure of, then I didn't know I knew him. Maybe that's hard to get, but that's the only way I can put it.'

'He was a queer old rooster,' said Cal Roundtree. 'I guess I knew him about as well as anybody ever did; I worked for him for sixteen years, and out on the range we slept together more than once, and we et together and got mad at one another. He was, to my notion, the finest man that ever walked in a pair of boots or forked a horse or got drunk or played cards or gave his money with both hands to folks that was in want, and he didn't ask any questions about their pedigree. Yep, I

145

knew old Early Bill as well as anybody on earth. Just the same, come right down to it, I ain't sure I knew him a damn bit! He was his own man; body and soul, inside and out, and you never could be sure of him. But this I do tell you: If he left his ranch and money to you, he knew you! He would make it his business to know you. And if old Doc Joe and the Judge say you knew him, well, then, you did. Maybe he went what you call—you know—maybe he went anonymous, so you wouldn't get any line on him and fish for favors. That would be like the damn old hell-hound. And if he left his belongings to Miss Ann, you can bet your damn boots he knew her, too.' He seemed to hesitate; he muttered under his breath, 'Most usual, when you'd think he was out on a limb, he had his ace in the hole, the old fox.'

'Somebody shot him?'

'Yes. I'm just hoping with all my hope-machinery that some day I'll find out who did that for old Bill.'

'Tell me about it; all that you know.'

Cal Roundtree told the story very simply; of the shot fired from the bushes in the early dawn while the old man was standing under his favorite pine; how old Early Bill made his way back to the house; how he stuck it out longer than most men could have done; sending for Doc Joe and the Judge, getting his affairs in shape. Before he had done, Cal had given all salient details that he felt free to give. If he

146

were holding something back, that was his business.

Cole Cody asked,

'When he came to making a will, then, he knew what he was doing? He wasn't delirious?'

'Not Early Bill,' vowed Cal Roundtree. 'When he stood up, aiming to die on his feet the same way he had lived, his damn old head was as clear as a bell. You could see it in his eyes. He had a pair of eyes like an eagle's.'

'Then how in blazes was it that at one and the same time he gave all he had to me—and gave the same everything to Ann Lee? I've seen both wills, man, and that's how they read!'

Cal shook his head. 'He was having him his fun, I reckon. Old Early Bill, come rain or shine, was always a great hand for having him his own fun in 'his own way.' He thought a moment. 'Say! It might be that this way he was making sure that you and Miss Ann would marry each other! Maybe that's the way he wanted it!'

'Then you're wrong about him not being crazy,' snorted Cole Cody.

They sat silent a little while, soaking in the sunshine. Presently they fell to talking of this and that as men, strangers to each other and thrown together, will, and so it chanced that the attempted stage robbery of the day before was mentioned. And so Cal Roundtree learned that the attack had been made against

147

Bucktooth Jenkins, and that Jenkins was now lying in bed at Bald Eagle, pretty well shot up.

'Did they get the money Bucktooth was carrying?' Cal Roundtree asked anxiously.

'They didn't get anything, unless one of them got a bullet in him. I couldn't be sure, it was that dark. We all wondered what Bucktooth was carrying that they wanted.'

'He was carrying ten thousand dollars in hard and folding money,' said Cal. 'It was money he had gone to collect for Early Bill, and he was bringing it home. I know because Early Bill showed me the letter Bucktooth had wrote him; the letter said he had collected all right but was staying over a couple of days to visit some relations of his at the old trading post down over by Tilton; said he'd be along on yesterday's stage, bringing the ten thousand bucks with him. But how the devil did anybody else find out about it? Bucktooth ain't a man to gab. Early Bill showed me the letter because when it came he was near blind with pain, and he just snapped at me like this, 'Oh, hell, it ain't anything if it's from that fool Bucktooth. Just about whether he did as I told him or fell down on it. Here, read it to me, Cal,' and he stuck on to that, same as usual, 'If you *can* read!' So I read it, and left it lying on his table when he chased me out to bring him a drink.'

'You left it on the table, huh? He probably left it on the table.—What do you know about this Rance Waldron hombre anyhow?'

'Nothing. Except I don't like the way he wears his face.'

'He could have found the letter and acted on it. Let's see; there were two hold-up men. *You* knew about Bucktooth's carrying the money!'

'You knocked hell out of me once this morning, Mr. Cody. I'd like to do the same for you right now, but you being shot up like you are I'll have to give you time to mend.'

Cody laughed and slapped Cal on the knee.

'I was just joshing and you know it, Cal. Forget it. But about Rance Waldron I'm not so sure. But if it was Waldron, who would be the other man with him?'

'Better pull your punches when it comes to joshing me about things like that, young feller,' Cal growled at him, 'or you'll get your ears knocked down. About it being Waldron, dammit, I bet it was! He's been in and out of Bald Eagle a time or two, and from what I hear he ain't got a two-bit piece to his name. And I wouldn't put him above hog-stealing. But where he'd find a side-kick in a game like this, him being a Johnny-come-lately hereabouts, I wouldn't know.'

'Just who is Bucktooth Jenkins anyhow? How come that Early Bill sent him on an errand such as that?'

'Bucktooth has been old Bill's handy-man for years. He lived in that little shack over yonder.' Cal pointed to one of the several

149

small *adobes* half hidden by the low drooping branches of a live oak. 'He's a good man and game, and always carried out orders the way he got 'em. Later I'll be riding into town to see how he's making out. If he gets well he ought to be back here, no matter who owns the place.'

'I'd sort of like to look the ranch over, to see what it's like,' said Cody wistfully. 'But I suppose, the shape I'm in, a horse would shake me plumb to pieces.'

'I'll hitch up the buckboard, if you say the word, Cody. A buckboard can go most any place, you know.'

It was while they were giving the matter thought that a man came riding to them from the country road, ignoring the ranch house and striking straight for the two on the log. First Cole Cody recognized the palomino, then the rider, and waved. Here came little Porfirio Lopez whom he had left last night in town.

Porfirio's white teeth gleamed in a wide grin as he pulled his horse up in front of them.

'*Buenos dias, Don Codito! Buenas dias, amigo!*' he greeted the two. 'The beeg, roun' worl' is nice place today, no?'

'Light down, Porfirio,' invited Cody, 'and make yourself at home.'

Porfirio swung down lightly, was introduced to Cal Roundtree who shook hands without getting up to do so, an unecessary effort anyhow, seated himself beside his *amigo* Cole Cody, and the three chatted. Porfirio had come, it appeared, for more than one reason: He wanted to visit the grave of the poor old Señor Beel Cole; he meant to pick some wild flowers by the creek and place them there with his own two hands. Also he had thought that he might find his *amigo* Cole Cody here. Third, his heavy black brows drawn down like the shadow of a thundercloud, he wanted to poke his nose into things here, to find out things for himself, to be like a hunting dog, maybe to learn what *cabrone* it was who had shot Early Bill.

'I would kill him like that!' he exclaimed and crushed an acorn with the high heel of his boot.

Cody explained to Cal Roundtree all about Porfirio.

'He sold his little ranch to come here. I'd like him to stay a while. If I take over, he's on my pay roll. Anyhow he might hole-up here a few days?'

Cal shrugged.

'Me, not owning the place, I can't hire a man,' he said. 'Likewise, not owning it, I've got no rights chasing a man off. As far as I go, Porfirio is welcome to stick around until his feet itch to be traveling.'

Porfirio smiled. 'But I do not travel on my feets, Señor!'

They fell to talking of all the fun old Early Bill, fun-lover, was missing. Speaking of the situation at the ranch house with three contenders moving in and sticking by their guns, of the shooting of Bucktooth Jenkins for Early Bill's money, they got around to Doc Joe and the Judge, each with five hundred dollars of Early Bill's in his grip, the two bound to be buying the drinks for Bald Eagle right now and beginning to whoop things up.

'It's a darn shame,' said Cole Cody, half smiling and half inclined to sigh over the thing, 'that the old boy can't be with us, watching all the little merry hell he's kicked up.'

Cal sat silent a little while, gently stirring the dirt with the toe of his boot. Without looking up from this leisurely occupation, he said quietly,

'Well, me, I don't know nothing about nothing nohow, which is damn good and convincing grammar when a man means he can't figger a thing out far enough to get started even. Now, me, I've got the fool hunch that old Early Bill is watching every damn move. Don't know, like I said. But I figger when a man dies a part of him is dead as hell; but that there's another part of him that lingers on, to speak to the point and poetic at the same time. The old coot as much as said when he kicked off that he was going to get his fun out of things. I wasn't drunk this morning; maybe I was half asleep and didn't know it, but I could have swore old Early Bill was somewhere real close by, and was chuckling to himself the way he always did. Hell's bells!

152

You can have a smelly rose in a room; you can take the rose out and go chuck it in the river; you can go back to the room and run square into the smell of the rose you've chucked away.' A broad if somewhat shamefaced grin widened his mobile mouth. 'Maybe someday I'll grow up to be an orator! Just the same, boys,' and he was altogether sober again, 'I believe what I just said. Now shall we creep into the shade some place? It's getting hotter'n the seven hinges of the bad place out here. And likewise, your horse and Porfirio's will want water and hay.'

'It's not a day for sitting still,' said Cody, and stood up. 'That's a great idea of yours, Cal, about the buckboard.'

'Suits me,' said Cal. 'Here we go.'

He roped two lively young bays in the corral, harness-broke, and after a minor tussle with them got them harnessed and hitched to the buckboard while Cody held the reins. Cal took the reins into his own hands, as he climbed up over the wheel, said to his train a quiet, 'Run, damn you, if that's what you've got in your hearts,' and swung them into the sketch of a road leading down into the valley. Porfirio Lopez, not to be left alone with his thoughts and problems, rode alongside.

It vwas a glorious morning such as early summer, still brushing fingers with springtime, brings to this land of gentle hills and small valleys under the steep and rugged barrier of the blue mountains, and the breeze blowing in their faces was sweet with the resinous incense of pines, the spicy whiff of sage, the "green smell" of rich young grass and wild flowers and the many green things growing. And the land itself had its variety of loveliness and grandeur; the femininely soft and fertile valley, the slender bright waterfalls, the stern and awesome mountains shutting all this in.

'And,' explained Cal Roundtree, stretching out his arm to point, then moving it in an arc of some forty-five degrees, 'the King Cole Ranch runs on and spreads out over a hell of a lot you can't see from here. You ride through Hot Springs Pass yonder and you come into Long Jim Valley, twenty thousand acres more or less of the finest land for grazing or for hay that a man ever wanted to see; then there's another smaller valley, but a honey just over that way across the hills through Sylvia Pass.'

'Sylvia Pass?' commented Cody. 'Funny name for a mountain pass. How come?'

'You'd have to ask old Early Bill; he named it. Maybe he sort of liked the name. *Quien sabe?*'

Well, old Early Bill Cole had lived a long life and a varied one, and no doubt there had been names to linger in his memory—quite likely that had been some one name that never gave over chiming like a little golden bell in his heart. Sylvia was a pretty name.

They noted the few grazing herds, cattle and

horses, all fine stock to be seen with a glance, yet few in numbers for a ranch of such abundance of forage and water. When Cody remarked on the fact Cal explained that old Early Bill, getting ready for the long trail, had the notion to put the bulk of his livestock into ready cash; let the new owner make his own decisions about things. Some folks nowadays, Early Bill said, were going in for other things; for hay and grain, for orchards; he'd leave behind him the ranch itself, clear of mortgages, and enough money in the bank to do most anything with.

'And I reckon he left a pile of dough,' said Cal. 'Take that ten thousand that Bucktooth just brought home.' He snapped his fingers. 'It wasn't any more than that to old Bill. Man! You should have saw him stack into a poker game with a bunch of big mining men!' He laughed; he had a soft, chuckling, pleasant laugh at times. 'I've saw him come home more than once with a bunch of scalps dangling at his belt, laughing his head off. Oh, there's been other times when he lost his shirt, britches, boots and hat; but those times were seldom. And damn me if he didn't laugh anyhow. He'd screw up his ugly old face and set his teeth and say without opening his mouth, "Cal, I'm just sweetening 'em up for the killing. It won't be long, either." And, most usual, it wasn't long!'

*   *   *

It was nearly noon when they returned to
ranch headquarters. Cole Cody left Porfirio
and Cal Roundtree taking care of the horses,
and made his way slowly up to the house. He
was tired from the trip which no doctor would
have consented to, and his present yearning
was for a quiet room with a bed in it. Passing a
window he got a glimpse of little Ann Lee;
their eyes met fleetingly and he marked in
passing that her eyes looked bigger than ever
and that her face was very serious. He lifted
his hat and went on to his corner of the house;
he had no way of telling that she had been
shocked by the deadly pallor of his face, its
haggard, drawn look—and by her stabbing
realization that it had been her hand to make
him like this. If he should die—

The hours had passed quietly, and yet there
was a tenseness in the air which the quiet did
nothing to relieve but, on the other hand,
accentuated. If only something would happen!
Then taut nerves would tauten further, to the
top notch, and perforce relax.

Of them all, Aunt Jenifer alone seemed as
cheery as any cricket. She went humming
about the house, dusting and sweeping—and
whenever she came near Rance Waldron's
locked door, she paused and listened. Later
she explored the kitchen and pantry and dining
room: She checked on supplies and dishes; bits

156

of broken crockery she dumped into a barrel at the back door; she sorted potatoes and apples, making her discards; she figured roughly how much flour and sugar were on hand. She went into the *patio* and used an old watering pot to water those flowers and shrubs which seemed to have a chance of pulling through. Back in the kitchen she found dried apples and dried apricots; she made half a dozen pies, and all the while she was singing little old songs which she had known at sixteen and which we know today. She made a batch of bread while figuring what she'd use for the main dish for dinner and supper.

Spasmodically little Ann Lee tried to help. But she was far better teaching her little school, or riding and dancing and even shooting, than she was at housekeeping, and Aunt Jenifer over pie-making was not to be trifled with, so Ann wandered away, and did little more than ask herself answerless questions, and daydream. She did think about Rance Waldron, and wonder what he was doing; she did have the repeated impulse to go to Cole Cody's room, knock softly and ask if there was anything she could do for him—if he was in terrible pain—if he was dead already— if he forgave her—for she guessed she hadn't really meant to shoot him but that that darn hair-trigger gun had just gone off of its own volition.

At noon Cal Roundtree came up to the

157

house to ask if anything was wanted that he could do; before leaving he went to Cole Cody's room, finding Cody lying flat on his back, his hands clasped behind his head, his narrowed eyes on the beamed ceiling.

'How're you doing, kid?' he said casually.

'Bully,' said Cole. 'Kind of weak and shaky, of course, but just from the loss of a couple of cupfuls of blood. A few beefsteaks will fix me up fine.'

'Why, I've got a half baby steer hanging in the spring house right now,' exclaimed Cal. 'I'd forgot all about it. And the rest of the folks will want some for dinner. Me, I never think about anything to eat until I get hungry; that's why I forgot it. I'll go bring up a chunk right now that'll make damn juicy, tender steaks.'

So presently Aunt Jenifer served a meal that she was not in the least ashamed of. Thick steaks with rich, brown, gravy; potatoes au gratin, because she had found a half cheese, not altogether moldy; fresh hot bread, good strong coffee, and any kind of hot pie you wanted so long as you wanted either apple or apricot.

Four lively appetites came to the table, which was quite as well, since the four possessors of these appetites hadn't much to say to one another. For her part, Aunt Jenifer was bright-eyed and frankly interested, yet comported herself somewhat after the fashion of one occupying a ring-side seat at a circus.

Then there was the fact that the three others claimed, each for himself, the entire Early Bill Cole estate and could not but regard the others as intruders and most unwelcome. When you added to that that Cole Cody had only today bloodied Rance Waldron's handsome nose and had knocked Waldron pretty nearly out of his boots, that Ann Lee had popped a bullet into Cole Cody, and that Cody had promptly taken her across his knees and administered a spanking which left her pink and tingling, even burning, you've got to concede that there was not to be expected a whole lot of give and take in bright badinage over Aunt Jenifer's most excellent dinner. They didn't even say, one to another, 'Please pass the potatoes,' if the length of their arms made it humanly possible to reach.

When they finished, demolishing one pie and leaving but a trace of another, they quitted the dining room all but wordlessly. Cole Cody, first to rise, ducked his head toward Aunt Jenifer.

'Excuse me, please,' he said. And then had the grace to add, 'It's a wonder to me how you could have served up such a corking meal. Thanks a lot, Aunt Jenifer.'

She smiled at him and returned his nod, and there were dimples in her pink cheeks.

In his turn, Rance Waldron, departing for his roost shortly after, made a polite little speech, but the man was on edge and his voice was gruff and his eyes unsmiling. Ann and Aunt Jenifer, left alone among the kitchen débris, looked at each other soberly a moment, then Aunt Jenifer began that soft laughter of hers and Ann had to smile.

'You were sick and tired of that little one horse school of yours, my pet,' she said. 'You wanted life, pulsing, red-blooded life in the raw; adventures like your Gramma used to have. Now you've got 'em. Mysteries in an iron box, the fun of shooting your first big game, the thrill of one of the nicest spankings I ever saw! And with a first class villain cut to measure, and with days coming along all shot full of question marks. If there ever was a girl who ought to be satisfied, it's Ann Lee!'

Ann said a trite, 'Is that so?' and they started together cleaning up the dishes. Most of the real work was done by Aunt Jenifer, again singing little old deathless ballads: 'There lived an Indian girl, The bright Alfereta, where flowed the waters of the blue Junietta': and of course, 'When the roses bloom again,' and 'My grandfather's clock was too tall for the shelf, so it stood ninety years on the floor; it was taller by half than the old man himself, but it weighed not a penny-weight more. It was bought on the morn that the old man was born. It was always his joy and his pride. But it stopped—short—never to go again, when the old man died.'

She washed the dishes and Ann dried them;

160

Aunt Jenifer could wash a plate as quick as a cat could wink its eye; as for Ann, she stood drying and polishing a coffee cup and staring out the window, and polishing her cup still more.

Thus they put in a good hour. Thereafter they wandered about the house, continuing Ann's cruise of discovery, and eventually they went out into the garden. Aunt Jenifer brought some knitting with her and sat comfortably on the carved green bench; Ann Lee walked up and down restlessly for a while, then,

'I'm going to take a little walk,' she said. 'Right up to the top of that little hill you can see from here. There are three lovely big pines up there and I am going to lie in the shade, and stop thinking about wills and ranches and men.'

So her first short stroll brought her to the three noble old pines which Early Bill had loved so long. She saw no signs of his grave; the ground had been flattened and patted smoothly hard with a spade; dry, rusty brown pine needles covered everything. For a space she even leaned against his favorite pine; its rough bark against her shoulder comforted her; it stilled the wild contradictory impulses surging within that tumultuous heart of hers. She looked with dreamful eyes out across the beautiful panorama of hill and valley; she breathed deep of the balmy sunlit air; but she could not know that she was drinking the view

161

which had been Early Bill's last, nor that what she felt now was but a small part of all that had ridden through his soul.

And in a little while she saw a man coming up the hill, a little, wizened dark man who might have been Mexican or Indian or both together. She wasn't afraid of him; at his first glimpse of her he lifted his sombrero and carried it in his hand; also the crook of his arm was filled with field flowers, red and yellow and some few blue ones, and many white. You couldn't be alarmed by a man like that, carrying flowers.

'*Señorita*!' exclaimed the gallant Porfirio; he spoke to every woman, young or old, pretty or not pretty, as though she were the queen, he her courtier. He did not humble himself, because to his way of thinking no man permitted in the gracious presence could conceivably be of lowly estate. '*Señorita*, I make you my respects. I am Porfirio Lopez, and at your services.'

Ann smiled at him, thinking him delightful.

'I shall remember, Señor Porfirio,' she said gaily. 'If at some time I am in great need of a gallant deed done for me, I shall send for you!'

'Gracias, *Señorita, con toda mi coratonz!* I am going to come when you want me like the wind blowing when it is a storm.'

'Your flowers are very pretty,' said Ann.

Porfirio sighed like a horse; immediately tears welled up in his liquid eyes and ran down his nose.

'I bring them to an old friend, one who is dead now.' He crossed himself devoutly. 'These are for the gran'est *caballero* that ever lived, the Señor Don Early Beel Cole. I come to put them on his grave. He is going to know that Porfirio remembered. Every year as long as I live, I swear it, I am going to do that, and Don Beel up there with God, will know and smile and say, "*Gracias*, Porfirio."'

He stepped softly not a dozen paces from where she stood; she saw then the two small stakes standing not over three inches above ground, set something over six feet apart, and realized with a queer, inexplicable feeling that she had been standing almost on Early Bill Cole's new grave. Porfirio scattered his flowers and stood a moment with bowed bead, hat in his hand; she could see his lips moving though no sound came from him. Then without a backward glance, without looking at her, he hurried away; when he clapped on his hat it was fiercely done.

She sat her back to the tree, Early Bill's pine with which he had talked a few times in his wild-and-gentle life, her eyes upon the strewn flowers and the pine-needle covered earth, and thought dismally, 'He is right here, so close to me. And I have come too late.—Oh, that man who killed him!'

*   *   *

163

The afternoon passed lingeringly. There was so much to think about, so little to do about any part of it. For the most part, Cole Cody lay in his room, fatigued and weakened by his jaunt in the buckboard; Rance Waldron kept to his rooms, seldom emerging and always, as Aunt Jenifer took pains to note, leaving a locked door behind him. Aunt Jenifer herself did a bit of snooping all over the place but mostly in the neighborhood of Waldron's quarters. As for Ann Lee, she sat in the *patio*, dreaming dreams of the future, thinking of the immediate past, musing about her benefactor, Early Bill. And again she hunted through the house, specializing on those rooms where signs of his occupancy were most apparent, trying from little signs and tokens to make out what sort of man he really had been. She positively thrilled when in the small drawer of an old desk, almost a secret drawer so unobtrusive was it, she found the picture of an astonishingly pretty young girl. A girl dressed as was the fashion fifty or sixty years before, dark and lovely, with large, expressive, long-lashed eyes and a mouth that even little Ann felt an impulsive urge to kiss, and slantingly across the bottom of the picture, in ink faded almost beyond deciphering, the words, 'To Billy, from Sylvia.'

'Billy! Oh, that was old Early Bill Cole! He was young then, maybe no older than I am now! And she *loved* him—and he loved her—

Oh, how I wish I had a picture of him then!'

Not long after the lamps were lit all gathered around the dining table when Aunt Jenifer rang the hand bell for supper. Again the meal was excellent and attacked as at dinner; again conversation died aborning. In fact, had it not been for Aunt Jenifer's few cheery remarks, there would probably not have been so much as a 'Please pass the potatoes,' remark. At the end of this feast of silence and flow of distrust, Cole Cody again said some sort of polite thanks, and went to his room. After Cody's departure, Rance Waldron sat a little while over his coffee, smoking a cigarette, and made some small endeavor to be agreeable. Aunt Jenifer did not like the man, and made him the curtest replies before she got up to clear the dishes away: Ann Lee seemed absent minded; she said 'What did you say?' twice to remarks of his; he was not long in saying his own good night and going to his room.

Ann Lee patted a yawn; they had been up early, it had been quite a day and she was sleepy already.

'Go to bed, Kitten,' said Aunt Jenifer. 'I'll do the dishes and follow along in two shakes.'

Ann got up listlessly and began helping with the scraping and piling of plates and carrying them to the kitchen sink. Aunt Jenifer washed them and Ann wiped and yawned and, once or twice, sighed. It seemed years before the work was done. She took up a lamp and said, 'Coming, Aunt Jenny?'

'You just scamper to your room and tuck into bed. You look as sleepy as a daytime hoot owl. Me, I'm young and strong and romantic, and I'm going out into the *patio* to look at the stars. At the moon, too, if there is any. Run along, Pet.'

Ann carried her lamp through quiet empty rooms where shadows seemed to come out of corners and from under tables and chairs, and scurry away like frightened things. In her room it was very still, and the starshine came in through the iron grilles of her open windows. She drew the shades down, undressed and slipped into her nightgown and into her big bed almost with one gesture. She left her lamp burning on her bedside table, snuggled her curly head deep into the pillow and passed gently from daydream to the land of night's dreams.

And Aunt Jenifer, as wide awake as any cat at any mouse hole, sat for a long while on the green bench, and her head was tipped at an angle that indicates the head's owner is listening intently for the slightest sound. Thus an hour passed; and the night was still. At even the slightest sound, she started; when she heard the faint creak of a board within the house, she clutched the edges of her bench with both hands, ready to spring up. But she knew the way of old houses; how in the night for no reason on earth that she knew, the ancient floorboards would creak like that; sometimes she had treated herself to the thrill of thinking, 'There goes a ghost!' Now she just sat back and continued to wait.

Long ago little Ann Lee was fast asleep, or she would have been out here seeking her. Aunt Jenifer stole out of her secret place and crept like an agile small shadow out to one of the big liveoaks not more than fifty yards from Rance Waldron's outer door. Under the thick branched tree, heavy with young foliage, it was black dark; here she established herself, seated on the ground, leaning back against the gnarled trunk.

At last even Aunt Jenifer began to yawn and her eyelids to grow so heavy that it required pounds of effort and the final exercise of her will power to get them lifted. But when at last she heard the sound she had waited for so long, her eyes flew wide open of their own accord and she was as wide awake as a child early on Christmas Eve.

The creaking this time was no ghostly creaking; it told of a door being slowly opened on rusty hinges. It was the door from one of Rance Waldron's rooms. And the steps she heard were no ghostly tread; two men, with the door softly closed and locked after them, were coming out, and one of the men walked scufflingly as though he dragged an injured leg after him.

167

She hid as best she could behind the dark old oak tree, peering out to see what she could see. The night was clear and there was light enough for her to be sure of two things: One of the men was a stranger to her, and he was hurt or sick. The other man was helping him along, and was Rance Waldron. She sniffed. 'As though he could fool me, with someone hid in his part of the house. Well, I know now it's a man and not some fool girl he's hiding out. And I'd bet my last bustle that there's a stranger in Mr. Waldron's woodpile!'

She strove with all her ears to hear what was said between them, but they spoke a few words only, those in lowered voices. She saw them move, one man lurching and the other supporting him, toward the group of ranch buildings at the foot of the slope, and furtively she followed them. She saw that Waldron had a couple of horses hid in a willow thicket just across the creek; she watched him help his companion up into the saddle; she saw them ride away, heading north, and hastening, then she turned and ran back to the house.

CHAPTER THIRTEEN

She went straight to Cole Cody's outside door and hammered at it hard with her knuckles. He was asleep but came awake instantly, and called out,

'Who's there? What's wanted?'

'It's me, Jenifer Edwards. Dress quick and come out here. Bring your gun, too.'

She heard his bare heels hit the floor. He slid into trousers, shirt and boots and, despite a sore stiffness along his side, went through his routine like a fire horse.

'Well?' he demanded when he stepped out close to Aunt Jenifer's shadowy form.

'I don't know,' she said calmly if eagerly. 'I don't trust that Rance Waldron; he's got a mean eye. All day long he has kept his door locked, and all day I've known that he had somebody he's been hiding. I've been watching, figuring with all this secrecy he'd be anxious to get his friend out of the house when he was sure everybody was in bed. Just now he and another man sneaked out and went to their horses that were saddled and hidden in a willow thicket.'

'What about it?' demanded Cody, about as amiable as most men rudely awakened from a deep sleep all for the sake of a mere trifle. 'What affair is it of mine? Or of yours, either?'

'Part of it is this: Rance Waldron has had this man hid in the house behind a locked door all day; that's a mystery, young man, and I don't like mysteries. Then it's shady, their sneaking out of the house this time of night, speaking in whispers. And someone shot Early Bill a few days ago; and in case there was no

169

will, Rance Waldron would have inherited ranch, cash, and everything. Another thing; the stage was held up yesterday by someone who knew that Bucktooth Jenkins was bringing ten thousand dollars in cash to Early Bill Cole. And you fired a few shots at the robbers and thought you hit one of them. And the man with Waldron limped so bad that he could hardly walk. Is that an earful, or just child's chatter?'

'Which way did they ride?' asked Cody, grown brisk now.

'Straight north, along the creek on this side.'

'You'd better get to bed, Aunt Jenifer. It's dawning on me that you're a pretty wonderful woman, but you can't keep going day and night.'

'You bet I'll go to my room, Bill Cole Cody, and lock my door. Darn it, I'm scared. And you come back as soon as you can; I'll hear you, and I'll creep out into the living room to make sure it is you. Now poke along.'

He caught her hand and gave it a squeeze; he came perilously close to hugging her. Then he hurried down to the ranch buildings for a word with Cal Roundtree, and a horse. He estimated that Rance Waldron and his companion would take it for granted that their departure had gone unnoted, and would not ride fast; with luck he and Cal could at least make out the general direction they took.

Cal Roundtree, waked and apprised of the situation, was out of the door still buttoning

170

his overalls and drawing his belt about his lean middle. Cole Cody was ahead of him at the stable; they saddled swiftly and took the trail Aunt Jenifer had specified, north along the creek.

'If they want to hide they can make themselves hard to find in this country,' said Cal Roundtree. 'The nights are not too cold up here as early as this, and they can hide out in any one of a hundred places. Just the same I knew the most likely place to look for them, since they must have thought that no one had seen their getaway, and so no one would be following them so soon. Likely they'll get under a roof tonight, anyhow, and maybe poke on tomorrow night.'

As they rode, Cole Cody told Cal in detail Aunt Jenifer's information, her suspicions and surmises. The two were inclined to believe that her contentions were grounded on imagination rather than fact, yet remained open-minded and were disposed to learn what they could. For one thing it developed that neither of them had the slightest earthly use for Rance Waldron.

'And I wouldn't put it beyond him to shoot the old man to keep him from making a will,' said Cal. 'And at that, seeing that he's got some other hombre along with him and is flat busted, I wouldn't say he didn't have a hand in the holdup. Miss Edwards is as smart as a whip, and there's the off chance she's right all along the line.'

171

Cole Cody nodded.

'We're thinking along the same lines, Cal. Let's hope we come up with them before Waldron sends the other man on his way; we can be pretty sure that Waldron will come back to the ranch, seeing a chance to hog the whole King Cole estate.'

Cal Roundtree slid a sly glance sidewise at Cody's face, starlit.

'I don't know the whole story,' he said, 'but I did help Doc Joe and the Judge with their buggy horse, and I heard a few words and learned a thing or two, and already knew a few things from what I had heard old Early Bill say before he died. The old devil was cooking him up some fun to last him after he had straddled the big black horse for the one way ride. Seems as though the game is in your hands, and that pretty girl, Ann Lee's. You two could get together—' He stopped, pondering the conventions which exist in the rough western country as well as in New York or London or any other place where women don peacock splendor and men squeeze into tails, and then said bluntly, 'Hell, the two of you might get married.'

'I think you mean well, Cal,' said Cody coldly. 'Let's let it go at that.'

'Sure,' said Cal agreeably, and they rode along in companionable silence. Cal led the way, and the darkness did not matter to him; moreover, his horse soon discovered where he

172

was going and thereafter needed no touch on the reins. They kept close to the creek for a mile, and though they rode swiftly they heard no sound of hoofbeats ahead. Then Cal swung to the right where a small tributary brook came tumbling down, and presently they passed into the mouth of a steep-walled ravine. Here it was darker than ever, made blackly shadowy by the tall growth of pines on the ridges and by the dense growth of alders and laurels nearer the bickering brook. But here Cal's horse was in no doubt whatever, and they continued to make rapid progress. It was about a half hour after entering the ravine that Cal Roundtree called softly over his shoulder,

'We've run 'em down, pardner. There's a log cabin up there at the head of the canyon where an old prospector used to hang out; nobody's been in it for three-four year, but there's a light there now.'

'It strikes me,' said Cody, 'that we've got 'em where we want them, where they can't run out on us.'

'It strikes me, Cody,' said Cal Roundtree, taking his time to think things out to some sort of logical conclusion, 'that it would be fair play and on the up and up if we played a dirty trick on them. We leave our horses before we get too close, and creep up on 'em Injun style. And we try our damnedest to hear what they are talking about. There's a lot of fellers I know that just can't help being blab-mouthed. If these two are like that, we might learn something we're hankering to know.'

'That sort of doings don't smell very sweet when you hear folks tell about them,' said Cody. 'But things don't smell very sweet, either, around the tracks Rance Waldron is making. How come he arrived here just at the right time to see old Early Bill die? How come he's been hiding somebody in the house all day? How come he sneaks him out after the middle of the night, goes whispering and heading up here? How come the man with him limps like he can hardly walk? You're damn' right we'll snoop and eavesdrop all we can. Me, I ain't even shamed of it. We won't hear anything bad if they're a couple of white angels; if they're a team of dirty dogs I hope we hear aplenty.'

'You've spoke it the way I was thinking it,' Cal said. 'Let's go on, *compañero.*'

They rode slowly, keeping their horses in the deep grass at the sides of the trail so that all hoofbeats were muffled. Thus they drew within a hundred yards of the log cabin. There Cal Roundtree gave a signal to stop, and both dismounted. They led their horses a score of paces into the thick timber fringing the creek, and removed their spurs to hang them on their saddle horns. Then walking in silence, lifting their booted feet as does a cat in wet grass, they drew near the cabin; they drew so near

174

that they could put out their hands and touch the rough log walls.

Right away they heard voices, but so thick were the logs of the walls, so thoroughly were the interstices chinked with clay, that only a mumble of sound came to their ears. So they moved cautiously, stepping around a corner, trying to do better at another wall. And so they did; they came to a place where the clay, dried out, had fallen from its place, and had left a long slit, a space fully the quarter of an inch wide, between two logs, breast-high.

A voice, not Rance Waldron's was speaking, and it was rough and querulous and came near being threatening.

'. . . and so, there you let me rot all day, damn you. I might of died! I might die yet for all the doctoring I'm getting. By God, Rance, I've got a notion and a damn good notion—'

'You'd better keep your mouth shut, Tom, old man, before you talk yourself into more trouble than you can ever crawl out of.'

There spoke Rance Waldron, and his voice was arrogant, contemptuous, revealing a man very sure of himself and of his own security, commanding and threatening a man in such fashion that those who were listening gained the impression that 'Tom' had been under Waldron's thumb many and many a long day.

But it would appear that all of a sudden the man Tom had slipped out from under the master thumb. He spoke up angrily, and jeeringly. He had said, 'I might of died! I might die yet . . .' It might be that he was in a fever. He said, and there was in his tone threat equal to Waldron's,

'Get it into your head, Rance, that things have changed like all hell! You had me down good and plenty, didn't you? You could have waggled your finger and sent me to the pen, couldn't you?' He laughed chuckingly. 'Not any more, kid!'

'You're crazy,' said Rance angrily. 'What I could have done for you any time during the last two years I could do tomorrow—tonight, as far as that goes! You're too badly shot up to make much time in a get-away, Gough. Think that over.'

Again Tom Gough indulged in his guttural, chuckling laugh.

'I've thought it over from all angles, Rance. You won't do any squealing on me because at the end you've let your foot slip; you'd be squealing on yourself the same as on me. What I've did you paid me for. The other job, with me getting shot up, you and me did together. *And I can prove it!*'

'Damn you—'

There was a breathless stillness there in the cabin. Then Tom Gough spoke again.

'Try it if you want to,' he said surlily. 'If you think you're quicker on the trigger than me and a straighter shot, try it now. If you can get away with it it might be your best bet. Try it,

176

you damn yellow dog!'

Again there was that breathless silence. Then Rance Waldron spoke again, and there was a marked change in his tone. All the challenge and threat, all the masterfulness and contempt had gone out of it. He said quietly, sounding thoughtful and quite unemotional,

'You are right, Tom. We have gone into this thing together and we had better see it through together. And I'll even grant you that I no longer have any hold on you; if you are big enough fool for it, you can leave me flat and go your own way for the rest of your life knowing that you don't have to be afraid of me any longer, because as you say I am as deep in this last affair as you are. It's your turn to speak up: Stick along with me and take orders from me and make yourself a big stake if I get away with this job, as I'm damn sure I will, with you or without you. Or tuck your tail between your legs and run out on me.'

That sort of talk, straight from the shoulder, evidently threw Tom Gough off his balance; he didn't have an immediate answer to make. To his listeners outside the cabin that silence after Rance Waldron's speech, made it clear that Waldron's was the driving spirit and that Tom Gough was the weaker of the two. That conviction became a certainty when Gough answered.

'I'm with you, Rance,' he said, and all the belligerent menace had melted out of his tone.

177

'In a way you've treated me pretty fair. From now on I know I can trust you or you'd tell me to get the hell out of here while the going is good. Now what?'

'You hole up here for a few days and give that wound a chance to heal. Nobody is apt to drop in on you; if they do you can say that you were prospecting up in the mountains and got a fall, and are resting up; they can't possibly connect you with the holdup. I'll manage to bring you some more grub; what you've got with you now will get you through until tomorrow night. Meantime I'll plan; I'll learn a few things I'm not sure of yet; I'll drop in on you late tomorrow night.'

'That's fair enough,' said Tom Gough. 'Be sure you bring me plenty coffee and sugar; I like a lot of sugar in my coffee. And plenty good grub, any kind, I ain't particular, so it's filling and sticks to the ribs. Thanks, Waldron.'

'All right,' said Waldron. 'I'll be on my way now. Keep under cover; watch out for any smoke from the fireplace; look for me some time tomorrow night.'

'Good night, Waldron,' said Gough.

Cal Roundtree had shoved Cody out of his way and was peering in through the open slit between the two logs. He saw Rance Waldron clearly in the candlelight, saw him go to the door and pass through and close the door behind him. And clearly he saw Tom Gough, a man of low, squat stature with a thick thatch of

178

black hair and a week's black bristly growth of whiskers; with a brutish, flat face and a pair of brilliant, close-set black eyes. And he took particular stock of Tom Gough's hat. *It was brand new.* Old clothes, ragged boots—and a brand new hat.

Rance Waldron went on his way to his horse tethered near by, then down trail returning along the way he had come. Cody and Roundtree stepped softly to the corner of the cabin and watched until the night swallowed him up, and still stood still until the sound of his horse's hoofs died away in the distance. Then they went to their own horses.

'That man in there, that Tom Gough,' said Cal, 'is the man that shot old Early Bill. He was made to do it by Rance Waldron. That's something I'm pretty damn certain of. And the two of them are the stage robbers; that's something else I'd bet my boots on.'

'You sound like you know what you're talking about,' said Cody. 'I gather the same idea as you do about the holdup. But how come you cinch the shooting of Early Bill on Tom Gough?'

'You don't see a man wearing a new hat every day, Cody. Early Bill, before he checked in his chips, told Doc Joe and the Judge how he had whanged away at the hombre that potted him; how he had shot the feller's hat off. He said, 'Watch out for a man with a hat with a hole in it, or a man without any hat at

179

all, or a man with a brand new hat.' Now we hear Waldron and Tom Gough talk like they're flat busted, and just the same Tom Gough had to spend a few bucks for his sombrero. That's sort of clear, ain't it?'

Cole Cody was shoving his foot into the stirrup, but brought it back to the ground.

'It's dead sure you're right all along the line, Cal. We step in right now and rope this Tom Gough. We take him with us back to the ranch and put our rope on Rance Waldron. Then we herd the two of them into Bald Eagle. They've got a jail house there, I reckon.'

'When I was a kid like you,' retorted Cal, and meant to sound calm and dispassionate and judicial, 'I used to go off half-cocked like that. I made me some fool mistakes, too. We're making us a guess that I'd bet on, but we ain't dead sure. If we was, we wouldn't drag these men into jail; we'd string 'em up by their dirty necks and watch 'em kick their lives out. Because taking 'em to jail wouldn't do any good; they'd get a jury trial and they'd go free because we wouldn't have any way on earth to prove anything. We leave 'em be for a spell; we know where they are; even if Gough moseys on a ways, it won't be far and we can round him up when we want him. This way we'll find out for sure, and when we've got 'em where we want 'em, we'll then do one of two things: Hand 'em over to the law, or burn 'em down ourselves. Now climb on your pony and

180

let's travel.'

*   *   *

And at the ranch house, while Cal Roundtree
and Cole Cody were giving their attention to
Waldron and Tom Gough, Aunt Jenifer was
busying herself in her own fashion. She
scurried post-haste to her own room, closed
the door and was going to lock it when she
discovered there was no key in the lock. She
hurried to Ann's room adjoining, carrying a
lamp turned low; Ann was asleep, and was
smiling; you knew from that smile of hers that
she was having a gay and lovely dream. Aunt
Jenifer went on tip-toe to Ann's other door; it
was closed but unlocked; no key there either.
Hmf! Of course old Early Bill wouldn't lock
doors; of course, during the years the keys, if
ever there had been any, had gone the way of
all keys.

But she thought, That Waldron man's door
is locked. He's got a key. There ought to be
others somewhere. So, carrying her lamp,
turned up higher now, she went prowling
through the house, key-hunting. She looked at
all locks *en passant*, she opened all drawers in
tables and dressers, she ran her fingers along
cupboard shelves. She came to a closed closet
and opened it to peer inside, and, of all places,
found a key in the lock within the closet. Hmf.
A funny place for a key; anyhow it's here

181

where nobody ever saw the darn thing, and I've got it now. Wonder if it will fit my door?

She tried it in her own lock; it fitted and she shot the bolt home. She locked herself in and went to Ann's door, the farther one opening upon the corridor. It fitted there, too. Another hmf! It seemed as though all the locks in the house were the same. And right then the inspiration and the temptation assailed her to try her key on still another door. If it worked on these locks, why not on Rance Waldron's?

She scurried with her lamp turned low again to that door through which Waldron had passed so many times, always locking it behind him. She was certain that he had not come back; she was equally willing to bet her best bonnet that Waldron's room or rooms were unoccupied. All she had to do was, as she expressed it to herself, get a wiggle on. And so she did.

And the key fitted the lock, and the door opened! She was thrilled with a sense of adventure and was also just a mite frightened.

'Keep your dander up, old girl,' she admonished herself. 'You didn't use to be anybody's scaredy-cat.'

She entered a bedroom that was in considerable disorder. She glanced at the bed itself with its covers dragging on the floor; then around the room until her eyes came to a full stop at a table on which there were some papers and a couple of penciled account books. She flipped over pages: Cattle bought and sold; numbers in various herds, cost nad sale prices; that sort of thing for the most part. Other entries of which she could make little in a hurry. Among the scattered papers, a few old letters which Early Bill hadn't bothered to destroy; one new letter signed by Andy Jenkins. She read it almost at a glance, so brief was it, yet her heart was going pit-a-pat before she finished the few lines. It said:

'Deer Bill, I done my job all right, better than you speckalated what I mean is I got the whole ten thousand and am bringing it with me only I am staying a day with my relations and will ketch the stage next day.
Yours truly,
Andy Jenkins.'

'So that's it,' Aunt Jenifer mumbled to herself. 'That Waldron devil found this letter and got busy, him and the man he's been hiding in here all day. No wonder he wanted to get rid of us! He's a villain and a fool; anybody but a fool would have burnt this letter or hid it.'

Then she fell to pondering; what was she to do with it now? It might serve as some sort of evidence if she kept it; also, if she took it with her, Waldron would know that someone had been in his room and, dollars to doughnuts, would say, 'Aha! That little snooping Aunt Jenifer!'

183

The matter demanded thought, quick thinking at that, since she wanted to take no chances of his catching her here. And there remained the adjoining room, its door wide open, for her to investigate.

She made up her mind in a jiffy. She crumpled the telltale letter in her hand and hurried into the other room and tried the door leading to the outside; again the key fitted. What a silly idea to have a lot of locks all the same! She closed the door again and began taking stock of this second room's contents. Another tumbled bed; the usual furnishings; the shade drawn as in the first room which she had decided was Waldron's—and something else. There was a splotch on the floor; a rug had evidently been drawn to cover it, then its edge turned over by a careless foot as the two men departed. And that spot looked to Aunt Jenifer like a blood smear. So she leaped to the same conclusion that had offered itself to Cody and Roundtree: The man who had been hidden in here was the man who. had been wounded in the stage holdup affair! No wonder he had hidden all day, then slipped away in the dark. She hoped Bill Cole Cody had caught up with him. She felt somehow that Cole Cody, single handed, was good enough to handle both Rance Waldron and the wounded man.

On the next step she was already decided. She would unlock the outside door again,

184

leave it unlocked, but closed, make her retreat through Waldron's room, slip out of his door that led into the corridor, lock that door and carry her key off with her. Then when he came home and found his outer door unlocked he would have something to think about; when he missed the Jenkins letter which he had been too great a fool to destroy or hide, he'd have still more matter for thought. But there wouldn't be the vaguest hint to make him think that this had been an inside job. And even though for one reason or another he did get the idea that Aunt Jenifer had had something to do with it, he couldn't really be convinced—and he'd be mighty careful about speaking of it to her, for fear of tipping his hand. And watch her play innocent tomorrow!

Now she wanted to hurry faster than ever, for she kept telling herself that she was in a den of murderers. Yet she kept telling herself also that now was her one and only chance to make a thorough search in these two rooms. She didn't really expect to come upon anything else of any importance, but she realized that if she went straightway to her own room without any further prying here, she would fairly writhe and squirm in her bed all night, calling herself as big a fool as Rance Waldron.

*   *   *

She had heard the old expression of the marrow turning cold in one's bones, and now

185

knew exactly what it meant. Her nerves were on edge, her heart was thumping and her whole body was quivering. It was hard to keep from bolting from the room and racing back to where Ann was. But once she had made up her mind, it took more than mere fear to turn Jenifer Edwards aside from her purpose. Pshaw, she told herself, Rance Waldron won't be back for an hour yet. You can bet your boots he took his wounded friend a good long trip from here. Don't go getting goose flesh old girl. Have yourself some fun while you've got the chance.

She rummaged Rance's room swiftly but thoroughly. There was a coat hanging on a peg; the pockets offered nothing of any consequence: a little loose tobacco, some matches, the stub of a lead pencil, a soiled handkerchief. She opened and examined every drawer in the room: for the most part they were empty. There was a suit of underwear, fairly clean, which she judged Rance Waldron's, one pair of socks, not new, a flashy checked shirt, a couple of bags of cigarette tobacco with papers, and that was all.

Aunt Jenifer nodded her head like an automaton.

'Dead broke, he is,' she told herself. 'Dead broke and bad in debt, I'd bet a man, and ready for anything from highway robbery to outright murder, just to line his pockets. I'm mighty glad Bill Cole Cody is staying here; I wish he was here right now!'

There remained the other room to be searched again, more meticulously. She returned to it, trying not to throw too much lamplight on the windows even though the curtains were drawn, and poked into corners, into the one closet, into drawers, as she had done in Rance Waldron's bedroom. Here after a pretty thorough search she found nothing of any interest—until she bethought herself of hunting through the bedding. There were no sheets, but there was a greyish-white blanket, and she was dead sure that the spot on it was a blood spot. It confirmed her judgment of the smear on the floor.

Well, she had done all she could now, and had better scamper for her own quarters.

So she did as she had planned, unlocked the outer door, removed the key and turned to retrace her steps through Rance Waldron's room.

And then she stiffened and almost dropped her lamp. Distinctly she heard rapidly oncoming footsteps outside.

CHAPTER FOURTEEN

For one stricken instant the adventuresome Aunt Jenifer felt as though she were paralyzed. The next second she leapt and ran like a frightened deer; her racing footsteps sounded extraordinarily loud to her own ears as she dashed through Waldron's room toward the corridor. Then an even louder sound struck her ears, a man in the yard running faster than she could run, making for the outside door of Tom Gough's room. She gained the door she was heading for and heard the other door snapped open, and heard a man's heavy boots come pounding on.

She fled faster than ever, carrying her lamp in one hand, her letter in the other. The lamp chimney was shaken off and crashed to the floor making a noise, it seemed to her, loud enough to wake the dead, but the flame, giving out more smoke than light, still burned on and showed her dimly the way she must go to gain her own room. She glanced back and saw the man speeding after her; it was too dark back there for her to make out clearly, but she knew it must be Rance Waldron, and she could imagine his hard hands choking her to death.

By about three yards she won the race. But by the time she could slip into Ann Lee's room and get her key into the lock, he was at her door. By the fraction of a second she shot the bolt before his hand touched the knob.

Then she sped through Ann Lee's room and to the door that gave upon the corridor, and as she heard him coming there, too, she got that door locked.

There was a heavy silence, then Ann Lee's

188

sleepy voice asking, 'Is that you, Auntie? What are you doing?'

Then Rance Waldron's voice spoke up, saying curtly yet not over loud, 'Miss Edwards, I think you had better let me come in. Or, if you like, you might step out here and give me a word of explanation.'

'Not tonight, Mr. Waldron, thank you,' said Aunt Jenifer with creditable calmness, considering the fright she was in.

Ann Lee sat up in bed, her hair in wild disorder about her piquant face, her eyes growing enormous as some part of her aunt's dread seeped into her.

'What is it?' she whispered. 'What has happened?'

Aunt Jenifer put her finger on her lips and shook her head emphatically for silence.

Again Rance Waldron spoke, more sternly this time.

'Miss Edwards, I won't stand for this sort of thing. You come out here and give me a damned good explanation or I'll smash your door down and come in.'

Aunt Jenifer told her pat little lie then.

'I still have Cal Roundtree's gun, Mr. Waldron,' she said quietly. 'Stick your ugly mug in here and I'll shoot it off.'

'I'll bust your door down, I tell you,' said Waldron. 'I know you haven't any gun. Cody pitched it out into the *patio* and I saw Roundtree pick it up and holster it and carry it

189

off with him. Going to open up?'

'No. Not on your life. And if you try it, I'll yell my head off, and I've got a voice that'll call the hogs home a mile; and the Cole Cody you mention will be here like a shot and will work on you the way he did this morning, only I'll bet my bustle he'll do a better and more lasting job this time.'

'That's something to think about,' said Waldron, and sounded reasonable and thoughtful. Then he fell silent. A moment later she could hear his footsteps, moving away.

By now Ann Lee was thoroughly frightened. She was sitting up, the bed covers clutched up to her throat as though for protection.

'Tell me!' she insisted. 'What is it all about, Aunt Jenny? What in the world has happened? What have you done?'

'Sh! I'll tell you later. I've been poking about in his room and he caught me. And when I said that I'd call to Cole Cody—Well, Cole Cody isn't in the house, I'm pretty sure. Maybe Rance Waldron is bluffed out—If he comes back we mustn't let him in. He—Oh, my God, Pet, I believe he'd kill us both! Now don't go shrieking or fainting, either! You just keep a hold on yourself, and if there's a rumpus, the two of us have got to handle it!'

For a moment the girl sat there in bed shivering, her eyes widening unbelievably with terror. Then that fine spirit that was a part of the fiery nature of her, drove out her fear and set up in its place a grim will to fight things out, anything that came along, with Aunt Jenifer. She sprang out of bed, shed her night gown in a jiffy and as swiftly donned a little suit she had brought along with her, a neat, rather shockingly boyish outfit which the times did not altogether condone yet which she loved, being a lover of heroes and riding. She began looking around for something to use as a weapon, some sort of club.

'He won't come back, I'm sure of it,' said Aunt Jenifer. Yet she wasn't sure, and he did come back.

That was only after he had pondered a moment, after he had returned to his room and Tom Gough's. He saw signs of the invasion; he marked the rug turned back showing the stain on the floor boards, he even saw the telltale spot on the greyish-white blanket. He looked things over in his own room—his papers had been tampered with— and the letter from Bucktooth Jenkins to old Early Bill was gone.

No man, even fool enough to have left that letter as he had, would be fool enough not to realize what its seizure implied. For a time he was at his wits' end; there was the off chance that Cole Cody would not hear Aunt Jenifer's and the girl's screams; a slim, slim chance on a quiet night even in so big a house. But there was still another chance! Slim, this one too, but a possibility. Cole Cody might not be in the house at all; he might have ridden into Bald Eagle during the evening, anxious and impatient about the will, seeking the Judge's counsel. At least it could do no harm to discover whether Cody were in or out.

He went swiftly yet on tip-toe to Cody's room. He rapped gently, saying, 'Cody, are you there? I've got terrible cramps; have you got a shot of whiskey with you?'

When he waited for an answer and got none, he tried the door. It was unlocked and he went in, striking a match as he crossed the threshold. There was no one in the room! No Cody to come running if Aunt Jenifer yelled her head off. And no likelihood of Cody returning this time of night.

So Rance Waldron returned promptly to Jenifer Edwards' room. There was grim determination in his voice as he said,

'I am going to shoot the lock off your door— or I'll go get an ax. You had better open up. As for calling that Cody hombre, it's no use. I've been to his room and he's not there. The chances are he's no nearer than Bald Eagle.'

Ann Lee whispered to her aunt, 'That isn't true!' But Aunt Jenifer nodded and drew down the corners of her mouth.

'Only it is true. I knew he had gone out and I knew he hadn't come back. It's likely he's down at the men's quarters by now, chinning with Cal Roundtree. But if we yelled our heads off they wouldn't hear; that's why Cal left you a gun this morning, to signal him with. Darn it, I wish we had that gun now! Well, anyhow, I've got all the keys I know about in this place, and it'll take a lot of ax work to batter one of these doors down.'

'Well, what's the answer?' demanded Waldron. 'I can't give you all night, you know, to make up your minds.'

Ann Lee put her lips close to Aunt Jenifer's ear.

'There are windows!' she whispered eagerly. 'We can slip through while he's battering at our door, and scoot like anything down to where Cal Roundtree is!'

Aunt Jenifer whispered back,

'Go take a good look at the windows, Goosey. This is a regular old Spanish house; every one of these windows has iron bars like a jail; if you haven't noticed, I have.'

'I'll give you about two minutes more to think it over,' said Waldron. 'That's because if I go shooting your lock off, I'm apt to wake that nosy Roundtree. I'll go to the kitchen and get a hand-ax; there's one by the wood box. I can handle that so he won't hear a sound. You've got until I get back to do your thinking. And I'll manage to keep an eye on your door so that you don't sneak out on me.'

They listened for his departing footsteps and didn't hear a sound. So they quite naturally decided that he was still standing before their door, trying to trick them into sticking their noses out when he'd be ready to pounce on them. But he had tricked them in another way. What he had actually done was remove his boots, set them down gently and hurry in his socked feet to the kitchen, get the hand-ax and return. The next thing they heard was his voice, at once angry and mocking.

'Fooled you that time, my pretty ladies,' he jeered at them. 'I pulled my boots off and made the trip, and here I am back with the ax. You had your chance to run, but it's gone now. Listen to this.'

The hand-ax crashed into the solid oak of the door.

'Open up now, and all I'll do is make you give me back something you stole from my room. Get pig-headed about it, and I won't let you off so easy. I'm willing to be reasonable about the whole thing, but nobody is going to burglarize my room and get away with it.'

The ax crashed into the wood the second time.

'What's the answer?' he demanded.

A voice, cool and impersonal, spoke out of the darkness, for it was dark where Rance Waldron stood; he had left his lamp in his room, making his way by striking an occasional match. The voice, cool and deliberate as it was, sounded like that of a man whom it would be just as well not to antagonize, the voice of Cole Cody, just now arrived in silence. The words were, merely,

'What's going on here?'

The answer came quickly enough; a thoroughly frightened Ann Lee forgot entirely for the moment her hatred of a man who had kissed her once in violence, to punish her, and had spanked her in anger; she screamed to him at the top of her voice,

'Oh, Cole! God sent you to us! That horrid Rance Waldron is trying to break our door down!'

'I can't see you, Waldron,' said Cody, his tone as steady and deliberate as before. 'From your ax work I can guess pretty close where you are, though. Want to shoot it out in the dark? Or stick your tail between your legs and get the hell out of here?'

Rance Waldron took his time in deciding how to answer.

'Shooting it out in the dark, Cody,' he said after due thought, 'is sheer luck. I haven't been over lucky of late; if it's the same with you I'd rather take you on by daylight.'

'Suits me fine,' said Cody. 'There's a light in your room, and the door is open. Suppose you step along in there and tuck yourself into bed for the night? Tomorrow is another day, you know.'

'And have you pot me in the back as soon as I step into the light? Are you a damn fool or do you think I am?'

'I'm no liar, Waldron. You're free to go to your room and shut the door, and I won't pull

195

a trigger. Take my word for it or try your luck in the dark.'

'Your word? You swear you won't shoot?'

'I won't shoot. Now make it lively.'

Rance Waldron dropped his ax. His gun was in his hand as he said, 'All right; I'm taking your word for it,' and started back down the corridor to his room. Cody was in the dark; Waldron, going to his own quarters was for a fleeting instant dimly outlined. He stepped into his room and slammed the door.

Then Bill Cole Cody stepped along through the darkness toward the rooms where Ann Lee and her aunt were imprisoned. He, like Waldron before him, struck a match or two. Arrived at his destination, he said,

'Will you ladies open up to me? It's in the cards, I think, that I have a word with you.'

It was Ann Lee's swift hand that unlocked the door; Cody, his gun still in his hand, since he trusted Rance Waldron in nothing, made no move to cross the threshold. His eyes, smoldering under his dark brows, took in all the loveliness of the trim little figure before him, gave no hint of his admiration, passed on to Aunt Jenifer.

'Do you care to tell me what the ruckus was all about?' he asked. 'It might be a good idea.' Speaking pointedly to Jenifer, he added: 'You were right in what you told me a while ago. Cal Roundtree and I have found out a thing or two.'

'Will you step in, Mr. Cody?' asked Aunt Jenifer. 'You're right welcome.'

'I'd be glad to do so, ma'am,' said Cody politely, and stepped briskly into Ann Lee's room. 'Being as I wouldn't put it beyond our friend Rance Waldron to take a pot-shot at me out of the dark. Thanking you, ma'am.'

Ann Lee began to laugh. That mercuric spirit of hers was ever ready to take wing, and this dialogue at such a time tapped her funny-bone.

'You two!' she cried, very gay because in a flash from the depths of near-despair she had risen to a place of absolute security. 'As polite all of a sudden as two French dancing masters! Why don't you bow prettily, Monsieur Cody, and you make your curtsy, Mademoiselle Jenifer?'

Cody's grin came and went without his knowing anything about it; Aunt Jenifer merely said, 'Hmf!' in her usual style, then closed and locked the door and wasted no further time giving Cole Cody, with Ann Lee all ears to take it in, her adventure of the night. She even handed the Jenkins letter to Cody who read it and then stood there frowning at it.

'I don't know what to do about it all,' he said at last. 'This letter found in his room, and the fact of his having hid a wounded man in his room all day, comes pretty close to pinning Mr. Rance Waldron's ears back. He—'

'A man hid in the house all day!' gasped Ann Lee. 'A wounded man? Tell me about it!'

'It's my notion,' said Aunt Jenifer tartly, 'and I reckon it's Cole Cody's notion, too, that Rance Waldron and the man he's been hiding, are the two that held the stage up yesterday. Right, Cole?'

Cody nodded.

'Right, Aunt Jenifer. And more than that, Cal Roundtree feels certain that Tom Gough—that's the man Waldron has been hiding out—is the man who shot old Early Bill. If all of us are right in our guesses, we'd better watch our steps. But if we round these two up and hand them over to the sheriff, what can we actually prove against them? We've got scraps of evidence, but it's mostly guesswork at that. Try a man for murder and let the jury find him innocent, and you can't ever haul him into court again. That's the law.'

'It's a big fool law, then,' said little Miss Ann, as sober and judicial as any Portia.

If by some off chance he thought that under the circumstances a contrite Ann Lee would break down and plead to be forgiven, he didn't as yet quite know his Ann Lee.

She could be very demure when it suited her. Her words now would have been aptly phrased in the Thee and Thou style of the Puritan maids. She kept her eyes down and her hands clasped before her, and said meekly,

'Perhaps, Mr. Cody, that the shot you

received this morning was sent by Providence to remind one that the spirit of man should never be proud, whereas if you stood out there in the lamp light and Mr. Waldron popped a bullet into you, it would probably only show that you are a bigger fool than he is.'

Cody started to swear, so did this girl get him down, then began to laugh. Aunt Jenifer hastened to turn the key in the lock. Ann Lee noted which way Bill Cole Cody's eyes were straying, and turned crimson and ran to the chair over which she had carelessly thrown her night gear. Cody grinned wider than ever, just to tease her.

Aunt Jenifer said crisply, 'Sit down, Mr. Cody. Seems as though you're always to save our bacon from falling into the fire. Let's have a bit of a war talk, shall we?'

'Auntie!' Ann Lee glared at Miss Edwards, using one of the highest-grade glares she kept in stock. 'For this war talk of yours hadn't we better step into your room?'

'This suits me fine,' said Cody, and sat down. And he noted that Ann Lee used still a more efficient glare upon her aunt, and that her small, shapely hands had hardened into fists at her sides. Aunt Jenifer began to giggle just as he was taking frank and approving stock of the girl's riding togs.

'There is merit in my niece's suggestion, Mr. Cody,' she said. 'You'll note if you look about you that her room is in some disarray; you see the dear child had already retired and was fast asleep when the fireworks started. My room you'll find as spick and span as I always am. This way, please.'

So the three went to the adjoining room and sat down, Ann Lee having returned to her own for the extra chair needed.

'Now for the war talk,' said Cody. He reached for tobacco and papers. 'You ladies don't mind, do you?'

'For my part,' cried Aunt Jenifer warmly, 'you can do any darn thing you want, and I'll love it if I hate it. If it hadn't been for you—'

'You'll get me started blushing if you talk at me like that, ma'am,' said Cole Cody, 'and when I get going good at the bashful business my ears get so red you could light a tallow candle at 'em.'

Ann Lee, scarcely audibly, said a small 'Hmf,' stolen from her aunt's arsenal.

'Here it is,' said Aunt Jenifer. 'While you all were away I thook into Rance Waldron's room; I found a letter there. Here it is; take it. Next I pried into the other room where he had his friend hid all day; I found blood on the floor, blood on the blanket. And I put two and two together, and being real bright at adding, I made about sixteen out of it.'

Cody had his cigarette rolled and lighted; Ann Lee waved her hand to keep the offensive smoke from her dainty nostrils as he made a move to return the letter to Aunt Jenifer.

200

Jenifer said, 'No. You keep it,' and he slipped it into his vest pocket.

'Cal and I figured the whole thing out about as you do. Cal thought it might be a good idea to hang the two of 'em right away, and save bother and fooling around. Maybe he was right. Yet come right dawn to it we don't really know a thing about either Rance Waldron or Tom Gough, and—'

'Tom Gough!' exclaimed Ann Lee. 'Why, I know him! That I've seen him and I know who he is?'

'Tom Gough,' said Aunt Jenifer, 'is a bad egg. He's lived for years down our way, and that's not over fifty miles from what used to be Rance Waldron's hang-out. I've even heard he and Waldron used to be friends once; that they fell out the same as thieves and worse are apt to do; then that there was a man killed and folks thought that Tom Gough did the killing, but they couldn't ever prove it. And there are those who say Tom Gough has been doing dirty work for Rance Waldron ever since— because Waldron's got the dead-wood on him, and so can tell Gough where to head in, or hang. Far as I know it's just all talk, like for a year folks has been saying my niece Ann Lee here is going to marry Dick Barnes, and Jake Umphries and Tod Tolliver and Hank Robins, and—'

'Aunt Jenifer,' said Ann Lee sharply, 'you stop it. You make me mad talking like that.'

Cole Cody chuckled. He said, 'It's a nice long list even if it's only started, but I reckon there's not much danger my name being tied on to the tail end of it.' Then, suddenly grave, chance cigarette smoke floating from his nostrils Ann Lee's way he remarked: 'Cal and I agree with your hunches all along the line, and it strikes me we're right. But I can't see much to be done on it tonight. It's kind of late and me, for one, I'm clean tuckered with the shooting-up this young lady handed me and the ride tonight. Suppose we talk this over, getting Cal in on it, in the morning and maybe sending for the Judge and Doc Joe to help give us a steer?'

Ann Lee looked her relief; Aunt Jenifer nodded and said vehemently,

'That's just the thing to do. Of course there's the chance that Rance Waldron may run out on us tonight—'

'That'll make us surer than ever that we're right. And he won't be hard to find in this country. Not with men like Cal and the Judge and Doc Joe setting the war dogs on him.' He stood up. 'I'm off to pick up on my beauty sleep.' He looked down on Miss Ann Lee, and had every appearance of being profoundly in earnest as he explained: 'You don't know half of it, how handsome a buckaroo I am when I'm all rested and my bullet holes don't hurt, and I've had a shave and have combed my hair and washed behind my ears. Better look out

202

that that string of fellers your aunt told me about don't all jump in the river. 'Night, Miss Jenifer. 'Night, Little Girl Child.'

Ann Lee was young enough to have still the impulse of sticking her tongue out, but in this case refrained and was merely haughty. She thought, much against her desire to think any such thing, There's something mighty fine about you, Bill Cole Cody, and if I was fool enough I could let my foot slip—both of 'em— and fall in love with you like nobody's business. But just the same I hate you and I'm darned glad I do.

'Mr. Cody,' said Aunt Jenifer, 'I want you to stay near to tonight. I've had the living daylights scared out of me. I'm scared stiff yet. I'll sleep with Ann Lee, and you take my room. Won't you?'

'Your key'll lock the door between,' he suggested.

'Darned if it will!' she flamed out at him. 'If I didn't trust you from below the boot heels to above the top of your hat, do you suppose I'd ask to be a neighbor?'

Cody rose and bowed; it was a rather graceful bow, thought Ann Lee as she and Aunt Jenifer rose also; she wondered, How many girls has he bowed like that to?

They passed to their room; he stepped after them to the door, closed it gently and said a very quiet,

'Thanks, ma'am. And good night, ladies.'

CHAPTER FIFTEEN

Cole Cody was first to awake the next morning, his habit of greeting each new day being not unlike Early Bill Cole's. He slipped quietly out of bed, dressed and tiptoed to his door, stepping through it, pocketing the key and going straight to Rance Waldron's room. He didn't stop to rap for entrance; from what he had heard from Jenifer Edwards he doubted that Waldron had a key; anyway he tried the knob, found the door unlocked and went in.

Waldron was gone and, obviously, whether or not for good and all, did not plan an immediate return, for he had stripped the covers from both beds, his and Tom Gough's, carrying them with him.

Cody lifted his shoulders in a high shrug. The chances were that Waldron had gone to join Tom Gough at the abandoned cabin where they had been last night, and could be found when and if wanted. Altogether, with matters as they stood, it was a relief to have the man out of the house.

Well, the first thing was breakfast—or was it a word with Cal Roundtree? Breakfast, of course: talk could always wait; and he'd noticed that the longer you waited to talk with a man, the less you found it necessary to say. He made his way to the kitchen and surrendered himself to pleasurable anticipations among routine activities. It's fun to make a wood fire in a big stove when you're hungry; fun to slice a half dozen slices of a lean, smoky side of bacon; to put on a big pot of water and to dump a handful of coffee into it. And there's a chiming music all its own—all this with the proviso that you're good and hungry—in the clang of pots and pans being strategically placed.

He hadn't gotten beyond the stage of bacon-slicing with a big, keen-edged butcher knife with a blade eighteen inches long, an instrument more like a weapon of the middle ages than a mere kitchen tool of today, when Jenifer Edwards, 'spick and span' in a new blue dress, with her hair nicely ordered, fluffed just a tiny bit about her invisible ears, and with lights in her eyes, came to join him, looking very gay and clean and fresh and friendly. She gave him a smile that had warmed many a: heart in her day, and presented him a bright nod along with her 'Good morning, Cole Cody!' and then added cheerily, 'Men are good for some things, the Lord knows what mostly, although of course they come in handy at rescuing yelping dames in distress, but I'll be darned if I'll have any man tinkering with my stove. Scat until breakfast is ready.'

He startled Aunt Jenifer until she came close to jumping out of her skin, by putting both arms around her slim little body, and giving her a good, hearty squeeze. Then he departed laughing, going to bring more wood. And she stood very still with a queer look on her face and then a very gentle little smile touched her lips and eyes.

He had brought ample armfuls of wood from the woodpile, breakfast was ready, piping hot and fragrant with the aroma of coffee floating far and wide, when little Ann Lee put in her appearance. She too was tricked out in a new little frock, baby blue with filmy white lace here and there, and her cheeks were as pink as a pink morning, and her eyes were both misty and bright, and she couldn't help smiling even though a thoroughly detested Bill Cole Cody was right there in plain sight. She thought, He is a great big brute and I hate him, but she thought also, Funny how such an ugly devil could be so handsome; just plain animalism, I suppose; and she thought further, He was brave last night and acted like a gentleman— just to show off, of course!

She tempered her morning smile a wee mite, and said a serene, 'Good morning, Aunt Jenny,' and then appeared really to notice Cole Cody for the first time and nodded her curly head while looking him steadily and unsmilingly in the eye, and offered a grave, 'Good morning, Mr. Cody.' Certainly, considering last night and for the moment setting aside all memory of past atrocities, that was the least any well brought up girl could do!

'Good morning, ma'am,' returned Mr. Cody solemnly, motivated by the inspiration that calling her 'ma'am' would annoy her. It did.

They sat at the kitchen table with its bright new red oilcloth—Early Bill for years had made a habit of a new red-as-fire oilcloth on the kitchen table at the beginning of every springtime—with Cody at the head, as was befitting, little Ann Lee at his right hand, Jenifer at his left when, after serving, she sat down. While all were sugaring their coffee, taking it black since Early Bill had never cared for milk, Aunt Jenifer remarked in an off-hand sort of way,

'I miss our other boarder, Mr. Rance Waldron. What news of him, Mr. Cody?'

'I won't answer,' Cody told her, looking stern, 'as long as you stick to that business of Mistering me. That's flat.'

Ann Lee chose to lift her eyebrows; she looked very pretty that way, with her big eyes making themselves bigger. Aunt Jenifer, Cody noted for the first time, had a way of dimpling which had the effect of cutting her years in half.

'I apologize, Bill Cole Cody,' she told him. 'What I meant to ask, Cole, is whether you by any chance happen to know anything of the whereabouts of Mr. Rance Waldron? And you don't mind me Mistering him, do you?'

'Serve him right. If it wasn't that there's

ladies present, I'm blamed if I wouldn't call him a varmint. Fact is he reminds me of a man I used to know who was so low down that he'd even tell the truth about a man behind his back! It's a fact.'

'Do tell!' said Aunt Jenifer. 'And now that you've read his title clear as a snake in the grass and a skunk in the chicken house, what about him this morning?'

'Gone,' said Cole Cody. 'Say, Miss Jenifer, the way that you can cook bacon and flap-jacks, and the coffee you make! Oh, Mr. Waldron this morning, yep, gone as clean as a whistle. And he took along with him all the bedding off his bed and Tom Gough's. And I wouldn't put it beyond him to have carted off a barley sack full of such things as beans and bacon, and all that sort of thing, which properly belongs to me!'

'I'm not surprised that he's gone,' said Aunt Jenifer, 'but I'll be mighty surprised if he doesn't show up again. He is dead set on getting this ranch and all that goes with it, and I've a notion that'll be a pile of cash money.' She looked shrewdly first at her aloof niece, then at an inscrutable Cole Cody. 'What with the two wills giving everything to two silly geese, so that the wills cut each other's throats, seems as though our Mr. Rance Waldron stands a first rate show of raking in the pot.' Then she asked quickly, before either the girl or Cody could answer, 'By the way, where do you two keep those precious, no 'count wills?'

Ann Lee looked straight into Cody's eyes when she replied to Jenifer's question.

'I've hidden mine in a safe place, not taking any chances on having it stolen.'

Cody returned Ann's penetrating look equably and addressed the questioner.

'I'm going to get mine into the Judge's hands and in the bank *pronto*. Around here it might get lost!'

'You—!' Ann began, furious.

'Pipe down, Kitten,' admonished Aunt Jenifer mildly. 'You started it, you know, and as I remember past happenings, there's a lot of things that you started that got finished by somebody else.'

Cole grinned and looked happy; Ann kept her eyes away from his and did not appear to have heard Jenifer's remark, but grew exclusively interested in her plate. As breakfast ended, silent from this point on save for the exchange of a few casual remarks between Jenifer Edwards and Cody, the latter said, rising,

'Thanks for the breakfast, ma'am; it sure was good. Now I'm stepping down for a word with Cal Roundtree; we'll see what his slant is at Waldron's walking out on us.'

. . . (If one could have had access to the page written in Aunt Jenifer's diary at the end of that day, he would come upon this brief commentary on the breakfast scene: 'That adorable little vixen of a niece of mine! And that mule-stubborn handsome young devil of a Bill Cole Cody! The two fools are crazy in love with each other since the minute he spotted her and piled aboard the stage, and haven't the sense God gave geese—they don't even know they were made for each other and will probably spend the next fifty years together trying to hate each other.') . . .

Cody brought Cal Roundtree up to the house, and the four of them discussed the situation brought about by the departure of Waldron, with enough bedding for two, and the inference that Waldron and Tom Gough, whom they all judged a killer, were sticking together. Cal scratched his head, and thereafter pulled reflectively at his ear, finally saying humbly and a shade ashamedly,

'I was wrong and you was right last night, Cody. We'd ought to have hung the two of them right then and there. Later, you're going to see, there'll be hell a-popping, if the ladies will excuse the swear words.'

'You were the one who wanted to hang them, sooner or later,' Cody reminded him. 'The worst I suggested was to stuff 'em into the *calaboosa*. Even yet I think we were right in keeping hands off until we could dig up some sort of evidence.'

'Maybe so,' agreed Cal somewhat morosely. Then he brightened. 'That greaser friend of yours, Porfirio, is like a bloodhound; he believes that that old cattle-thief, Early Bill Cole—'

'Mr. Roundtree!' exclaimed Ann Lee. 'Don't you dare—'

'Now don't you be silly, Pet,' put in Aunt Jenifer mildly. 'These men, Cal and Doc Joe and the Judge, they all knew Early Bill a heap better than you did, and if they all want to call him a hell-snapper on wheels, let 'em alone. What's the rest of it, Cal?'

Cal was looking with admiring and approving eyes on the indignant Ann Lee. He withdrew his gaze promptly, and finished what he had to say about Cody's friend of mixed bloods.

'That *hombre* Porfirio,' he said, 'has got his teeth, so to speak, in the idea that it's quite a job for a man to make a hat disappear in a hurry; to make it vanish off the face of the earth for good and all. He says a hat's hard to burn in a great big hurry; maybe a piece of the brim will burn and the fire will go out. You can throw it away, into a patch of brush, but if a man's got eyes like Porfirio says his eyes are when he's praying in his heart to avenge a friend like that old—like Early Bill was—he can see every horse track and every boot track, and a black hat hidden in the bushes. And he says if you dig a hole and bury a hat, no matter how you scatter leaves over the place, eyes like Porfirio's are going to notice something funny about it. And even if you stuff a hat under a

211

rock, there'll be some little something to show that the rock was moved. And Porfirio is going to find that hat or spend the rest of his life hunting it.'

Ann Lee could hardly keep still for him to come to the end of his long winded dissertation on the Porfirio-hat affair.

'What in the world are you talking about?' she wanted to know instantly. 'What hat? Whose hat?'

Cal expelled a long breath.

'I'm talked out,' he told her. Then he said to Cody, 'You tell her, Cody.'

'No!' exclaimed Ann Lee in her vehement way. 'You started this, Cal, and you finish it.'

Later on that same forenoon, Doc Joe and the Judge drove out to the ranch in the Judge's top buggy; they had discarded shafts for a pole and came whizzing out like the leading rig in a harness race. Arrived at the ranch house they made a brave noise of pounding at the front door; without waiting for anyone to answer, they opened it and came with a sort of martial stride into the living room where the conference was still in session; as one man they swept off their broad-brimmed, ragged old Stetsons; they wore the most genial of smiles; Doc Joe's bald head gleamed as brightly as if it had newly been shellacked and polished, and the Judge's snowy mane of hair and flowing beard were fluffed out in a glorious sort of fashion; and altogether they were two bright and beaming old souls seeming about to explode with youth and springtime.

The Judge bowed gallantly to Ann Lee whom, of the ladies, he chanced to note first, then with a brightening and suddenly warmly approving eye, he made Aunt Jenifer a bow so profound as to be labeled as of the first order. Doc Joe stiffened into erect and frozen dignity, then, like the Judge before him bowed to the girl and thereafter almost bent double before Aunt Jenifer like an over-ardent courtier before his liege lady. Ann Lee looked at them in amazement; Aunt Jenifer positively tittered; both Cody and Cal sniffed the air suspiciously. Yes, these two old porch-sitters brought along with them an exhilarating fragrance like the very bouquet of spring or anyhow of Kentucky bourbon.

'We come to greet you at this early, pearly hour,' said the Judge sonorously, 'because we have been thinking of you, talking of you, pondering the problem of the two wills drawn up by that old scion of sin, Early Bill Cole.' At the outset it appeared that what he had to say was addressed to the two legatees, but before his poetic, 'early, pearly hour' phrase was out of his oratorical mouth, his slightly humid eyes were full upon Aunt Jenifer. 'We sat up late last night giving the matter our best thought—'

'In fact, ladies and gents,' put in Doc Joe, his words slicing into the Judge's flow like a sharp knife through butter, 'our hearts were so much with you, our every thought so much bent upon your welfare, we sat up all night! We did, didn't we, Judge?'

And, as if seeking an answer not from the Judge but elsewhere, his bright regard was directed to Aunt Jenifer.

'Now you look here, you, Judge and Doc,' spoke up Cal Roundtree good humoredly yet firmly, 'you two step along with me to the kitchen; we're going to have a cup of good strong, black coffee. Come ahead; we've got all day to talk in.'

They weren't drunk, the Judge and Doc Joe, not they. But during their night of drinking many a toast to their departed friend, Early Bill, spending Early Bill's money the way they knew in their tough old hearts he'd want it spent, breaking dozens of glasses that none of them ever be used again to serve a purpose less sacred, tossing off enough bourbon to paralyze any other ten men in Bald Eagle, they had arrived at a condition which may be described as a genial glow. They were here to stand loyally by Early Bill's heir and heiress, their purpose pure and noble. And it would appear that another emotion motivated them; it would strike the casual observer that they had found something mighty attractive and appealing in Ann's Aunt Jenifer, and they were bound to pay her tribute.

'Do you know,' spoke up Aunt Jenifer,

beginning to sparkle, 'I believe that I would like another cup myself! I'll make a big coffee pot full, and we'll have some flapjacks and jam, too! Kitten, if you'll set the table in the dining room—'

'Yes, Aunt Jenny,' said Ann Lee quickly, and the two departed.

The Judge and Doc Joe, having spoken their few words about being sorry to put the ladies to so much trouble, turned, together to Cole Cody and Cal. In a lowered voice the Judge spoke.

'Gents,' he said solemnly, 'yesterday we won a couple of bets from the dead and gone old reprobate that folks called Early Bill—called him that, I may say at last, because he always got up before daylight, that hour suiting him best of all for his trade of horse stealing. We had a drink or two, as perhaps you may have guessed without being told, to the aforementioned hell hound. We have done more; we have, outside in my top buggy, a full jug—'

'You're a liar, Judge,' said Doc Joe. 'But I'll grant you it was full when we left Bald Eagle, I grant you that.'

'To hell with technicalities this morning, you damn hairsplitter,' said the Judge, still keeping his tone lowered. 'It is merely my suggestion that, while those two lovely ladies are preparing us a very proper morning drink, we steal a march on them and step out to where the jug is.'

'It's a great little idea, Judge,' said Cole Cody, and you would have thought that he meant it. 'First though, we want to tell you something and ask your advice. Rance Waldron sneaked out last night—'

'The hell with Rance Waldron and all like him. The thing is—'

'And,' said Cody sharply, 'last night he took a hand-ax and tried to break down the door to the rooms where your two lovely ladies had locked themselves in.'

'What!'

After that there was no further mention, just as there was no thought, of the jug in the buggy. The two old porch-sitters had to be told in detail all that had happened: Of Tom Gough's hiding in the house—both of them knew Tom Gough—of his departure attended by Waldron, of all the rest of it.

And Aunt Jenifer's voice called from the dining room:

'Hot coffee! Come and get it!'

CHAPTER SIXTEEN

They all had coffee together, Aunt Jenifer, gentle but firm and pleasantly vivacious, seeing to it that both the old boys had three cups, and then they adjourned to the *patio*. There were outdoor hickory chairs there, and the old green benches, and the *patio* was warm and fragrant with roses, where honeysuckle trailed from one arbor and a Mission grapevine from another, and where humming birds thrummed. One looked out along the hill slope and saw Early Bill's three tall pines, and a monster white oak, lower down, where the woodpeckers with their constant 'Ickety-ickety-ickety' were already busy using their small bright red heads for hammers and their bills for drills in the hard wood. The small part of the world encompassed within the King Cole Valley was steeped in peace and yellow sunshine, and only harmonious sounds drifted through it on a soft, dry breeze.

'It's so lovely here!' Ann Lee said in a small, hushed voice after a deep breath. 'I think it's the loveliest place in all the world.'

Cal Roundtree, head down while rolling a cigarette, muttered:

'It's going to be hell-and-all if that dirty devil Rance Waldron gobbles it up.' He raised his head to stare narrowly at the Judge. 'How about it, Judge? You ought to know, being a lawyer and a banker, too. Old Early Bill had to have himself his fun, dead or alive, I know that; but what I hear about his two wills makes me think they kill each other, and Waldron, being nearest of kin, takes the whole kit and caboodle.'

The Judge cleared his throat, but Cole Cody

cut in. He extracted one of the two wills, twice folded, from his vest pocket and handed it to the Judge, saying,

'Here, Judge, you take care of mine, will you? You'll know how to handle it. I suggested yesterday that you take safeguard of my interests; suppose you're retained right now to do that for me? Is it a go?'

The Judge accepted the document, unfolded it and smoothed it out and pocketed it.

'You're dead right, son,' he said heartily. 'I'll take care of it for you. You can depend on me to take all the necessary legal steps. As to the fee, we'll talk about that later on; it's all tomfoolery to take the ten percent you mentioned. But we'll come to a proper business understanding.'

The dreamy ecstasy fled from Ann Lee's eyes and a bright determination came into them. She jumped up and ran into the house; not a word was spoken before she returned, bringing her own precious document with her.

'Doc Joe,' she said, and was for the moment like a pretty little girl-child, very trustful, innocent and irresistible, 'won't you keep this for me? And won't you see that I am not cheated out of my rights? You know that Mr. Early Bill Cole wanted me to have everything that was his, don't you? You will protect me, won't you, Doc Joe?'

Doc Joe fairly snatched the paper into his

218

hands. He spoke to her while he glared at the Judge.

'Miss Ann Lee,' he said sternly, 'I do know that old Early Bill wanted you to have everything that he has willed to you here. I witnessed his signature; I talked alone with him a spell; he gave you the ranch and a lot of other truck, and by the jump—the jimminy you're going to have it!'

The Judge spoke to Cole Cody, the while returning Doc Joe's glare.

'Don't you worry about what this old galoot says, Kid Cody,' he said. 'He knows less about law than I know about China. I might say he knows almost as little about it as he does about his own trade as a medicine man, but maybe that's going too far.'

This made Aunt Jenifer, today in one of her merriest moods, start laughing, and her laughter drew the attention of both Doc Joe and the Judge, and at once the battle look was swept clear of their old faces, to be replaced by expressions hinting at a condition not unlike that of very young men in a state of calf love. A small sniff came from little Ann Lee; it seemed very silly to her for men as old as they to cast calves' eyes at a spinster of the antiquity of Aunt Jenny.

Cody again mentioned Waldron and Gough; the two old fellows knew a good deal of Gough, nothing to his benefit, and vowed to get busy learning a lot more of his intimacy with Waldron, and what lay behind that power, gone now, which Waldron had held over him. Both, too, knew something of Porfirio; having dwelt these many years in Bald Eagle, being, as they were, veritable aces of porch-sitters, they knew a good deal about every man within fifty miles of their gossipy little town. They agreed for once on this particular day in declaring that if Porfirio Lopez had set out to run a man down, or a hat, in order to come at his man, Porfirio would never swerve from his purpose until he achieved success, or died.

'There is one other matter which we merely touched on yesterday,' said the Judge, 'that we might as well nail down right now. No matter which way the cat jumped you two young folks, Miss Ann Lee and William Cole Cody—who, by the way,' he injected into his speech, obviously by way of strengthening the case for his new client, 'was named 'Cole' in honor of old Early Bill himself, since Bill Cole Cody's daddy was the best friend old Early Bill ever had on earth—Where was I? Oh, yes—'

'You're a liar, sir,' snapped Doc Joe. 'The best friend Early Bill or any other man ever had was a man named Busty Lee, and he was the daddy of Miss Ann Lee, and that's a fact.'

The Judge snorted and went on with that other matter which demanded attention.

'Like I said,' he continued, 'you two young folks, no matter what happens to these two wills, have a lot of cash money in bank, and it's

220

in my bank, and it's deposited there subject to your orders. I'd have to check to find out how big the pile is, but it's right considerable; shucks, just yesterday Bucktooth Jenkins brought in an extra ten thousand bucks to add to it, and Bill Cole Cody and Miss Jenifer's niece can take it any minute they want.'

He reached into his pocket and drew out a small check book and tossed it into Cole's hands. Those listening to him, all but Doc Joe, watched and waited for the other check book. It appeared there wasn't any.

So in the end Doc Joe explained.

'Miss Ann Lee,' he said, and sounded apologetic, 'this whole set-up is a mess. The money is there in the bank, if the Judge hasn't stole it. Fifty thousand, maybe, maybe a hundred thousand or a whale of a lot more. Fact is, I'm no banker and the Judge here claims to be, and for some fool reason, Early Bill trusted him. But here's the joker, like there is in every brand new deck: The account is in the joint names of you and this here Cody. In short, if either of you wants to draw a cent or a thousand dollars or anything, you both got to sign the same check! That was so ordered by the late Mr. William Cole, known by some as Early Bill, by others as Old King Cole himself. You two have just simply got to get together.'

Of course Cole Cody and Ann Lee had to look at each other then, and of course that taunting, gleeful grin of Cody's came flashing

back—and little Ann flushed up and bit her
lip. For just a thin slice of a second she felt
that she could have slapped old Early Bill's
face. Then suddenly she jumped up as once
already she had done, and ran into the house
without a word. She sped to her own room and
went down on two softly rounded knees and
buried her face in her hands, and prayed.

'Dear God,' plead little Ann Lee, 'forgive
me! I am a wretched little beast; I wanted to
slap—' Tears wet her hands. She jumped up
and hurried to the kitchen and at the sink
splashed water on her face. She returned to
the *patio* in a gay, almost dancing sort of way,
and finding silence awaiting her there,
exclaimed gaily,

'I am going to draw out a thousand dollars
today! A whole thousand! Oh, Aunt Jenny,
think of the things we are going to do! We can
spend a thousand dollars every day, if we want
to!'

No one said anything, not even Cole Cody
who was in no hurry to seize an opportunity.
Out of the silence Ann spoke again, saying to
Doc Joe,

'I can, can't I?'

'Of course you can, my dear girl,' Doc Joe
assured. 'Only of course, you and Mr. Cody
will have to sign the checks together, like I just
told you.'

Ann looked at Cody. He looked back at her
and for once his face was as blank as a slate

222

just out of the store.

'Mr. Cody, I haven't the slightest doubt,' said Ann lightly, 'will be wanting some money! So he will sign with me; that's clear enough.'

Cody could have taken this as his cue to speak, but did not grasp the opportunity. In fact he sat still, and his face remained new-slate expressionless.

Doc Joe spoke up then, his voice sharpening.

'Mr. Cody, sir,' he said, 'Miss Lee has just asked you a civil question.'

'I didn't hear her,' said Cody serenely. 'I did hear her say something about me, nothing to me.'

Ann Lee thought that if on earth there had ever been a more infuriating creature, he must have been gathered in to draw crowds at a circus side show. She smiled, and did her best to make the smile icy.

'I am sorry, Mr. Cody,' she said sweetly, 'that I failed in the courtesy due you. Will you sign a check with me this morning?'

'Why, now!' exclaimed Cody, and sounded friendly and hearty. 'It's an idea! As a matter of fact I could do with a little money myself. Here; I'll write the check right now, and we'll give it to the Judge to cash and split two ways for us. Where's pen and ink?'

'I'll show you,' said Aunt Jenifer, and Cody followed her into the house. They were not long gone.

Cody had written and signed the check; he handed it with the pen and ink bottle to Ann for her signature *below his*.

She started to sign, then stiffened her small figure, and her lips were compressed and her eyes blazing. He had written in the amount: Twenty Dollars.

'I said a thousand!' she said.

'Shucks,' said the good humored Bill Cole Cody. 'Twenty bucks is a lot of money. You take ten, I take ten—and there you are.'

She crumpled the check and threw it at him.

'When sometime you want to draw out some money, Mr. Cody,' she told him, 'say a considerable amount, for some emergency, maybe—Why, just come to me for my signature, won't you?'

Right there the *patio* conference broke up. But on its heels came another. This was a sub-rosa affair, engineered by none other than Miss Jenifer Edwards who managed without the least difficulty to draw her two latest ardent admirers aside in the dining room. There the three, become conspirators in a second, spoke to the point.

'These young fools,' said Aunt Jenifer, 'are going to ruin everything unless we can find some way to stop them. After all I guess the wills are worth their weight in bologna sausages; one alone would be approved in a law court, the two would have to be thrown out. Am I right, gentlemen?'

224

'We don't know for sure,' said Doc Joe. 'Maybe, with so much money at stake, we could buy the Judge. You never can tell until you try. But it looks bad.'

'Why the deuce,' asked the Judge, 'don't they quit bickering anyhow? They've a common interest. They're just cutting their own throats. They're crazier than two jay birds. What they ought to do is run to the preacher and get married. That's what that old snake in the grass wanted anyhow; it shows a mile off.'

'The judge is right,' said Doc Joe. 'Why don't the two hurry up and fall in love? She's about the sweetest little thing that ever was; and young Cody himself ain't so bad. That would be the end of all this nonsense.'

Aunt Jenifer smiled.

'I'll tell you a secret,' she said softly. 'They are in love, heels over head in love, already. They've been that way from the first minute they saw each other. But love's a funny thing, I've found out. Either they don't know they're that way, or they do know, and it makes 'em mad. There's nothing we can do about it, I reckon; just let Time and maybe the devil work it out.'

But the Judge and Doc Joe were intrigued, in part with the obvious problem, that was sure; in part by Jenifer Edwards. They were willing to steep themselves in coffee and more coffee, to forego and even almost forget the demijohn in the buggy, in order to while away

225

a few more bright moments in her vivacious presence.

They suggested a formal conspiracy. Maybe if they kidnapped the girl and hid her away in some mountain ravine—and let it appear that a gang of desperadoes—Rance Waldron and Tom Gough, murderous hounds!—held her at their merciless mercy! Or if somehow they made her think that he, riding alone in the wilderness, had been dangerously hurt! A fall over a precipice—a treacherous shot in the back by none other than the deadly Tom Gough or the villainous Rance Waldron!

'We'd make her think he was dying,' said the Judge. 'That he was gasping her name—'

Presently the Judge and Doc Joe wended their homeward way, to lift their jug at the outset with a remark made by the first jug-grabber that was seconded by the other: 'Hell's bells, we've drunk enough to that old rapscallion; this here drink goes to a lady that is a lady, lively, lovely and lovable: Miss Jenifer!'

And at that moment the lively, lovely and lovable spinster, Jenifer Edwards, was having the law laid down to her by her niece who had once been a school teacher, and who of a sudden resumed the air of a petty dictator. She looked at Aunt Jenifer severely.

'Aunt Jenny!' she exclaimed. 'How could you! Oh, for shame, for shame, Jenifer Edwards!'

Aunt Jenifer was for once taken aback and flushed up guiltily. She leaped to the conclusion that little Ann Lee had been eavesdropping and had heard the whole of the conspirators' plottings.

'So you've been snooping, have you?' was the best she could think of.

'For shame again, that you should think that I would lower myself by listening at keyholes! That wasn't needed; I couldn't have stood any more! Those two old men ever since they came have been making love to you, and you know it! And you are actually leading them on! And at your age!'

So that was it! Aunt Jenifer tittered and, it seemed to a watchful and suspicious Ann Lee, blushed.

Meantime Cole Cody and Cal Roundtree strolled away, heads down, hands jammed deep down in their pockets, sat under a tree down near the barn and were silent together for a long while.

*   *   *

Young as the summer was, it was a lazily languid day by now, and both the Judge and Doc Joe were inclined to a sort of dreamful ease, the horses had expended their first, early morning zest, and the homeward journey lacked the speed and dash marking its first phase, from Bald Eagle to the King Cole

227

Ranch. Now the sun was higher and warmer, now the two old cronies were drowsy and pleasurably sentimental, their eyes heavy-lidded from last night's indulgence—and in a spot where the narrow road wound down into a cool and shady ravine both men were rudely startled when a man on horseback cut unexpectedly into the road in front of them and issued his orders. The man wore a mask improvised from a bandana handkerchief, and his voice was a strange muffled voice—he might have had pebbles in his mouth—and his few, briskly spoken words were to the effect that the Judge and Doc Joe were to stop where they were and not reach for any guns provided they carried such articles—as, naturally, both did.

'Dammit,' snorted the old Judge. 'Who the hell do you think you are, telling us where to head in?'

The man wearing the bandana mask was not inclined toward prolonged conversation. His words were few and to the point, and the gun in his hand was slightly raised, its ugly looking muzzle threatening both of the old fellows with the cold menace of a rattlesnake about to strike.

'I want everything in your pockets,' he said, 'and I want it quick. If you make a fuss about it I'll kill the two of you inside ten seconds.'

Men like the Judge and Doc Joe knew when the cards were stacked against them, when a

228

man would be a plain fool or worse to start argument. They reached for their purses and tossed them into the dry, dusty grass alongside the road.

'There you are, Stranger,' grumbled Doc Joe. 'Take it and go to hell.'

He was about to drive on when he got the rest of his orders.

'I said I wanted everything in your pockets,' he was reminded in a voice which rankled long in his memory. 'Every damn thing you've got.'

'That's all we got,' roared the Judge, his hand itching to reach for the Colt he hadn't gone without for many and many a year, but never stirring an inch toward it because he knew better. 'Unless you want our smoking and chawing tobacca.'

'Get a move on, you two damned old fools! Turn your pockets out. '

The Judge looked at Doc Joe and Doc Joe looked at the Judge. There was nothing on earth they could do about it. This free-riding gent had simply beat them to the draw. To argue the matter would be exactly like trying to win a jack pot on a pair of deuces against a straight flush. They emptied their pockets.

They strove to fumble and to hide the papers they had carried, that given Doc Joe by Ann Lee, that entrusted to the Judge by Bill Cody. But the steady eyes bent upon them were too watchful.

'Everything, I tell you! Empty your pockets

229

to your nose rags and tobacco. Everything you've got. Pitch it out and drive on—and get a move on doing it!'

This time they couldn't look at each other.

Doc Joe had a pet corn, and pretty nearly every man, woman and child in Bald Eagle knew of it; for one thing, Doc Joe could foretell rain with it; for another he was apt to slaughter a man who trod on it. And certainly none knew about this corn better than did the Judge.

And now the Judge trod heavily and deliberately on Doc Joe's corn. And Doc Joe, already stung almost beyond endurance, caught the signal and was glad to have the Judge with him, and like one man the two of them went for their guns.

CHAPTER SEVENTEEN

Well along in years they might be, those two old cronies of the departed Early Bill Cole, but they were not the type of man whose coat tail you tread on with impunity any more than you go poking a stick at an old rattlesnake. Not as fast on the draw, not as quick on the trigger, not as sure of eye as they had been a couple of score years earlier, yet there was a deal of life in the old dogs yet and their fangs had never been drawn. It was a sight to see as Arthur

Henry Pope and Joseph Daniel Dodge went into action.

Actuated by the same instinctive impulse, alike not caring for their present position on the buggy seat, as they snatched at their side arms they threw themselves clear, over the wheels into the road, landing anyhow, sprawling. Doc Joe sat up and began firing at the masked rider; the Judge rested on his knees and loosed his own screaming bullets, their way greased along the airway for them by the Judge's bellowing curses.

Their horses, left to their own devices, startled by the crash of gun-fire, bolted, headed straight toward the man at whose command they had been halted. He, too, was firing, rapidly yet not so rapidly as to bespeak any nerve-storm; wasting no time, yet spacing his shots coolly.

His horse started to lunge, as the frightened team almost ran him down; his bandana slipped; both Judge and Doc Joe saw who it was.

'Rance Waldron!' roared the old Judge and, his shooting skill not being quite what it had been once upon a time a long time ago, shot Waldron's horse through the throat. The beast reared and screamed and fell, pawing the air with flailing hoofs; Rance Waldron leaped clear.

A sharp cry of warning burst from Doc Joe.

'Judge! Look out! There's another of them

231

hid in the bushes—Like when they held the stage up the other day!'

The runaway team went thundering down the road. Taking advantage of a moment of confusion, the Judge strove to scramble behind a big pine. Rance, on foot now was firing again, and bullets came whizzing from the man whom Doc Joe had glimpsed joining Rance's attack from a point of some small shelter. The Judge got a good clear view of him and, steadying his hand and taking time for it, drove two bullets into Tom Gough's body. Doc Joe saw and squealed with delight as Gough sagged and clutched at his saddle horn, and slowly slid down, out of sight, in the underbrush.

The Judge had but half a dozen paces to go, to come to his big pine, but never made the short distance. Rance shot him through the upper body, and the old fellow sprawled on his face and for a moment lay there, clawing the dust.

Doc Joe couldn't spare time off to look at him; he could only yell, 'Get up, Judge, and give 'em hell! You're all right, you old fool.' But he couldn't help but see how little puffs of dust rose from under the claws which his old crony's hands had become, and how the lean tall figure writhed, seeking to roll over, to get back into the fight, his strength failing him.

'We got one down!' panted Doc Joe. 'We'll get that Rance varmint in a minute.'

But somehow his eyes weren't as clear as they used to be; he had to blink them once. And there was a tremor in his hand, no matter how steady and firm his will. Rance, unafraid it would appear, and contemptuous, laughed at him and fired and sang out all together,

'That for you, you meddling old fool!'

Old Doc Joe spat back at him with verbal vitriol and hot lead, knowing himself for an old fool, himself and the Judge for two old fools trying to fight it out with the game against them from the outset, yet somehow glad to be fighting—even though he knew the Judge had not as yet risen. Doc Joe himself surged up to his feet at last, but only in time to drop again, his weapon falling from his sudden limp grasp, and when he fell, lying crookedly on his side facing the Judge yet failing to see him or anything else on earth, the reason for his fall was written in a bright red dripping smear upon his temple.

Rance Waldron stood stone still where he was, save for the swift, sure movement of his fingers reloading; his eyes were hard and bright and suspicious, bent shrewdly upon the two old men lying one in the dusty road, the other at its side. He saw that there was never a twitch in Doc Joe's body; he marked how feebly the Judge struggled, still face down, still unable to turn over. Then for an instant only his hard bright eyes flicked toward the brush down into which Tom Gough had spilled.

233

'Tom!' he called. 'Tom! Are you all right? Or are you done for? Playing possum, to keep out of the fight, or dying? Speak up man!'

He sounded impatient, angry.

There was a little silence; only the faint breeze stirred in its lazy, summer style through the grass and whispered as if under its breath through the trees; the silence lasted on a little longer, while Rance Waldron stood watchful where he was. Then a blue jay called harshly, and then Tom Gough's voice, scarcely to be heard above the gush of the breeze, spoke.

'I'm all shot to hell, Rance. Help me, quick; I'll bleed to death.'

'You're always getting yourself all shot to hell; you're always bleeding to death,' grumbled Rance. 'What the hell are you good for? Bleed and be damned to you.'

He stepped along then, not toward Tom Gough but toward the two old men in the road, a fully loaded gun in each of his hands. He came first to Doc Joe, stopped and stood looking down at him, then moved on, muttering, 'Deader'n hell, and a good job, too.'

The Judge, as a final spasm of strength swept along on a final spasm of pain, sat up; he even groped for his fallen gun and found it. All the strength he could summon was needed to lift the heavy Colt .45. But there was living murder in his eyes and, though he did not speak, he cursed Rance Waldron down to hell and back again.

Deliberately, not hastening, Rance Waldron shot him square between the eyes . . .

He turned then, still deliberate, and broke his way through the brush to where Tom Gough lay with his shoulders wedged against a rock, his hands pressed against his chest and side. There was a terrible look in Tom Gough's eyes, a look of fear and of dumb agony and of wild pleading, a hopeless pleading for there was no spark of hope in those dulling eyes.

'So you're done for, are you, Tom?' said Waldron. He didn't exactly taunt, didn't exactly smile, but there was the stamp of infinite cruelty, callous and unfeeling, in his look. He said quietly, no emotion whatever tinging his tone, 'Here, I'll lend you a hand.'

Heavy man though Tom Gough was, Rance Waldron lifted him easily and bore him the short distance to the roadside. There he put him down, not more than a score of paces from where the still bodies of the Judge and Doc Joe lay.

'Those two are dead, Tom,' said Rance. 'Folk'll say you stuck 'em up, and you three shot it out—and all three of you cut one another down.'

'For God's sake, Rance!'

Rance shot him twice through the body. It wouldn't do to have all three men shot through the head!

235

He emptied the pockets of both the Judge and Doc Joe. He glanced at the two wills and put them into his pocket. He gathered up the rest of their personal effects, money and watches, and dropped the lot close to Tom Gough's outflung hand. Then he went to Tom Gough's horse and rode away into the thickest of the wooded hills, leaving his own horse, not dead yet, but dying slowly, to kick its life out.

CHAPTER EIGHTEEN

It was a sweet day, averred young Gaucho Ortega, idling homeward from Bald Eagle, a day in the late afternoon not so much like summer come again as like the *hasta la vista* kiss of springtime, lingering and tender, promising not to go so far away that she could not come tripping back again; that same young Gaucho whom not so long ago old Early Bill Cole had despatched into Bald Eagle to summon the Judge and Doc Joe to aid in his final ante mortem arrangements. Gaucho had gone to town for tobacco—Well, tobacco was as good a reason as any. And there was not much to do at the rancho these days, with nearly all the herds sold, with everybody just waiting to see what was going to happen next. And in town he had had a couple of ice-cold *cervezas*, and had found a new pretty girl, the

236

daughter of an ugly old woman, newly arrived, who was growing wealthy taking in washing. And the girl had flashed the boy a white-toothed smile before melting shyly into the house, and the cool beer had warmed within him, so that he felt like singing, and did sing softly under his breath, quite as though it were moonlight, and rode slowly, one foot in its stirrup, a leg about his saddle horn. So on such a day and in such a mood he came first of all upon the wreckage of brutal tragedy.

Only three or four miles from town, where a canyon debouched upon the valley on the farther rim of which Bald Eagle sunned itself, he saw the runaway team, running no longer but hung up in a roadside growth of brush and small trees, the buggy leaning crazily with one wheel high on a boulder and the pole snapped in two, with the horses stopped by a young pine, one on either side, in a tangle of harness. He recognized the horses with a sweeping glance: Doc Joe and the Judge had had a runaway. But where were they?

Nowhere in sight; nowhere in hearing, for he shouted at the top of his voice. He snapped out of one mood into another and into action; he whipped his leg back over the saddle horn, jammed his boot into the stirrup and gave his mount the spurs. And as he sped along, headed still toward the ranch, since obviously it was from the ranch that Doc Joe and the Judge had been traveling, he kept looking

237

everywhere and now and again shouting.

Then, a couple of miles farther on, he came upon the three bodies asprawl in the road or at its edge.

'Holy Mother of God!' gasped Gaucho, and turned sick, horror struck. After a moment of stupefaction he spurred his frightened animal as close as he could; he sat staring down at this blood-spattered scene of murder; he crossed himself, his face dead white, the sweat running down his cheeks. 'Three men dead! And the old Judge and Doc Joe two of them!'

When his wits returned to him he thought straight to the point: It was less than half a dozen miles back to Bald Eagle, more than twice that distance to the ranch. And this thing should be made known in town anyhow; here was a job for the sheriff, for all men who could wear guns. For a doctor, too! He sighed and shook his head; too late for that. But anyhow the town must know. So he rode back toward Bald Eagle like a dark streak through the afternoon sunshine.

And it was the same Gaucho—Not quite the same Gaucho, rather, for he had forgotten his ice-cold beer and his new pretty girl, and now had big tears hanging on his long black lashes, for he, whose heart was so open to springtime and quick smiles, had loved those two nice good old men—who brought the heavy tidings to the King Cole Ranch.

Aunt Jenifer and Ann Lee were in the *patio*,

and when Gaucho burst upon them they stared back at him, speechless. At first, so great was the shock, that they felt nothing; they couldn't make his running words make sense, there was no reality in what he was voicing so wildly. The Judge and Doc Joe, dead? Dead! When so little a while ago?

And they didn't say a word, didn't ask a question, didn't even look at each other until Gaucho sped away to find Cal Roundtree and the other boys and tell all that had happened. For one thing, there was nothing to ask, so complete if hurried had been the boy's details. And there was nothing to say.

Slowly their impassive faces changed and their eyes met. The dazed look had gone and in its place came horror, then grief splashed with sudden tears. Those two fine gallant old men, dead!

Ann Lee wept softly then, her face hidden in her hands, her body rocking, convulsed. Aunt Jenifer dashed the tears from her eyes and sat very straight, her head up, her eyes steady now with almost the glint of steel in them, bent upon far away distances. Presently she spoke very gently, but she did not stir from where she sat on the old green bench.

'They were two fine men, Ann darling; they were old; they had to go sometime; like Early Bill they had had their fun.' Her lips thinned to bleak silence; then she added crisply, 'And they killed the murderer who shot them down!

239

That's something.'

'I could have loved them to death,' said Ann faintly. 'Already we were friends; they were, as you say, fine and good—Why, they were friends of dear old Early Bill! And now—'

She sprang up and, like her aunt before her, swept the wetness from eyes which were blazing now.

'Is there to be nothing but killing and robbery?' she flared out. 'Early Bill the first, then the stage robbery, with two men nearly killed, now the Judge and Doc Joe? And it's all Rance Waldron's doing! I know, I know, I know it!'

'Sh! Don't storm at me, my pet. And this time it seems it isn't Rance Waldron but some other man—the man they killed, defending themselves, and who was lying there in the road with them.'

Ann was hushed, but not for long. Hope that will not down without a death struggle sprang up in her breast.

'Maybe they are not really dead!' she exclaimed excitedly. 'A man can be shot, he can be badly hurt, unconscious even, and yet live!'

And she started running. Jenifer called after her, but the flying Ann did not stop or glance back or answer; she was on her way as fast as her flying feet could carry her to the men's quarters, to send a man, if they didn't have sense enough themselves, racing into Bald

Eagle to get a doctor in all hot haste; to save somehow the lives of Doc Joe and the Judge.

She came upon a small knot of men, Cole Cody and Cal Roundtree and Porfirio and two others, grouped in a sort of circle, their heads down, their boot toes for the most part scraping in the dirt, as they listened to Gaucho's words. She screamed at them before she reached them to hurry for a doctor, to do what they could to save two lives which otherwise might be lost even while they stood here doing nothing.

The men looked at her gravely as she came running to them; no one answered her; she thought Cole Cody's eyes were horribly indifferent, cold and unsympathetic, and that Cal Roundtree listened as though not particularly interested.

Cody said, not to her but to Gaucho,

'What was he like, the man who killed them? The other dead man in the road?'

Gaucho screwed up his face. It is a hard thing, making you see a man the way he really looks, drawing pictures with words. He did his best which was very bad indeed; one gathered that the man had two legs, two arms and eyes, the usual complement of features—Oh, yes; he hadn't had a shave for a week maybe; he looked like a sick man, but maybe that was because he was dead. He had big hands with lots of black hair on them, like hair on a tarantula. Yes, his face was kind of square, and he wasn't a very big man up and down, but wide—

Cody and Roundtree looked at each other and nodded: Tom Gough, for a bet, sent to do the job for Rance Waldron. But why? Not yet had either of them and not yet had Ann Lee thought of the two wills the old men were carrying, for safekeeping, to Bald Eagle.

Cal turned on his heel.

'I'm off to town, boys. I'll take care of things if anything's needed. Come along, Cody?'

Cody shook his head.

'Later maybe, Cal; in the buckboard, if I do come, so you better not wait.'

Cal went his long-strided way; the small group, broke up; Cole Cody and Ann were left standing together. He looked down upon the soft loveliness of her curly hair as she, blinking her eyes furiously, looked unseeingly down at the ground and the queer designs the men's boots had made.

'I—it's so terrible—' she said, her voice quivering, and he saw how her breast filled to a deep draught of air.

'It's hell,' said Cody simply.

'Yes, it is hell. Everything has been hell, hasn't it? Since—Why, since you and I first saw each other, Cole Cody! And somehow you and I seem to be to blame for it.'

'To blame? You and I?' He shook his head, tucking in the corners of his mouth. 'Don't let yourself go off on a trail like that, young lady.

242

These things have just been in the cards.'

'Why should that man have tried to kill them? They couldn't have been carrying much money—Not robbery, then—someone who just killed for hate! Oh!'

'Not robbery, no—' he began. And then, for the first time he did think of the two wills, and a new light flashed into his eyes. 'Maybe you and I *are* somehow to blame,' he said, and she looked up at him swiftly, near-frightened by his tone. 'And maybe it was robbery. And maybe two men had a hand in it, and one of them got away!'

'What makes you talk like that?' She drew back a step or two from him; his eyes fascinated her, holding her gaze hypnotically. 'You said it wasn't robbery and now you say maybe it is—and that you and I maybe—'

'It just dawned on me,' he said, cutting across her rush of words, 'that you gave a certain document to Doc Joe to keep for you, and I gave—'

'Rance Waldron!' she gasped, and forgot herself and her pet feud so far as to clutch his arm, tight in both hands. 'The first thing I thought of when I heard, was Rance Waldron!'

He studied her a moment intently.

'If you guessed right, you know what this is going to mean, don't you?' he said.

'I don't understand. What do you—'

'If Waldron staged this affair, it was because somehow, though I'm hanged if I can figure it

243

out, he learned that the two old boys had the two wills along with them. And if he got away with them—' He shrugged, yet all the while was watching her upturned face for the slightest change of expression, 'Well, then it's goodby for keeps to any hope of yours of ever coming to own this outfit!'

'Darn the outfit and all that goes with it!' she exclaimed passionately. 'I don't care what happens to it now. It's just those two dear old men—'

'Why, shake!' cried Cole Cody, and shot his hand out, and before she knew it her hand had sped to a meeting with his, to be clasped tight, held hard.

Hand in hand, there was almost a smile in their eyes, though trouble lay back of it. Slowly their hands fell apart and her eyes drifted away.

'I guess I'll drift along into town too,' he said. 'I'll take the buckboard and make pretty near the time Cal's making on horseback.'

He was turning away when she called after him, sounding excited.

'Cole! It was Rance Waldron! I knew it at first and I know it better now! And I know how he found out about the wills! I told him myself! Oh, I was right about that other thing: Somehow you and I, or one of us, seem to be to blame for everything! When Rance Waldron was battering at our door, I called to him that I going to hand over my will to Doc

244

Joe the very first chance I got! I wish I had bit my tongue out first! Don't you see? He couldn't have known that the Judge—'

'But he would figure that if he had the one only, yours, he could maybe dicker! But don't you go blaming yourself, Ann Lee girl. I tell you things like this are either in the cards or not, and that's all there is to it.'

'And Rance—'

'Right now he's got the game by the tail with a good old-fashioned, down-hill drag! All he's got to do is set a match to a couple of pieces of paper and sit tight. If he can get away with it! You run along up to the house, Ann; you and Aunt Jenifer will be all right; in the first place Waldron isn't apt to show up here again in a hurry; besides I'll have Porfirio stick around with you.'

He headed toward the corral. She started toward the house, once in her life obedient simply because she hadn't thought to be otherwise, but glanced back over her shoulder. She thought that Cody's eyes, despite their sternness and flash of fierceness and that hidden, gentle smile of his, looked haggard, and that there was an unaccustomed pallor under his rich bronze tan—and she bit her lip and muttered to herself,

'Ann Lee, you little spit-fire, what a nasty little beast you can be!'

For she thought, too, of how she had shot him, and she shuddered there in the warmly glowing sunlight as though with cold; how she had shot him, half if not quite meaning it, and how she might have killed him.

Then she saw that he was not going for the buckboard at all. She watched him rope a horse in the corral, lead it into the barn, come out sitting in the saddle. She called sharply, her hand at her throat, for already she guessed a change of purpose in him:

'You are going to town?'

He hesitated, then shook his head.

'I've thought of another place to ride first,' he said lightly, and waved at her and rode away, striking into a trail that led up along the creek toward the canyon-cleft mountains.

She stood with her hands clenched at her sides, her chin up, her eyes steady, watching him out of sight. But there was a throbbing in her throat and her lips began to tremble.

CHAPTER NINETEEN

Bill Cole Cody rode straight to the lonely, abandoned cabin in the mountain ravine to which he and Cal Roundtree had followed Rance Waldron and Tom Gough. He had no great hope of finding Waldron lingering on here now that the Judge and Doc Joe had been cut down and robbed, now that Tom Gough was dead and in all likelihood would be

246

judged the sole highwayman and killer. Yet Rance must be somewhere, and Cody meant to find him, and here was as likely a place to look as any.

The shadows were long across the mountain slopes, the pines growing black in the deep dusk in the ravines, and there was no sign of life, no up-drifting smoke from the rock chimney when Cody came within sight of it; no horse browsing; nothing to break the sway of solitude and silence.

Cody called and his voice echoed against the granite cliffs and throbbed away into the returning stillness. He dismounted and went to the door, his hand on the butt of his gun. The door was ajar, he threw it open and looked the place over, staring frowningly into its thickening gloom. He saw a pile of blankets on the one bunk; other blankets on the floor; some scraps of food on a sagging shelf. That was all.

He went back to his horse, rode out of the ravine and into the golden sunshine again, crossed the creek and struck across country toward town. It was his thought that he might possibly have word of Waldron there; if not, he could join Cal Roundtree and discuss the new set-up with him.

He rode slowly; his wound, slight as it was, irked him somewhat, and besides he felt no need of haste. If Rance Waldron meant to hide out, well then, he had had time already to slip into some secret lair. And in time he would return; the stake at the King Cole Ranch was too big to be passed up, and certainly Rance Waldron, holding the cards, would not drop out of the game.

It was early dark when Cody rode down out of the hills along an old rutted wagon road and onto the valley rim from which he could see Bald Eagle glimmering with pale lamp lights. This was an idle hour for most men, verging on supper hour, with the day's work done and the night too young yet to be inviting to festivity. But tonight there were many men on the single street; they stood in small, compact groups or moved silently from one place to another. Some talked; others listened attentively. Voices were not loud; they didn't need to be. Men were thoughtful, and a deep hush pervaded the place. Yet there was something strangely electric in this quiet.

Cody dismounted in front of the hotel, tied his horse at the hitching rail and moved softly and silently as others were moving, seeking some sign of Cal Roundtree. He was conscious of eyes following him and knew that he drew interest here at this hour because he was a stranger; because these men, steadily gathering in numbers, were distrustful of strangers. So soon after someone had shot down old Early Bill Cole, Early Bill's two old friends had been likewise shot down. And the three, Early Bill and the Judge and Doc Joe

248

meant very much to little Bald Eagle. There were men who had to clear their throats when they spoke, and whose voices, low-toned though they kept them, were harsh, rough with emotion. And in the houses there were many wet eyes.

Cal Roundtree was turning into a saloon, two friends flanking him, when he saw Cody; he said a word to his companions who went on into the Spread Eagle, and turned back to Cody.

'It was Tom Gough, all right,' he said. 'The Judge and old Doc fought it out with him like he'd know they would if he knew them at all. All three dead, but here's a sort of funny thing: The shot that killed Gough must have been fired the same split second that he finished off either Doc Joe or the Judge: both the old boys was shot through the head. Hell, man, their bullets, the last, the ones that did the killing on both sides, must have passed one another in the air!'

'Listen, Cal,' said Cody. 'Tom Gough wasn't the only killer out after the old boys; it's like the stage holdup; there were two of them. Tom Gough for one, sure. The other? Rance Waldron and don't you fool yourself. Early Bill's two wills—the one to Ann Lee and the one to me—They haven't turned up, have they? Not in the Judge's and Doc Joe's pockets, were they? Not in Tom Gough's?'

'Me, I don't know. I don't even get what

you're driving at!'

Cody explained swiftly and Cal began to nod before he had finished.

'Rance Waldron is in town right now,' he said, his brows puckering tight as he tried to make heads and tails of things. 'He's in a back room at the hotel playing poker. I saw him there a while ago. Come ahead in and have a drink before you start anything. This wants a bit of thinking—Dammit to hell, I wish the old Judge and Doc Joe was here to lend a hand— and old Early Bill, too! Come on, kid; a drink first and we'll see what we can see. For one thing, Rance Waldron's not in hiding; for another, if he pulled this job, he's got nerve and he's sure of himself. You and me'll go slow for a minute, Cody.'

Cody nodded without saying anything and the two entered the saloon together to range up along the bar with Cal's two friends. They downed their liquor, the four of them, and stood rolling their cigarettes, grave, thoughtful men. Most of the space in the big barnlike room was given over to games of chance, faro, roulette and the like, with a restricted bare space for dancing. The tables were deserted; true it was early, but more than that, Bald Eagle wasn't thinking of such pastimes tonight.

'We might mosey over to the hotel and see what things look like,' suggested Cody.

This time Cal Roundtree nodded. He bethought him of introductions: 'Cody, these

250

boys are friends of mine, Red Johnson and Hap Davis from the Broken Arrow.' They shook hands with their formal, 'Glad to know you,' or 'Please to meet up with you.' And Cal added, 'You boys might come along; it ain't far over to the hotel.'

'Sure,' they said amiably, though they, too, were grave-faced, having caught something of Cody's and Cal's mood. 'What's up?' Hap Davis asked as they passed through the swing doors.

'We don't know yet,' was Cal's answer.

There were several men in the hotel lobby, a greater number in the bar upon which a door opened at the side. The four men passed into the bar; at its rear was another door, standing perhaps a quarter open. It was a small room in yonder, private or semi-private for gentlemen who wished to withdraw for draw or stud; a nickeled swinging coal oil lamp could be seen, and one man's side and shoulders and elbow, and the brim of his hat.

With a look Cody asked of Cal Roundtree, 'In there?' and with a look Cal answered, 'Yes.' Cody went to the door and pushed it open, Cal and the others keeping three or four paces behind him, stopping when he stopped.

'Hello, Waldron,' said Cody.

Rance Waldron looked up from his game; he was playing with four other men, all strangers to Cody, and none of them particularly fastidious looking nor handsome;

four of the toughest looking gents he had seen in a tough town.

Waldron put down his cards and shoved his chair back; he didn't make a move to rise and didn't remove his hands from the table top.

'Hello, Cody,' he said. 'What's wanted? If there's anything wrong with your eyes, I'm playing cards.'

'The Judge and Doc Joe were killed today, Waldron,' said Cody. 'It was an ugly sort of killing from what I hear. Murder, folks are calling it.'

'I heard about it,' said Rance Waldron.

'Another man got his come-uppance the same time; a man name of Tom Gough. Maybe you knew him?'

Rance Waldron took all the time in the world answering, yet it could not exactly be said that he hesitated. Cody was very deliberate; Rance Waldron's was as cool a deliberation.

'Maybe,' he answered.

'Friend of yours?'

'Who wants to know?' Waldron cocked up his brows, and though his eyes had narrowed until they were grown icy slits with a cold anger like the chill of steel, his lips affected a tolerant smile.

'Been in town all day, Waldron?'

Rance laughed. There were two ways to take a thing like this; he had his choice. Rather than recognize the broad implication seriously,

252

he elected to greet it as funny.

'I'd like to get along with the game, Mr. Cody,' he said, sounding now like a man who meant to remain patient as long as he could, but whose patience was fast running out. 'No, I haven't been in town all day. I rode in about—' He turned to two of the men at the table with him; all were very still, very watchful, more than half expecting an explosion. The two to whom Rance Waldron now addressed himself were a big, bristly, burly half-breed Mexican and Indian; and a lean-visaged, pale-eyed, furtive looking youngster who looked like the dissipated wreckage of youth's 'teens. Rance Waldron said, 'You boys, what time was it I ran into you at the edge of town?'

'Two o'clock,' both said promptly.

Cody heard Cal Roundtree's snort; those two sure had the thing down pat. And Cody was tempted to ask them if they carried watches! Well, there was Rance Waldron's alibi, as tight as a rain barrel: He had been all afternoon, of course, in the company of these gents—with them in or near Bald Eagle while three men were being killed.

'Now, Cody,' said Rance, and chose to laugh again, 'I'll thank you to get the hell out of here.'

Cody obliged him.

'Nothing to do, nothing you can put your mind to,' grumbled Cal Roundtree as the four turned away from the poker room. 'Waldron's nobody's fool; he could make him a good living training snakes.'

'Kind of too bad all three men, old Doc and the Judge and the other, was plumb shot to death,' said Red Johnson mournfully, but then he was a man with a mournful voice.

'And kind of funny, too,' added Hap Davis. 'Three men to get into an argument, all three to get wiped out, two of 'em shot through the head. Pretty damn kind of funny, if it comes around so you ask me.'

They had progressed as far as the lobby when a sharp, petulant, eager voice called,

'You, there, Roundtree! Cal! I want a word with you.'

The speaker, wiping his mouth as he came out of the bar behind them, was a youngish man in high lop-sided boots, with a bristle of a scrubby little black mustache, coatless, with his sleeves rolled up on a pair of brawny, hairy arms, with large, dark and strikingly intelligent eyes.

Cal explained to Cole Cody, 'It's Dr. Parke Evans. They sent for him over to Rim Rock as soon as word of a shooting got out, Doc Joe for once not being on tap here in Bald Eagle,' and turned toward the Rim Rock doctor.

'Anything private, Doc?' he asked. 'I got friends with me.'

'Yes. It's private. And I'm in a hurry.'

He led the way, rolling down his sleeves, to the stairway leading upward from the lobby,

254

and Cal climbed along after him, wondering as others wondered, what Parke Evans could want with him. Half way up the staircase he called down to Cody,

'Stick around, Cody, and wait for me. I won't be long; then we'll ride out to the ranch together.'

So Cole Cody waited. He stepped out onto the porch; there were two rocking chairs there, and he thought that never in all his born days had he seen chairs, or anything else, that looked so empty. Men coming and going looked at them quite as Cody did; no one sat down. He stood leaning against a post, smoking a thoughtful cigarette, gazing abstractedly at the brightening glitter of the stars hanging over the hills rimming the valley.

Time passed, he didn't know how long. At last he sat down on the top step, leaning against the post supporting the porch roof. He ought to be getting along, he thought; Ann Lee and Aunt Jenifer would be alone, and the hour would bear down oppressively upon them. A queer, half humorous and half sad smile stirred on his lips; he was remembering those two old boys paying court to Miss Jenifer Edwards! And little Ann Lee hadn't liked it a bit! How that girl's eyes could snap! How they could sparkle, too, when she tipped her pretty head back and laughed; how soft and warm and tender they could be at rare, oh, very rare times—and what a cute trick they had of crinkling at the corners when she smiled. Yes, he'd better get along; he could leave word for Cal; no sense waiting all night.

He stood up, not quite decided yet on the verge of going.

*   *   *

Rance Waldron with his two alibi-liars at his heels came out and ran down the steps onto the sidewalk; Waldron flashed a glance at Cole Cody where he stood in the lamp light streaming out through the hotel door, and said something in a low voice to his companions; the three laughed.

Yes, might as well get along back to Ann Lee—to the ranch, he meant. There was no telling about Rance Waldron; he might be headed back that way himself. He had his chin in the air tonight.

Cal Roundtree came out. He looked to be in a daze; he was like a man walking in his sleep. His eyes were wide open; they stated straight at Cole Cody; their expression, or lack of expression rather, did not alter. He looked at Cody and did not see him.

Cody thought, He's been hit over the head!

He said, 'Cal! What's come over you, man? You haven't gone and got yourself pie-eyed drunk this quick, have you?'

'Hello, Cody,' said Cal dully. He stopped

and removed his hat and ran his fingers through his hair. Slowly his eyes narrowed to normalcy, but there remained a queer, troubled look in them. 'Come ahead, kid,' he said. 'Let's go get our horses. Let's pile out of here for home.'

The two strode along side by side and got their horses. They swung up into their saddles and headed down the road. By starlight nothing could be made of Cal's face, but his heavy silence was disquieting. Cody however held his peace. If a man wanted to keep his thoughts to himself, that was his affair.

'I got to do a bit of thinking,' said Cal presently. 'And, dammit, I can't! I'm all tangled up; I'm rattled like no man ever was before. I got to tell you something, Cody; I got to tell somebody or I'll bust, and I'd rather it was you. But, hell take it, I don't know how much to spill and how much to hold back. Because I can't tell it all, get me? I got to hold part back! Maybe I'll go get somebody to cut my tongue out. Shut up a minute, and let me think; let me anyhow try to think.'

Cody leaned out of the saddle and clapped the perplexed man on the shoulder, and made no other answer.

They rode for ten or fifteen minutes, out across the floor of the valley, striking into the little rolling hills, before Cal spoke again.

'Like I said, Cody, I can't spill the whole sack o' beans, though I wish to God I could!

And I could kill that hell-roaring, hyena-laughing, Hell's favorite, old Early Bill Cole—only the son-a-gun's dead already! Whoa! There I go again. Well, here's what I can tell you, and you better pull leather whilst you listen good, else you're apt to fall out'n your saddle.'

And here is what Cal Roundtree held himself free to tell:

Dr. Parke Evans had led the way upstairs to a locked room; he had unlocked the door, motioned Cal Roundtree to go in, had then closed the door and stood outside, guarding against any interruption. On the far side of the room, with his back turned, a man was standing. The lamp was turned low; Cal did not make out at once who it was. But when the door had been closed, the man moved to the table where the lamp was and turned up the wick.

Right then Cal Roundtree sat down. There was a chair and a bed; he sat on the bed because it was handier. The manner of his sitting was like that of a man whose legs had been chopped off under him. He goggled as his first stroke of bewilderment smote him. Here in the flesh, looking very much alive and in fact as he had looked for the twenty years Cal had known him, save for a terrible grimness on his face, was old Doc Joe.

Doc Joe lifted a sudden warning hand to forestall any explosive utterance from the astounded Cal Roundtree.

'No loud talking, Cal,' he said incisively.

Cal swallowed.

'Me? Me, I can't talk at all!' Then a tinge of color, angry color, came into his darkly weathered face. 'What in hell's this mean?' he demanded.

Doc Joe pulled up the chair close to the bed and spoke softly, throttling his voice down to a near-whisper.

'For one thing, I ain't dead now, never was and don't intend to be for a spell yet,' he said. 'Get that in your head, Cal. Don't go thinking ghosts.'

Cal snorted.

'You don't look anything like what I might suppose a ghost would look,' he said curtly. 'Now, let's get after this: What in the name of blazes you been playing dead for?'

'For a spell, I had to,' said Doc Joe. 'If I hadn't, Rance Waldron would have killed me sure, like he did the Judge and Tom Gough. He nicked me side of the head.' He put his finger gingerly to a bit of taped gauze over his temple. 'It sort of dazed me. I lay on my side and saw him step over to the Judge. He shot the Judge between the horns before I could wiggle a finger. Then he looked at me. I hope I never have another man look at me like that again, not with me laying in the road and him standing over me with a gun! Maybe I sort of fainted a minute; I don't quite know or rec'lect

259

or give a damn. I was scared enough to faint anyhow. He came back dragging Tom Gough. He shot Gough twice; he took Tom's horse and rode away. I tried to get up. I got dizzy and sure did faint for good. When I woke up and the boys hauled us into town, I was out cold. They thought I was dead. Me, I got to thinking. I let 'em keep on thinking so. Nobody knows but Doc Evans; you and him, now, Cal. And you're both going to keep your mouths shut until I give the word.'

Cal came bounding to his feet at that.

'Like hell I am,' he began shouting, but old Doc Joe clapped a hand over his mouth and admonished him, 'Shut up, you blasted fool! You're supposed to be in here with a dead man. And you're going to—'

'Rance Waldron is downstairs right now,' said Cal, stubborn and eager. 'He killed the Judge, you say. And you saw him? And it's almost a dead certainty that either him or his hired hand, Tom Gough, potted old Early Bill! And you say I'm going to keep my mouth shut! Like hell, Doc Joe! You can go lay all the bets you want that inside a quarter hour from right now Mr. Rance Waldron is going to be kicking his heels high up in empty air! Lemme out o' here!'

'Shush, you bull-headed lummox! You remind me of a boy I knew who when he was nineteen years old couldn't get promoted to the second grade. You—'

260

'That boy wasn't you, was he?' snapped Cal, and put a heavy hand on old Doc Joe's shoulder. 'I'm on my way.'

'Shut up and sit down and keep your shirt tail tucked in! Now, listen. The Judge and me, we had those two damn fool wills that old jackass Bill Cole drawed up. And Mr. Rance Waldron's got 'em now. You can bet your last bottom dollar he's got 'em hid, hid good and proper—'

'You're crazy, Doc! That bullet must have scratched your brains! Hell's bells, Waldron, once he got his hand on those papers, wouldn't have wasted two minutes doing away with 'em. He'd have ducked over the first hill and burned 'em to ashes, and kicked the ashes all over a ten acre wood-lot. Don't you realize that that's all he's got to do—to—to—'

And Cal came to a dead halt and his face began to redden and he looked downright foolish. So foolish, in fact that Doc Joe stared at him wonderingly.

And now Cal Roundtree, telling this to Cole Cody as the two jogged along, came again to a halt. Then he began to swear explosively. And in the end, grown quiet after his struggle with himself, he muttered disgustedly.

'Hell, Cody, I don't know which end I'm standing on. There's something I know that I got to keep under my hat, like I been doing; I almost blew my top off and let the cat jump with old Doc Joe; I'm damn near doing the

261

same thing with you.

'Why not, Cal?' said Cody quietly. 'You and I haven't known each other all summer, but— What's on your mind, old timer?'

'No,' Cal growled. 'Let me be, dammit. Let me go on now and tell you the rest that I can; what old Doc Joe has got in his mind. He says Rance Waldron is smart like a whole herd of foxes; he says, No, Waldron won't destroy those wills right off; he says Waldron will play safe, and hide 'em damn good, where the devil himself can't find 'em, until he sees for sure which way the wind blows. He claims to be next of kin to that hell-twisting, trouble-making, pestiferous, gen'rally no-'count Early Bill Cole, darn his ornery hide. But, says Doc Joe, Waldron not being any man's come-on-Charlie will figger there's slips between the mahogany and the gullet, and many a full glass o' licker gets spilled. Maybe other heirs might turn up; they always do when there's a pot of money dangling. And it might take years and some more years before Rance gets his teeth into the property, and by then the lawyers would have anyhow half of it. That's what Doc Joe says, and I guess you got to admit there's a speck of sense left in the old devil.

'What he says, is this: Waldron will try to gobble the King Cole Ranch and anything else left hanging. If he makes a go of it, he'll burn the papers. If there's any slip-up along that trail, well then, with the two wills in his war

262

bag, he can dicker. Dicker with you; dicker with Ann Lee. He could make threats; he could try bribes. He'd be holding a good hand. Says Doc Joe. Now, if we strung him up, and had ourselves a good time watching him choke to death, he'd be dead, and the wills would be the same as gone forever. This is Doc Joe's jabber, mind you.'

Cole Cody, when Cal's vehement utterances were at an end, thought the matter over from all angles—from all angles, that is, which it was given him to glimpse. There were things he did not know. There was something that Cal Roundtree did know and would not put into words. It was something that had to do with old Early Bill Cole. Was that old hell-hound as those who had known him and loved him termed him over and over with many a salty oath, dead and buried as he most indubitably was, no make-believe dead man like old Doc Joe, still ordering lives? Still 'getting him his fun' as he had sworn to do, dead or alive?

After a long while Cody asked,

'What does Doc Joe plan? How long is he going to play dead?'

That started Cal Roundtree off again. But he got himself in hand ultimately and explained some part of Doc Joe's plan.

'Late tonight the other doc, Parke Evans, will find a paper in Doc's room, signed by Doc Joe himself, dated a couple of years ago, saying when he's dead he yearns to be packed up and shipped back to his boyhood's home which is in dear old Tennessee!' Cal spat far into space. 'So Doc Evans will pack him in a box, and haul him off with him tomorrow, going back to Rim Rock, and to the railroad at Christmas Forks. They'll ship some sort of a bundle and Doc Joe will hide out for a spell with Doc Evans. Later he'll get a chance to creep back thisaway by the dark of the moon. Meantime we're to watch and wait for Rance Waldron to be making his play. And Doc Joe says, just for the hell of it, having watched Waldron shoot down the old Judge, then plug his own pardner, that he wants to be in at the hanging-bee; he wants a hand on the rope and he wants to spit in Rance Waldron's eye and tell him it was him that out-foxed him and got him hung.—Say, my throat's dry! Let's fog along; there's a bottle hid behind my bunk and I need it.'

Cole Cody, content with silence and his own thoughts, said to himself, Well, old Early Bill sure fixed things up to have him his fun after he was dead! He has made more things happen, longer after they dug him under, than lots of men stir up in a good long lifetime.

The two wills, while available, cut each other's throats nicely, and started trouble to boot. Gone, or as good as gone in Rance Waldron's hands, there went with them all hope of Bill Cole Cody ever coming to own any part of the King Cole Ranch—and he was

264

already by way of falling in love with its broad, sweeping acres under the long shadows of the purple range. Gone, too, were all Ann Lee's bright hopes.

Little Ann Lee! Cody filled his lungs to a long intake of air and Cal looked at him sideways. That sounded like a sigh. Well, why not? But Cal couldn't know that of a sudden Bill Cole Cody was thinking more of little Ann Lee's coming bitter disappointment than of his own.

CHAPTER TWENTY

Arrived at the ranch they unsaddled, cared for their horses and said good night, Cal to turn in at the bunk house and no doubt tilt his bottle to a long gurgle, Cole Cody hastening up the slope to the ranch house. In the starlit *patio* he came upon Porfirio lounging on a bench, waiting for him. Porfirio's glowing cigarette described a quick, small arc in the gloom as Porfirio came to his feet.

'That is you, Don Codito?' he asked softly.

'Yes, Porfirio. Everything all right here? No visitors?'

Porfirio assured him that all was well; no, no visitors. And the ladies? Just now they had come out to him; they had brought him hot coffee and a whole pie, and *caramba*, eet was a

265

good wan! Not five minutes ago, or maybe ten, no more, they had gone to their rooms.

'I'll see you in the morning, Porfirio—'

'But wait!' exclaimed Porfirio excitedly. 'And look! Ah, better light a match to see good! I have found it, like I said I was going to do. You see it, Don Codito.'

'What the devil is it?' muttered Cody, stooping to see better. 'Not a dead cat, is it? Somebody's old black tom—A hat!'

'*Seguro qui si, Señor!* You are damn' right she is a hat! An old black one, *tambien,* and with a hole of a bullet in it! Better we go inside and have a lamp; you are going to see something. It is the hat of the man that killed *mi amigo* Señor Early Bill Cole, and it is the hat of the man I am going to kill!'

Cody led the way into the living room; while he was lighting a lamp Porfirio explained how his persistence had brought him to his discovery. From the place where the man had hidden when he shot Early Bill, Porfirio on horseback had ridden a score of times, following each time a slightly different path, thinking, Now if it was me, and I was riding like the wind, I'd go this way; thinking, And I would get rid of that hat *muy pronto.* And he had looked at all the possible hiding places, had looked even for signs of a small hot fire. And then at last his keen eyes had seen a stick, a small dead pine limb, its end sticking out from under a sizable boulder!

Aha! He had it! For how could a stick get itself shoved under a rock like that? If a man had moved that rock now, and had been in a hurry settling it back, and in a hurry to ride on, he might with a careless boot have kicked that stick where it got caught under the stone! Porfirio sweated over the boulder, moving it—and found the hat.

Yes, there was a bullet hole drilled through it. There was more. There was everything; Cole Cody could only regret that its message came too late. In the sweat band were the initials, tooled through the leather, 'T.G.'

'Tom Gough, that's who it was, Porfirio,' he said as he tossed the hat, now of no interest, to the table. 'But Rance Waldron—Look, Porfirio, Tom Gough is dead already. He's the stick-up gent that fought it out with the Judge and Doc Joe.' Porfirio began cursing softly in the tongue of the south. He started to the door; he said good night sullenly—Then of a sudden he whirled and cried out 'Dead, the *cabrone!* And so he gets away from me like that, does he, Don Codito?' He laughed, and it was an evil sound when Porfirio Lopez laughed that way. 'Look, Señor. Some day I am going to be dead, too, no? *Bueno!* But I don't forget, not even when dead, I don't forget *mi amigo*, Señor Don Early Bill Cole. And some fine morning when I'm dead not very long, you know what I am going to do? I am going to pop right down to hell where that

267

Tom Gough is, and—and—and—'

His voice trailed away and he himself departed in silence. He was scratching his head, Cody saw: Just what a man could do when he came up with his quarry in hell— Well, there was food for thought for Porfirio.

Cody, not yet of any mind for bed and sleep, started a quick blaze in the fireplace and dragged a big comfortable chair in front of it. It wasn't cold, yet the night air had freshened so that there was the hint of chill in it, and besides a man brooding alone finds companionship in a living fireplace. Sunk deep into Early Bill's pet chair, rolling what he thought was to be a good night cigarette, he did not hear a door open and close softly, nor did he hear light oncoming steps. What he heard first was a subdued voice saying,

'Hello, Cole Cody. Mind if I join you and the fire a minute? I can't sleep—can you?'

He rose and drew up a companion chair; the young firelight, catching at a stick of pitch-pine, flared up and shone brightly on his face and little Ann Lee's as they stood a moment looking seriously at each other; it shone in their eyes and made them bright.

She smiled a little then, a fleeting, sad wisp of a smile that he wasn't dead sure was any smile at all, that it wasn't merely the effect of the flames flickering. He saw her eyes clearly, with the light dancing in them, and was sure that she had been crying. Impulsively he shot

268

out his hand; hers snuggled into it and he gave hers a strong, warm squeeze. She nodded her head understandingly as she slowly withdrew her hand. They sat side by side and watched the flames in silence, each seeing reflected there what was uppermost in his own mind.

He thought resentfully, That confounded Doc Joe! I could strangle him! Here she's been crying her eyes out for him and the old Judge, slaughtered; and there in Bald Eagle is Doe Joe no doubt getting half drunk and beginning to bubble with the fun he's going to have with Rance Waldron when he gets good and ready. If, instead, he'd just step in here now, Ann Lee would be so glad she'd even forget for a while that the Judge wasn't alive, too.

A burning stick rolled out on the hearth, sending its thin spout of blue smoke out into the room. He kicked it back into place and, while astir, put on a larger log. Ann Lee, with her hands lying loose in her lap, her fingers curling and pink with the fireglow so that they were like flower petals, watched every move he made; when he sat down and glanced at her she again smiled at him, and he thought it a brave little smile this time. And he wanted to reach out for her hand again—but didn't.

'Ann Lee,' he said after a while.

'What is it, Cole?' she asked. Both their voices were quiet, hers hushed.

'You realize by this time, don't you, that there's not a chance in the world of either you or me ever coming to own any part of the King Cole Ranch?'

'Yes.' She spoke very simply, not seeming or sounding in the least concerned; scarcely interested. He heard her long, quivering sigh before she added, 'Maybe it's funny, but I don't seem to care any more. After what has just happened—those two dear old men—'

Darn your hide, Doc Joe! It was hard for Bill Cole Cody to keep from violating Cal's confidence, just as it had been a man's job for Cal to keep from blurting out something else he knew, something he felt bound to keep to himself.

The long silences which fell between words broken off, a sense of remoteness, the young summer night breathing into the room, perhaps something of the spirit of the fire in the old black fireplace, brewed a sort of magic. Cody smoked an inch of his cigarette, flipped the thing into the fire, sat with his elbows on his knees, his chin in his hands, his eyes and their expression hidden from her. She could see only the flat plane of his brown cheek, flushed by the fire, the clean-cut, purposeful jaw, where his thumb did not quite hide it all, the dark thatch of hair, in disorder now and inclined to break into curls here and there. Hair like that could be a temptation; it was made, she thought, for some girl's fingers to go stealing softly through. She wondered, What girls does he know? And is there, somewhere,

270

a girl—

Little by little, out of these drifting silences, they fell to talking briefly and sketchily about each other, about themselves. He knew so little of her; she had taught a country school, she had her Aunt Jenifer to live with, her parents were long dead; her father had been one of Early Bill's closest friends. She knew so very little of Cole; a young man who lived alone, who had his ambitions, who had been rancher and mining engineer; he, too, had had a father who was a lifetime friend of Early Bill.

They laughed a little together, and came closer to each other than ever before, when they started to speak at the same instant and with the same thought:

'Why, your father and mine, too, must have been great friends!'

Cody made himself another cigarette and, instead of smoking it or even remembering that he had made it to smoke, sat rolling and rolling it with his lean, strong fingers. He said without looking up,

'I could almost be glad—in a way, I would be glad if it wasn't that Rance Waldron might come to profit by it—that those two wills are, anyhow for the present and maybe for good, out of the picture.' Then he did straighten and look at her, and she saw his eyes, keen and steady, bent upon hers. And then he laughed again. 'All we've done, maybe all we'd ever do, is fight like cat and dog over the darned place!

Maybe now—Well, maybe we can get along without fighting! It might be fun for a change, Ann Lee?'

'I'm a beast most of the time, I'm afraid,' she said contritely. 'And I try so hard not to be! Honestly, Bill Cole Cody, I try terribly hard. And—and I really didn't go to shoot you!' Her eyes dilated; she leaned close and clutched his arm tightly. 'You'll believe that, won't you? Please do! That d-darned gun of Cal Roundtree's—'

He put his hand on hers; she permitted the contact for a long moment, then gently slid her fingers out from under his and, palm upward, let them curl again on her lap.

'I guess I shouldn't have spanked you—so hard, anyhow!'

'I deserved every bit of it—and harder!' But he saw that the hot color in her cheeks now was not altogether the affair of the fire.

He wondered if she could blush any hotter than that? If by an incredibly long chance she could look any prettier? He made his voice sound contrite, anyhow almost contrite, as he added, with an eye still upon her,

'And I guess I oughtn't to have kissed you on the stage—the way I did!'

Her face *did* flame redder. And, darn it all, she *was* prettier!

'Let's not quarrel any more, ever,' she said hurriedly. She lifted her eyes to his. 'We have been friends, in a way, haven't we? We do like each other, even after all that's happened; I know we do.'

He said soberly, 'You're being mighty sweet, Ann Lee. I never knew a girl like you!'

'Oh, yes you have, Mr. Cody! Bushels of 'em. There are lots of girls like me.'

'No.'

'I love fireplaces! One like this; look how the coals are forming now! Do you like to find pictures in them? Of course, everybody does. The fireplace is one of the things that makes me love this room.' She stirred slightly and sighed; she moved her arms, crossing them, her hands on her shoulders, giving herself a little hug; she said, 'Dear old Early Bill, he did try, didn't he? Tried so hard to "have him his fun" and at the same time do something splendid for you and me, for his old friends' son and daughter. Well, I've a tiny fireplace all my own at home, and when I go back to teaching—'

'Ann! What are you talking about? You haven't forgotten, have you, the money he left for us in the bank, fifty-fifty? We know that Bucktooth Jenkins got that ten thousand into the pot; you heard the Judge say there was a whole lot more! And you talking about teaching!'

Her sudden laughter, gay and gleeful this time, surprised him.

'Honestly, cross my heart and hope to die,' she exclaimed, 'I had forgotten all about that part of it! Why, there are thousands and thousands there, all yours and mine! For us to take and use any minute we like! It's like a fairy tale, isn't it, Cole Cody?'

'What'll we do with all that money?' he asked, glad to keep her in this gayer mood.

She made a face at him.

'I could have killed you! When I said that I was going to take out a big round thousand, all at once, and you cut me down to ten dollars!'

He chuckled. 'You asked for it, you know you did, Miss High and Mighty, that day! Say! Tell me something: When we whack up what's there, dividing it all up even-Stephen, what do you think you're going to do with your cut?'

'Well, let's see.' She settled back deeper into her big chair, lithe and graceful as a kitten curling itself into laziest comfort. 'There'll be a trip to a town; some big town with lots of big stores, Aunt Jenifer and me. We'll drive in a fine carriage with the finest horses and a hired driver with a fine suit and a whip with a red ribbon on it. There'll be dresses, trunkfuls. And—'

'The biggest town you can find,' mused Cody aloud, 'with the biggest and best stores. No matter how far away—'

'And there's a little old lady I know; I call her Granny; you'd love her to death; and she's, oh, terribly poor, and her children are all grown up and gone away and they're not very good to her, and it's the dream of her life to go

274

back to her girlhood home in Georgia before she dies, and—Oh, there are lots of things! Millions!'

'Did you ever see the plug come out of a keg of beer, and the beer start spouting? That's the way thoughts spout out of my old head tonight! I've got an idea that you might call— Shucks, a fancy name for it would be Inspiration!'

'Sounds exciting! What is it, Bill Cole Cody?'

'Maybe,' drawled Cody, tantalizing her with his over-accentuated deliberation, 'maybe I've hit on the right thing to do. Take all that money in the bank, now; add to it your notion to go running off hither and thither, as the feller sez: going fast and going far, and maybe forgetting to ever come back. Now, suppose we let that money stay right where it is, the way it is! Then, when you felt like a spending spree, you'd have to come tell me about it! Because unless I signed the checks with you—'

'Cole Cody!'

Aunt Jenifer cleared her throat considerably in the far, dim end of the long room.

'Mind if I come in, you two?' she asked, and came straight ahead. 'I'm close to getting the jim-jams, all alone in my room. And I got to thinking about a pot of coffee and—You two fighting again?'

Cody gave her his chair, squatted on the

corner of the hearth and started a fresh cigarette. Ann Lee began to laugh.

And thus began on the King Cole Ranch a short period of time into which entered many a pleasant moment, with moments of quiet peace, moments of spontaneous happiness, flitting all too swiftly because always the shadow came back, moments when Ann Lee surprised a look in Bill Cole Cody's eyes which he did not know was there, which no other girl ever put there; and times when he, trying to read what lay in her mind, what she felt deep down in her heart even, dreamed his dreams.

They rode together hours on end, memorizing the lovely details of the vast King Cole Ranch. There were times of nooning, with sandwiches and clear, cold mountain water, in the hidden secret places among the hills. Once Ann Lee, as they came to the crest of a rise of land from which they could look for miles across a glory of undulating panorama, exclaimed breathlessly, 'Oh, Cole! If this really could be ours!' And he repeated within himself, not looking at her but into the farthest blue distance, his jaw hard and his eyes narrowed, 'Ours!'

And his thoughts switched swiftly, as so often they did, to the vanished Rance Waldron. For since that night in Bald Eagle, none at the ranch had seen or heard of him; in town Cal Roundtree, who seemed to have some mysterious business of his own which carried him there daily, could get no news of him. Rance Waldron had simply faded out of the picture, leaving no inkling of where he had gone or why or for how long.

And so the days drifted by, with summer ripening, and Cole Cody and Ann Lee with Aunt Jenifer lingered on. It was pleasant here, pleasanter than anywhere else on earth; here the grass along the creeks was greener and fresher and the wild flowers gayer; here the blue bowl of the sky in the early morning and the late afternoon was the blue of deep, clear water; the sunrises were master canvases splashed with living, shifting colors; the stars were blue and yellow and amethystine jewels, and when the full moon came surging up over the black eastern ridges and swept up and up, the nights were ineffably serene and also vaguely troubling to young warm hearts.

There were days which Cole Cody and Cal Roundtree spent together, Cody for the most part inclined to long silences; Cal moody, given to brooding spells and to inexplicable flares of temper, of a sort of petulant irritation. At times out of their silences he would burst into sulphurous ranch swear words; boiled down and sterilized his utterances would be something like this:

'Damn that old Doc Joe! I could cut him wide open with a hand-ax and rub salt on his pestiferous gizzard!' Or, 'Damn that lying, grinning, trouble-making old Early Bill Cole!

Lucky for him he's dead already; I'd like to rig the hide off him, was he alive, and wrap it around him and set him in the sun for the hide to shrink so it would strangle him to death!'

Those were the days when Ann Lee remained in the big, still old house. She moved softly through the dim rooms, the shades drawn against the glowing outside heat. She trailed her fingertips along table tops, along the backs of chairs; she smoothed the time-darkened walls with the palm of her hand. 'I love you, Old House,' she sometimes whispered when quite alone. 'You've got your secrets, haven't you, Old House? All sorts of memories; heaps of 'em. Good ones, and bad ones, too, I bet! Dear old Early Bill was young once here, wasn't he? What was he like then, Old House? Why can't you tell me? And who was 'Sylvia'? Did something happen to her, did she die, long and long ago? When she was just a young girl like me? And did young Billy Cole, before he got to be old Early Bill, love her terribly? Did she love him, too, and was she, oh, so faithful and true to him?'

Dear, dead, faded rose leaves of romance, these were what she was finding everywhere. Folks thought that they knew old Early Bill from the crown of his ragged old Stetson to his spurred boot heels—but they didn't know him the way she did—the way 'Sylvia' had known him when both were young.

'I love you, Early Bill! You're an old

darling, that's what you are!'

And sometimes, alone in an early morning hour or in a hushed twilight, she would stand or sit very still, and would whisper,

'I know you are what folks call 'dead,' Early Bill—but I don't believe you've really gone away, not for one minute! I can *feel* you right here somewhere. Why, you're even near enough for me to reach out and touch—if only I could *see* you! And is Sylvia with you, too? You're laughing, Early Bill, you old scamp! I know you are!—Oh, why couldn't I have come sooner? Why couldn't I have known you?'

She wandered up to the three pines, Early Bill's beloved pines under which that part of him which no longer lived lay at rest; the body of an old man, wearied, now resting. She put her arms as far as she could around the biggest of the pines and pressed her cheek against its rough bark. Those long, long years ago young Bill Cole and Sylvia had loved to loiter there together. Sylvia loved dawns, too, the way he did. But somehow never could little Ann Lee feel his nearness here as she could in the *patio* or under the red-tiled roof.

And it was in the *patio* of early mornings and in the summer magic of the long, lingering twilights that she and Bill Cole Cody grew into the pleasant habit of meeting, to speak little, to dwell in a warm awareness of each other that was a glow like that lying about them over the hills and valleys; sometimes they looked at each other, each seeking what lay deep down in the other's eyes, a little searching their own hearts. Aunt Jenifer spied on them at times from a safe, secret distance, then went her quiet way smiling.

Thus they had been sitting on a particular evening, with even fewer words and with longer glances between them than ever before, when three occurrences burst upon them with the effect of sudden, unrelated and unexpected explosions. They sat tonight on the same green bench; the first stars were coming shyly into the sweep of the clean, richly blue sky; Cody put his hand out and very gently touched her fingers.

'Ann,' he said. 'Ann Lee—'

They had heard no sound of footsteps, so enwrapped were they in the concerns of their world which at the moment was as far away from their immediate surroundings as was the star from which the girl's eyes came now so swiftly to try to read through the shadowy half-light what was written on his face, when of a sudden Porfirio stood before them.

'Don Codito!' he burst out in some tremendous excitement. 'Come quick! For the love of God, Señor, come as fast as lightning! No, no, no! Not the *señorita*! You are to come alone. You won't believe it—I cannot tell you—It is a miracle, Don Codito!'

'Are you drunk, Porfirio?' snapped Cody.

Porfirio caught him by the sleeve and fairly

heaved him up from his place at the girl's side and willy-nilly, short of a fight, Cody had to accompany him some few steps. Then Porfirio began whispering in his ear; and then Cody understood and went willingly enough, hurrying long-stridedly, eager and glad that one sequence of a tragi-comedy, a farcical one at that, was at an end. At the darkest corner of the house where a great live oak almost swept the ground with its lower branches, Porfirio brought him to Doc Joe.

CHAPTER TWENTY-ONE

When almost immediately Cole Cody came rushing back to Ann Lee, all but breathless, he found her standing in the *patio*, her slight body rigidly held, her hands at her sides, her chin lifted, her eyes on the stars. She hadn't known that he was really coming back at all; Porfirio's abrupt appearance had startled her, she was vaguely frightened—and for some reason her heart was pounding.

Her hands must have come up toward her breast when she heard him hurrying back to her. At any rate, even in the faint uncertain glimmering of star-glow his hands found them, both of them, and caught them firmly.

'Ann! Something wonderful! Listen, Ann— don't let it bowl you over—'

Aunt Jenifer was just on her way to join them; she stopped, as yet unseen though within earshot, about to withdraw. She sniffed, though smiling. To herself she commented,

'That's the darnedest way for a man to start telling a girl he loves her!'

Perhaps Ann was thinking the same thing. Neither knew how Doc Joe had just told young Cody to go ahead and prepare the ladies for his coming; the thing was to be done gradually, with tact, yet in a hurry, too! It had to be gotten over with before an interruption came, and Doc Joe was by way of knowing exactly what interruption was on the road.

'Go slow, young feller, but hurry up with it!' was about the burden of Doc Joe's exhortation.

'Cole! What is it?' asked Ann Lee, leaving her hands for the present where they were.

'Come into the house; quick. And get Aunt Jenifer. There's something I want to tell both of you; it's just about the most wonderful news—You won't be able to believe it. Only hurry, please!'

Aunt Jenifer's appearance, were the two young people less taken up with themselves and with the as yet unspoken glad tidings, must have smacked of magic; there she was as they came, hand in hand, into the lamp-lighted living room.

He released one of Ann's hands then and took one of Aunt Jenifer's. She saw how earnest and eager he was; she said quietly,

'All right, Cole. It's something to surprise us, but we won't be silly about it, especially since it's good news. We can take heaps of that, Ann and I.'

When he told them, Aunt Jenifer sat down right in the middle of the floor; Ann reached out and clung tight to him and didn't seem to note that he had an arm about her.

Then Doc Joe came in.

Jenifer scrambled to her feet and kissed him. Ann Lee deserted Cole Cody and put both arms about Doc Joe and gave him a mighty hug.

'Oh, Doc Joe! Doc Joe!' she kept saying over and over.

Doc Joe beamed all over. He made them each a bow; he kissed first Jenifer's hand, then Ann Lee's.

'Ladies!' he exclaimed throatily, his face red. 'I never thought anything could make a man so happy! It would have been worth it to be dead for sure, just to know that you cared like you do! I'm powerful happy and proud. Proud, ladies—Shucks, that's no name for it.'

Aunt Jenifer's little laugh, meant to conceal her fluttering, only gave her away still further, as did also her hurried,

'That fool ankle of mine, I turned it on this pesky floor and fell sprawling just when I should have been like a lady in a play, graceful and dramatic! Howdy, Doc Joe; we're real glad to see you looking so well—'

'Aunt Jenny!' cried Ann Lee.

'Listen!' cut in Cody. 'Doc Joe wants us to hide him a little longer; for only a few minutes or a few hours, I don't know. He knows a lot about Rance Waldron; he'll tell you what it is. And while we didn't know where Waldron had gone, he knew and was having him watched all the time. And he knows that Waldron is on his way right now to the ranch and ought to be here any minute. So it's up to us to get Doc Joe under cover in a hurry, then be ready for Waldron's coming.'

'That's it, my boy, that's it!' said Doc Joe hurriedly. 'I don't want any beans spilled until I do the spilling. Get me out of sight, can you, ladies? I'll try to do a mite of explaining to you while we wait. And that Waldron dog will be showing up in a jiffy. He's not to know I'm alive until I can up and tell him he's as good as dead. Where'll we go?'

'Into our rooms!' said Aunt Jenifer, and started leading the way. 'That's the safest place.' Then she said, 'Shush!' and all stood at attention, straining their ears. Through the silence which shut down about them they heard distinctly the thud of hoofbeats not too far away.

'Hurry along,' said Cole Cody. 'I'll be in the main room. If it's Rance Waldron, I'll find out what he wants.'

'He wants the King Cole Ranch,' snapped

284

Doc Joe over his shoulder, as already, between Aunt Jenifer and Ann Lee, he was being steered toward the safe harbor of their rooms. 'He wants all he can get. And he's come to feel pretty dead sure the world is his with a red ribbon around it and a downhill drag.'

Yes, Rance Waldron wanted the ranch and meant to have it and, as Doc Joe had said, already counted it as good as his to have and to hold or to coin into good hard money and toss where he liked, the way the wind tosses dead leaves. That was ever Rance Waldron's way.

He didn't knock; why should he, coming home, returning to his own place? He shoved the door open and strode in; his thumbs were cocked into his belt, his hat was far back on his thatch of hair, his eyes were bright and arrogant as they condescended to traffic with Bill Cole Cody's.

'So you're still here, Cody, are you?' he said curtly. He was wearing riding gauntlets, new, ornate and expensive ones. His hands looked white and well cared for, the hands of a gambler whose fingers knew each card in the deck. He drew his gauntlets off, whipped them against his leg, tossed them along with his hat to the big table and sat down in the old comfortable chair before the fireplace. 'Still hanging around, eh, Cody?'

The sight of a reptile, of a tarantula, say, of a rattlesnake, of any spider or make—with

285

some men it's a naked knife—can move a man tremendously, shooting into his blood a turbulence which may be compounded of abhorrence, of fear, of hate, of sheer animalism, of a tangle of complex instincts. Right now, looking at Rance Waldron's not unhandsome face, Bill Cole Cody's bloodstream was ruffled all but beyond endurance; it ran cold and it ran hot, and queer, blazing streaks of fire, like miniature stabs of lightning, shot through him. Here was the man who had killed the good old Judge, killing him as a man may tread under his careless boot heel some creeping thing he hardly notices. The Judge! Here was the man who had connived at the death of old Early Bill Cole, who had engineered, who had the same as shot the old man down, shooting him in the back. The man who had cold bloodedly murdered his own henchman, Tom Gough, and though Gough had undoubtedly needed killing, perhaps even he did not deserve his death the way he got it, the way this damned Rance Waldron, so cool now and contemptuous and sure of his high destiny, had meted it out.

Cole Cody's throat constricted. He came close to choking on his gorge. He didn't say a word. Within himself, and in his own fashion, he was praying, 'Make it quick now, Lord! I can't stand it much longer.'

'You know,' said Rance Waldron, stretching

his long legs out, reaching indolently for his tobacco and papers, starting to build himself an insulting cigarette, 'you're a damn fool, Cody, for sticking around in any hope of catching any few drops that might spill out over the top of the bucket. Because, if you listen to me, there won't be any drops spilled over. It might be a good time if you tucked your tail between your legs and got to hell out of here.'

He licked his cigarette, slid a match along his thigh, held the small steady flame up before his eyes thoughtfully a moment, lighted his cigarette and drew the first draught of smoke, letting it merely trickle out of his slowly distending nostrils. Then, before he went on he hooked his thumbs back into his belt, and his hands thus were very close to his guns.

'Let's get down to bed rock, Cody,' he said, and his voice changed, getting as hard as flint, no longer merely mocking. He stood up, coming lithely to his feet, standing firmly, balanced nicely. 'You haven't any claim here. It's common knowledge, told in every saloon, that you had some sort of a trumped up "will," a faked thing—and that you haven't even got that now. So you can get to hell in a hurry, Mr. Cody. Am I right?'

Cody swallowed. He answered very quietly, very slowly.

'Waldron, if I'm taking a big dose of you

287

now, you'll know why later on. Suppose, until that time comes, you keep your mouth shut? I'm not asking the hell of a lot; the breath of the thoughts you think—stinks! *Shut up!'*

Waldron chose to laugh, and never was there a man who could put a nastier sneer into laughter which should be a pleasant thing and which can be detestable beyond most sounds.

'It's hard to swallow, huh, Cody?' he jeered. 'Thought you had an edge on the situation, didn't you? Thought I'd take it the way you dished it out! Thought that if you couldn't take it any other way,' he said, and jeered, 'you'd gobble it along with that nifty piece of girl-meat, that little cuddly, pink-and-white female thing Ann Lee, that a man can buy a dozen of in town for—'

Cody struck the way lightning strikes. He had no sense of volition, there was no more plan within him than there is in a bolt of lightning. His action was like that of a blazing match set against anything highly inflammable. His force was the clean brutal force of an unleashed avalanche.

Rance Waldron, with his belted thumbs, had his fanwise fingers brushing the grips of his guns. Bill Cole Cody, thinking of nothing on earth, didn't think of guns. He had hands, capable, rather gloriously strong male hands, and he used them. He used them as a swordsman uses his sword, as a serpent uses its fangs, as a scorpion uses its sting, as a shark uses its teeth. As a primordial man uses his hands.

Glorious hands.

Hands that, when four years old had tied intricate knots into strings, and had untied them; hands that, belonging to an adolescent youth, had argued the case before the bar of *lex naturae* with a seven year old timber wolf, the case dismissed with a barlow knife sawn desperately across the wolf's throat; hands that were somehow sensitive and artistlike, though sinewy and brown and as hard as granite. Hands now grown octopus-like, grown like a Neanderthal's wicked bludgeon, hands acting of their own volition, as though twin brains resided within them, beseeching a certain cock-sure, revolver-sconded Rance Waldron. 'Come hither, Rance Waldron. Bring your hardware; make yourself at home; you're mighty damned welcome. Let's go, you man I hate!'

Leaping yards across the floor, Bill Cole Cody swung with his left hand and struck a blow for any hard-striking man to be proud of. Only—Rance Waldron wasn't there, wasn't at the end of that perfect short arc. He was three or four quick leaps behind it, jerking out his guns. And he was in high heaven, with full provocation to burn his man down. Attacked without warning, he had every right to go for his guns, to kill his man. And it would be so easy! If there were only a witness to his predicament, that of a man defending himself against a murderous attack.

That witness he had, but he knew that only later. It was Ann Lee who had stolen a-tip-toe from the room in which Doc Joe and Aunt Jenifer, two sentimental old fools, were explaining and talking two-at-a-time, and blinking against fat tear drops; a tremulous Ann Lee who was wondering where a certain William Cole Cody—'William,' she thought; 'that must be his real name; the name his mama and papa gave him'—had betaken herself. She heard and she saw, and she nearly dropped dead, hearing and seeing.

Now as Bill Cole Cody had leaped forward and the watchful Rance Waldron had leaped back to be out of his reach, Waldron fired and Cody struck again—and little Ann tried to scream and tried to shut her eyes, and could do neither. In a sort of trance she saw how it was that Bill Cody struck: Not with his fist this time, since that would have been too late; but as a bullet clipped through a loose fold of his sleeve, he struck with his whole body, launching himself like a long lean catapult with bullets ripping the air where he had been a split second before. And as his feet left the floor and he became a sort of giant's arrow in horizontal flight, and his head struck Rance Waldron in the middle, his long arms with those tremendously gripping hands of his grappled with the man he sent toppling and crashing to the floor.

Now, Bill Cole Cody didn't miss all the bullets which swarmed about him like angry bees. Two of them scraped him, barely, laid the skin back, and their effect was to cause him to lose all temper which he hadn't had time to lose already. There was a scratch along the top of his head, and blood ran down into his left eye; there was a twin scratch six or eight inches long down the back of his left shoulder. Ann Lee saw the blood and thought he was surely dead, and came running; she'd grab Rance Waldron's guns and shoot him all to pieces!

But no intercession was needed. As Waldron spilled back on the floor one of his guns flew out of his hands; Bill Cody, though with one eye dimmed, could see that. The other gun swung in its brief arc to blow his brains out, but Cody's hand swung quicker. He caught Waldron's wrist; he all but broke it in the power of his grip; slowly he twisted it so that the muzzle of Waldron's gun was against Waldron's temple. And then Bill Cody spoke his little speech:

'Pull the trigger now, Waldron, if you like. Or drop the gun—and drop it damn quick!'

The gun fell from Waldron's fingers. Little Ann Lee, standing so close to them both now, caught it up, ran for the other, backed off and stood in a corner with both weapons in her hands. The two men stood up. She said,

'Rance Waldron, I think I am going to kill

you. I know I'll never be sorry if I do; I may be sorry all the years of my life if I don't!'

That made Bill Cole Cody laugh. In his turn, his own laughter was scarcely more pleasant on the ear than Rance Waldron's had been just now.

'No you don't, Ann Lee!' he called to her and sounded at once commanding and oddly gay. 'I don't want Rance Waldron killed right now, especially here in the house where he'd make a mess of things. Why, I'm not even going to kill him myself—unless, mind you, it's just accidental.'

Then his grin faded and his tone hardened and he stepped closer to Waldron.

'You asked for it,' he said curtly.

They fought all over the room; they fought until Ann turned deathly sick; they fought until Aunt Jenifer and even Doc Joe, half hidden behind her, looked in through a half open door. Neither Cody nor Waldron saw any one of their spectators; they saw for the most part only their opponent's eyes and battered, infuriated face.

Bill Cody fought clean and fair, feeling no need of anything beyond his clubbing, strangling hands. Once Waldron strove to snatch up the heavy fireside poker; once he caught up a solid oaken chair. These things did him no good; Cody was too lightning-fast for him, too recklessly contemptuous of the threat of any weapon on earth. And once Waldron fell, going over backwards, and lay there a moment, and Bill Cody stood patiently waiting for him to get up. By now Waldron's face was a bleeding pulp, his eyes mere bright, malevolent points of light sunk in ugly folds of flesh.

He stirred but again lay still. It was hard to make out his words when he spoke.

'All right,' he said. 'I know when I'm licked. I quit, Cody.'

Cody shook his head. He was thinking of the old Judge, of old Early Bill, even of Tom Gough shot like a dog. He said quietly,

'No, Waldron, you're not licked yet. Stand up.'

'Like hell I will!' gasped Waldron.

Cody came closer and drew back his boot, poising it to drive it into the fallen man's body.

'Stand up, I say,' he commanded. 'If you don't I'll bust your body open with the toe of my boot. *Stand up!*'

Waldron stood up. New rage reddened the pin-points of his eyes, new strength flowed into him and perhaps new courage. He charged like a bull—Bill Cody struck the one blow then that was like a *coup de grâce*. It took Rance Waldron on the point of the chin; it seemed to lift him inches from the floor. And this time when he fell, whether taunted by words or threatened with further bodily punishment, he was beyond rising.

Ann Lee thought him dead. So did Aunt

293

Jenifer. So, for that matter, did Doc Joe.

In the kitchen, 'Oh, Cole Cody! Your poor dear face!' gulped little Ann Lee. 'Your poor eye!' and tears began spattering like summer rain.

Bill Cody caught her in his arms; he forgot the unloveliness of his battered face and crookedly leering eye; he drew her tight and tighter and kissed her. And it is of record that Ann Lee returned his kiss exactly the way it was received, a fact to be sworn to if necessary by Cal Roundtree who, just then bursting into the room stood a moment transfixed on the threshold.

But they heard him and whirled about; and Ann Lee turned scarlet and Bill Cody's good eye glowed more fiercely than it had just now at the end of the battle with Rance Waldron.

'Look here, Roundtree—' he began stiffly.

Cal virtually brushed Ann Lee aside, grasping Bill Cole Cody by an arm, yanking him close, then whispering into his ear.

'I bet Rance Waldron's here, from the looks of you,' was what he said. 'And, Cody—'

'No secrets from Ann Lee,' said Cody, pulling away. 'Sure he's here. And so is old Doc, and both Ann and Aunt Jenifer know that, too.'

Cal emitted a mild whoop and came as close to the execution of a war dance as either of the amazed onlookers had ever dreamed lay within his possibilities.

'Keep Waldron from getting away; lead me to old Doc Joe!' was what he had next to remark.

Rance Waldron was in a small room with iron-grilled windows and with a murderous looking Porfirio, a gun in his belt and a wicked looking knife in his hand, riding herd on him. Doc Joe and Aunt Jenifer, hearing voices, came into the kitchen.

'Keep all this dark from Waldron until tomorrow,' said Cal Roundtree. 'That's all I ask.'

'That's fair enough, Cal,' nodded old Doc Joe. 'Only just what is it that we're to keep dark?'

But at that Cal closed his mouth after the fashion of buttoning it. Then he shook his head. Finally he said,

'Tell you at sun-up. Just keep Rance Waldron alive and handy. 'Night, folks.'

For a time after Cal's abrupt departure there was a deal of speculation, but since it led nowhere, such talk died away. Presently Bill Cole Cody and Ann Lee found themselves alone in the kitchen; it was really a very lovely kitchen, a pleasant and satisfactory place to be. She put compresses on his bruised face and he appeared to like it; she found a piece of sticking-plaster and mended a long cut on his check; she kissed him above a swollen eye with the softest, gentlest warmest lips in the world and made the place well.

295

After a while, in the hushed house they talked with hushed voices.

'We've lost dear old Early Bill's ranch, his home place, Bill,' said Ann, 'and that makes me sad; I know he wanted us to have it; both of us. But we've found something else, haven't we? You're not too terribly disappointed, are you, dear?'

Somehow she found herself on his knee; it didn't quite seem to her that she had got there through her own volition; he couldn't have sworn that he had scooped her up and set her there; rather it seemed just one of those wonderful and altogether inexplicable phenomena.

'I love you so much that it hurts,' said Bill Cole Cody. 'I love you more than anyone on this earth ever loved anyone else! Twice, ten times as much!'

'Why, Cole Cody! You can't say a thing like that! I love you every bit as much as you love me—More! From the first minute I ever saw you. You couldn't love anyone the way I could—the way I do!'

'Couldn't, huh?' demanded Cody. 'You look here, Ann Lee Cody—'

'I'm not Ann Lee *Cody* yet, Mr. William Cole Cody—! And if you dare for a minute to insinuate that I'm one of those colorless little creatures that doesn't have the power to love—'

'I didn't say that!'

'You did! I hate you.'

*   *   *

Before sun-up all in the house breakfasted, even to a savage, sullen Rance Waldron, save Doc Joe alone who as yet wanted Waldron to know nothing about his presence, about his still being above ground. Yet Waldron, though battered and angry, had a certain malicious grin in his eye. Over the coffee he said with a dash of his old cock-sure arrogance,

'My lawyer's coming out this morning. The sheriff will be with him or close behind. This place is mine, is going to be proved mine, and every damned one of you interlopers is going to clear out, bag and baggage.'

Cal Roundtree came up from the bunkhouse. He carried an open envelope in his hand. He cleared his throat, forgot all about saying good morning, and announced a bit of news that came pretty close to knocking several people out of their chairs.

'Me,' said Cal, 'I just got a letter last night. It's a letter from a guy by name of Mr. William Cole, known far and wide as Early Bill.'

The first to gasp out a word was Rance Waldron, hastily on his feet.

'You fool! Early Bill's dead and buried! Are you crazy?'

'Nope, I ain't crazy. Yep, the old devil's dead and buried; me, I saw him die and I

297

helped bury him. Just the same he wrote me a letter and I just got it last night.' He tossed the missive to the table. 'Here, Cody, you read it,' he said. 'Read it right out loud.'

Cody caught it up, whipped the letter out of its envelope and stared at it a long minute. He stared from face to face, then back at the letter.

'Here's what it says,' he said slowly, 'and it's in Early Bill's handwriting.'

And he read:

'Dear Cal, you old sinner, me being dead and dug under ground, my old bones sort of feel cramped. I'd sort of like if you'd dig me up, soon as you get this, which I'm writing sitting on top of a nice big pink-and-white cloud sort of learning to get the hang of a harp; and I want you to shift me over where I told you. Now get a move on, and me, I'm having me my fun yet.

So long Cal, *gracias, amigo*.

Wm. Cole, alias Early Bill.'

Rance Waldron pretended to laugh. The thing of course was some sort of hoax.

'No, it ain't,' said Cal soberly. 'This letter just come, like I say, into Bald Eagle by stage last night. It was sent in another envelope from a feller I'd heard old Early Bill talk about a time or two, a feller that used to be friends with him. I reckon Bill sent it a round-about

298

way to get here when he wanted it to.' He cleared his throat again and added, 'As for him squatting on a cloud twanging a harp, it's a lie, and I'd tell him so; most likely he's shoveling coal down hellwards. But never mind; I got Porfirio outside, and Gaucho and a couple shovels, and we start doing what the old fool said do. Come ahead.'

Out under the three pines, hushed and wondering and with a touch of awe, at Early Bill's favorite dawn hour men went to work with their shovels. So exclusively were they occupied in what was going forward, none particularly remembered Rance Waldron, who, sneering after his fashion, hands on his hips, stood a few steps withdrawn—none, that is, except old Doc Joe who had taken his chance to slip out of the house and follow on, and who now peered from behind the farther of the three pines.

Little Ann Lee, her face very white, her eyes enormous, clutched Aunt Jenifer's arm tight in both hands, and Aunt Jenifer put a comforting arm around her. The sods flew under the strongly wielded shovels; the soil was light and loose; very swiftly the excavation took form, some seven feet long, half as wide, two or three feet deep—

'I'm going to the house,' murmured Ann. 'I—I can't stand it!'

Cal Roundtree, down in the excavation looked up and said sharply, 'You stay right where you are!'

And an instant later he exclaimed triumphantly,

'Here it is!'

He reached down, scratched in the loose soil with both hands and unearthed a small iron box; a box exactly like the one which Cody and Ann had opened together with two keys! He tossed it up to them, to Cody and Ann both, and said, 'You'll see this one opens with two keys just like the other. You two better open it! Old Early Bill ain't here at all; hell, me and Gaucho moved him the night after he was planted here. That box is for you, because that's what he told me, making me swear to keep my trap shut. *Open it!*'

With trembling fingers they did get it open. There were folded papers within. The top one said briefly, 'This is my Ace in the Hole; me, I always figured to hold one in any game like this!' Then there was a letter addressed to Ann Lee. There was one for William Cole Cody. There was a lone, sealed envelope, and it was addressed to them together.

And next was a picture, a fine likeness of an old, lean, devil-may-care man with a humorous gleam in his eye. And it was inscribed, 'To Ann Lee and Cole Cody from an old friend, Early Bill.'

And Ann came close to shrieking out, 'Why, I knew him! Aunt Jenny, look! Don't you remember that old man who came to our house, and he was broke and sick and sad-looking, and we took him in and—'

And Cole Cody, a queer catch in his voice was muttering, 'So that's Early Bill, huh? The darned old rascal! I played poker with him; he let me skin him out of his eye teeth; he stuck around and let me stake him; he even asked to borrow money from me—If I'd have known who he was I'd have chased him off the ranch!'

They read their letters hastily; Ann was crying softly and Cody was making rough noises in his throat.

'Open the big envelope,' said Cal. 'That's Bill's Ace in the Hole.'

Again they found a brief note for them both:

'I've had my fun I reckon. I thought as how, knowing the two of you pups, you might fight a while, then fall in love and get married; I'd like that fine. But maybe things will go some other way, and maybe that damned sneaky varmint name of Rance Waldron might throw a monkey wrench in the machine; I've a hunch he's the bozo hired somebody to shoot me down, him being too foxy and maybe scared. And now here's my third will and, by gravy, my last: And you'll find it leaves everything I've got to you two kids, fight or don't fight, marry or don't marry. And honest, kids, I did have a good time—and I'm still having it right

301

now. So long.'

And there was the will!
And there was Doc Joe.
'Grab that Waldron hombre,' he shouted. 'He's going to hang; and me, I'm going to see that he does.'
Waldron whirled. His face went as dead white as Ann's had been. He could have had no thought for that first instant save that he was looking on a dead man, one he himself had murdered. Then he was quick to know he had been tricked, and he was quick to snatch out from his belt a gun that no one had seen, that no one dreamed he had, that no one ever knew where he had come by it. He swung it, murder in his eyes, upon Doc Joe.
Very neatly Porfirio, as watchful as a cat, shot Rance Waldron through the back of the head.
And Bill Cole Cody very gently put his arm about little Ann Lee and led her away, led her clinging to him, back to the *patio* into which the early sun was just entering.

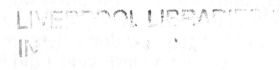

We hope you have enjoyed this Large Print book. Other Chivers Press or Thorndike Press Large Print books are available at your library or directly from the publishers.

For more information about current and forthcoming titles, please call or write, without obligation, to:

Chivers Large Print
published by BBC Audiobooks Ltd
St James House, The Square
Lower Bristol Road
Bath BA2 3SB
UK
email: bbcaudiobooks@bbc.co.uk
www.bbcaudiobooks.co.uk

OR

Thorndike Press
295 Kennedy Memorial Drive
Waterville
Maine 04901
USA
www.gale.com/thorndike
www.gale.com/wheeler

All our Large Print titles are designed for easy reading, and all our books are made to last.